BOURBON & BLOOD

THE VOODOO BASTARDS MC
BOOK 1

A.J. DOWNEY

BOURBON & BLOOD

The Voodoo Bastards MC

Book I
by A. J. Downey

BOOK ONE

Published 2022 by Second Circle Press
Text Copyright © 2022 A.J. Downey
ISBN: 978-1-950222-38-4
All Rights Reserved

No part of this book may be reproduced in any form or by an electronic or mechanical means, including information storage and retrieval systems, without written permission from the author, except for the use of brief quotations in a book review.

This is a work of fiction. The names, characters, businesses, places, events, and incidents are either the products of the author's imagination or used in a fictitious manner and are not to be construed as real except where noted and authorized. Any resemblance to actual persons, living or dead, or actual events are purely coincidental. Any trademarks, service marks, product names, or names featured are assumed to be the property of their respective owners, and are used only for reference. There is no implied endorsement if any of these terms are used.

The author acknowledges the trademarked status and trademark owners of various products referenced in this work, which have been used without permission. The publication/use of these trademarks is not authorized, associated with or sponsored by the trademark owners.

Editing & book design by Maggie Kern @ Ms.K Edits
Cover art and Indigo Knights logo by Dar Albert at Wicked Smart Designs

DEDICATION

For my rage-filled little darlings who have had it just about as much as I have for the system and for the rules that keep us down. In the famous words of Margaret Atwood's characters, "Don't let the bastards grind you down" – but please do let my bastards grind on you a little bit. I promise it'll be so worth it.

PROLOGUE

*L*a Croix...
 I sat on the picnic table, scuffed boots, leather eaten and some of the shine of the steel toe on the left one shining through under the strings of bare lightbulbs. They were strung up around the inside of the slatted fence of the club's front courtyard. It was hot – a sweaty, muggy, NOLA night – and the boys were partying hard inside.

 I wasn't interested. The mood felt forced and wasn't all good – but things had been declining for a while like that.

 I took a sip outta my flask, the rich, smoky, good, bourbon a rolling fire against my tongue and all the way down. I didn't want no part of the festivities no more. I found myself out here more often than not... but then again, I had a good reason.

 I squinted up past the glare of the streetlight at the window on the third floor of the old building across the way, at the woman between the curtains and the fall of her red hair over her creamy shoulders, hiding her pale back under a straight shining copper fall that was damn near to her waist. She wore a green tank top, the kind that clung tight to her and cut a straight line across, just above where the band of her bra should be. The bra was a neutral beige. I could see the straps around the thin ones of the tank.

Soundlessly, her voice encased by the window glass and insulated from my ears by the brick walls of the old place, she laughed as a boy picked her up and she hung over his shoulder, beating her fists against his back ineffectually. She had the most perfect heart-shaped ass under her beige panties, a match for the bra. Cotton, though. Nothing fancy or satin…

Still, the underwear matched. She planned to fuck him.

I grunted and put the freshly rolled spliff between my lips, fishing my lighter out of my pocket and swiping it twice, once down and once up, against the rough denim of my jeans at my thigh.

"Figured I'd find you out here," Hex called out from behind me as I sucked in a lungful of green.

I grunted in acknowledgment of his presence, didn't need much beyond that.

He sighed and dropped onto the bench by my booted feet and leaned back, with an "*ahhh.*"

I knew that sound, and without a word, I passed him my flask.

"Thank you kindly," he muttered and took a healthy swig.

I stared at him, waiting him out, waiting to hear how bad it was.

He glanced up at me, handed me back my flask, and wordlessly held out his hand for the joint in my other hand. I passed it silently and felt myself frown.

He took a puff off it and handed it back.

Through his held breath, he said, "It's bad, brother. I think we're past a no-confidence vote. Ruth is off his fuckin' rocker and the boys are gettin' restless."

He didn't sound happy about it. Hell, I wasn't happy about it, either. Still, I had to say, "Don't sound like no confidence in there to me—"

"Yeah, well, still gotta let off steam where you can, but the vibe in there ain't great. I imagine that's why you're out here – no?"

I glanced back up to the pixie-like woman through her window. I liked to watch her. She was all that was sweet and good in this world and easy on my eyes. I didn't know her. Like, I didn't know her name – at least not really. Just what was on the label next to her apartment number on the buzzer. At least what I thought was her apartment number. I'd never been inside the building to look, but if I had to reckon, she was in apartment 3A and the name on 3A was A. Bouchard.

"Boy, you even listening to me?" Hex rapped his knuckles on the toe of my boot like he was knocking on a door.

I swung my gaze down from the girl's now-empty window and fixed my gaze on Hex who leaned back and said, "Alright, damn. Y' ain't gotta turn that creepy stare on me, brother."

I blinked and frowned. I hadn't realized I'd looked at him any type of way, but with the inked sclera of my eyes, hell – probably any look was scary as fuck, which was sorta the whole point.

I took another hit off the joint and grunted again, and he sighed.

"I *said,* I don't know how much longer this is gonna roll until the goddamn wheels come off."

I nodded. I knew Ruth wasn't in his right head and I also knew we were past it. That he was too far gone on that shit he'd been breathin' and poisonin' himself with.

"What d' you want me t' do?" I asked and I turned and looked at Hex again. He looked troubled.

He sighed finally and shook his head, dropping it so he could look at his own booted feet.

"I don't rightly know," he confessed. "All I *do* know, is that whatever it is, the time come, it ain't gon' be pretty."

I looked up at the girl's window. The only thing that was pretty on this block was her.

"I ain't here for pretty," I reminded him. "That's not what y'all keep me 'round for."

He sighed again, and it wasn't happy.

"We don't 'keep you around' for nothin'," he said and I snorted. "We don't. You're one of us, our brother, at least that's how this is *supposed* to work."

I chuckled darkly at that. With Ruth at the helm, that's hardly how it worked. He was the king of his fucked-up little kingdom, alright – but he wasn't no benevolent king. Not like Cutter and his boys seemed to work.

I looked to Hex and sighed.

"You want change," I said and it wasn't a question.

He nodded judiciously. "We all do, I reckon."

I grunted in agreement to that one – problem was, what form that change would take.

"A coup, then?" I asked.

"Think there's any other way?" he demanded.

I shook my head and ran a hand over my bald head, the stubble of the hair just starting to grow, rasping my rough palm like sandpaper. I scowled.

"You got a leader picked out?" I growled.

"Was kinda hopin' it'd be you," he said and I hocked and spit, giving him a down and dirty look.

He held up his hands in surrender and said, "Okay. Don't shoot the messenger."

I cocked my head. "That what the rest of them boys want?" I asked.

He looked at me a little startled and said, "You really ain't got no clue, do yah?"

My scowl deepened and I growled a little and he laughed, climbing to his feet, and slapping me on the cut that covered my back.

"Only man in this club they respect more 'n Ruth and fear just at much… is you," he said. "Now, they might respect me, but they don't fear me the same way they do you, and sometimes in moments when the respect runs thin, even momentarily, you gotta have that fear or somethin' else to fall back on."

I lowered my head, shook it and said, "Call a meeting on the down-low. I need to hear it from them."

Hex nodded and asked me, "You don't want it, do yah?"

I glared at him, and he nodded to himself.

"Tells me you might just be the right man for the job, then."

"Fuck outta here," I grumbled and took another deep hit off the spliff while I unscrewed the cap off my flask for another pull off it.

I looked up to the window again, hoping for another glimpse and felt my brow crush down even harder.

All that long red hair was pressed to the glass as her boyfriend plowed into her.

It wasn't the show I was hoping for. Instead of the calm I usually felt at seeing her, all I felt was more rage. Especially when his hand appeared over her shoulder, pressed to the glass.

"Fuck," I muttered, and flicked the remainder of my marijuana cigarette away. I downed the rest of what was in my flask in three long swallows and got up.

I turned, shaking with rage, and walked back toward the club. I'd either slug it out or fuck it out and nobody'd better get in my fucking way.

CHAPTER ONE

*A*lina...
   Moving day.
   You would think I would be happy about it, and in some ways; yes, I was, but in others...
   "Hey, you, are you okay?" I looked up at Dorian, smiled and heaved a big sigh. Dorian was a good guy, a fellow bartender down in the Quarter at the bar we both worked at, and hey – he was here to help which automatically made him a good friend. There were friends, and then there were friends who would help you *move*. And the friends who would help you *move*? Well, they were *gold*.
   "Yeah, just a little bit in my feelings, you know?" I asked.
   "Ah, yeah," he said, crow's feet fanning out from his eyes as he smiled. He was younger than me, which was to say mid-twenties, to my late-twenties – so only a few years, but he looked older.
   Of course, *everybody* looked older than me. I pretty much looked like I was perpetually sixteen due to my petite size, but most people I guess were too nice to say it. I tossed one of my thick red braids over my shoulder and heaved a big sigh.
   "It's just my first apartment, and I'm gonna miss it," I whined. He

laughed and put an arm around my shoulders, giving me a sideways hug.

"Yes, but on to new adventures, right?" he asked, giving me a little shake.

I rolled my eyes.

"I mean, I'll certainly be closer to work, and it *is* a smaller place," I said.

"Cheaper, too, and away from Patrick," Maya said, coming up to us and making a face. She was a Creole Queen – light skinned, sure, but with a glorious crown of curls and a descendant of some distant cousin of Marie Laveau, New Orleans' Voodoo Queen herself. Or so the "legend has it" and the rumor mill liked to say. Maya had a flair for the dramatic though, and let the rumors run rampant. She laughed at all the silliness with me and was an absolute riot about it. She was my best friend and we were – what she liked to call – sisters of the heart.

I sighed and nodded. Patrick Cahill was my very ex-boyfriend and had wound up being a cheater and an absolute dog.

I felt a wave of nausea roll through me at even the mere mention of his name.

"Sorry," Maya said with a shrug of her perfect shoulders. She was trying to break into modeling, and if she could, she would go so very far. She was beautiful in that way that wasn't quite real, you know?

"It's fine, but can we please just relegate him to 'the nameless one' or something?" I asked meekly.

"Sure," Dorian said and let me go. With a gusty sigh, he asked, "You ready to tackle this couch then?"

I groaned.

"No," I said. "But let's do it."

We wrestled the three-seater overstuffed thing all the way down from the third floor and over to the moving van.

"Okay, hold on, hold on, hold on!" Dorian cried, and I panted and braced my end, my arms shaking with fatigue as I pivoted and tried to rest it against my hip – Dorian yelling from the other end, "Wait, wait, wait, wait, wait! Don't shove it in yet!"

"That's what she said!" Maya called over the back of the couch where she steadied it.

I snorted and yelled back, "I'm not! I'm just trying to—" The weight was just gone, like magic and I startled and whirled, looking up into eyes that were wall-to-wall midnight. I blinked, my mouth falling open in shock as the big, and I do mean *big*, bald, and heavily tattooed man looked down at me. His face was impassive and hard as stone. He jerked his head to one side and I moved out of the way, my feet feeling like they barely touched the ground as a shiver went down my spine.

And no, I wasn't cold. There was no such thing as being cold in New Orleans, standing outside on the summer sidewalk.

"Alina, you got it?" Dorian called. He straightened up and said, "Oh, hey. Thanks, man."

The big man holding the end of my couch up off the ground with one hand didn't take his eyes off me, as though he was committing my face to memory.

"Uh, right," Dorian said after a protracted silence that was interrupted not only by Dorian but by the subtle laughing and chuckling out of three more bikers standing nearby, watching the strange spectacle as a cicada screamed in the near distance.

The big man in the leather vest finally tore his eyes off me and looked to Dorian, raising his chin as though to silently ask if Dorian was ready.

"Yeah, put it in," he said.

Maya snorted and said again, "That's what she said."

The rest of the bikers spectating all had another good laugh.

The couch went into the back of the van and the big man turned back to me to stare some more.

"You good?" a voice called from the three bikers off to the side.

"What? Me? Yeah," I said finally, tearing my eyes from the big man staring me down. There was something wrong with his eyes. I mean, there was no white. They were just black as midnight, black as pitch, the inkiest darkness I had ever seen – which is when it dawned on me. It *was* ink. He'd tattooed the whites of his eyes – which made me shudder. I couldn't even *imagine* what that'd felt like, and *no*! Just no. Mm-mm. *No, no, no, and nope.* Didn't want to think about it too hard. I was good.

Jesus!

"Anything else, darlin'?" the same biker from the pack of them off to the side asked. I shook my head no.

"No, that was the last thing," I murmured. Still wide-eyed and transfixed by the giant – or at least giant to *me* – bald man who was absolutely *jacked,* who hadn't budged from his spot in front of me. A coldness radiated off of him despite the muggy heat socking us all in.

"Thank you," I said and he gave me a slow, single nod before turning and walking back up the sidewalk and joining the rest of his friends. They all turned and walked across the street and through the gate of the Voodoo Bastards' compound.

"Alina?" Dorian called and I turned and looked from him to Maya who mouthed, *What was that?* at me. I shrugged and mouthed back *I don't know!* Then I looked back to Dorian who looked just as mystified as both me and my bestie.

I'd lived right outside their compound for three years, now. Had a view from both my living room and bedroom window right down into it even. But I'd really never paid them any mind except for the roar of their bikes when they'd drunkenly drag raced up the block on wild party nights and the times the music had been almost too loud to think – but I wasn't dumb. I never called it in or complained or anything. The Voodoo Bastards weren't something you messed with out here. Not if you didn't want to become gator food or whatever.

Still, in the last three years, this was the first time I had ever had an up-close encounter with any of them… and I was suddenly glad it *was* moving day. I wasn't sure I ever wanted another encounter ever again. They were scary!

CHAPTER TWO

*L*a Croix…

"What was that all about, boss?" I ignored Axeman and walked right past him, Hex, and Saint.

I could almost feel Axe and Saint exchange a look and shrug behind me, Hex falling into step beside me. He probably already knew what I was thinkin'. Hex was the real brains of this fuckin' outfit, not me. I was president, sure, but in name only. A ploy. I was the biggest and baddest motherfucker in the yard and if I got taken out, it would suck to be me, but the club? The club would do just fine because it was *Hex* who was the real brains of the entire outfit. I mean, this was all his design. I wasn't stupid, just not as smart as he was. It was a good leadership model as far as they went. What president didn't have his trusted cabinet?

Ruth had thought he was smart but he'd let the drugs fuck him over. A few too many bad decisions later and he had the rest of the club questioning his loyalty. As in was it to the club and the rest of us, or just himself? A few more bad decisions later and it was clear. Ruth had to fuckin' go.

The coup had been easy, almost too easy. It had me and Hex

watching each other's backs for a minute. We'd quashed some shit a few months later and that'd tightened things right up.

We'd been thirteen under Ruthless, but that'd dropped to eight. We didn't like the even number, but it couldn't be helped. We had a prospect, and he wasn't far from earning his colors. In fact, we were sure it'd be any day now.

I went for our office once we were inside. Yeah, I know it was supposed to be mine – but it was Hex's *and* mine's and truthfully, I preferred to think of it that way. It'd been a year and some change and I still couldn't quite get my head around the whole thing – me bein' the president and all. Still didn't feel real.

"Looks like your little redheaded obsession's movin' on out," Hex said once the door'd been shut. He gave me a bit of a sly look and a wink. I scowled darkly and he chuckled, opened the door back up, and yelled for our prospect, Louie.

"Yeah, boss?" Louie called from somewhere out there. I didn't pay it no never mind.

"Might wanna get our fearless leader a bourbon, boy," Hex called out, reading my mind.

"You got it. Anything else?"

Hex looked back over his shoulder at me as I dropped heavily into the seat behind the big ol' battered desk.

"Yeah," he muttered. "Better make it a double."

"You got it, boss," Louie declared and hustled his ass back down the hall unseen.

Hex leaned his back against the wall by the slightly open door, waiting for my bourbon to show up.

"You wanna talk about it, man?" he asked.

I shook my head. Talking never got me anywhere. Just a bunch of bullshit and excuses as my daddy always liked to say, usually before he cracked me in the mouth as a kid. Silence was always better 'n bullshit in my book.

"Learn anything new, gettin' a look up close?" he asked.

"Her name," I answered, knowing he wouldn't let it the fuck go until he dragged something outta me. I knew how he worked.

"You mean all this time you ain't learned her name?" he asked after barking a laugh.

I kept my mouth shut. The prospect's boot tread loud on the concrete floor out in the hallway.

"I say god*damn* prospect!" Hex shouted, taking the bourbon from the kid. "You keep walkin' around like that, ain't a fuckin' soul in NOLA ain't know you comin'. Good way to get yourself shot, dipshit."

"Shit," the kid said chagrinned. "My bad."

I frowned.

"Take off your boots," I ordered. "You can have 'em back when you learn t' be quieter." Wordlessly, the kid complied, pulling off one then the other as I jerked my head at the empty corner of the room. He tossed 'em there and I said, "Now get out."

Hex brought the glass of bourbon over and set it in front of me. I sipped it and stared off into space, thinking about Alina, *Alina Bouchard*.

"I know that look," Hex said sighing. "You ain't fixin' to do something foolish now, are you?" he asked. I flicked my gaze from that indeterminable point in space back to his and growled.

"Fuck me," he muttered. "You want me to put a call into Radar? Have him do some o' dat hoodoo magic computer shit he do?" he asked.

I shook my head.

I'd do it myself.

Later.

Some things were just too personal, and for whatever reason, Alina had become personal for me. Never mind I didn't actually know her from fuckin' Eve.

"What business we got to attend to?" I demanded, changing the subject.

Hex chuckled and cocked his head.

"Not a damn thing," he said. "We're gravy."

I grunted.

"Then get the fuck out," I told him and he barked a laugh.

"Alright, then. Have fun." He waved over his shoulder dismissively on his way out and shut the door behind him.

I sat for a while, in the stale warmth of the small office and frowned slightly when the swamp cooler in the painted-over window kicked on to try and cool it. It was struggling, the press of summer hot and heavy. Reminded me of the time I pressed a motherfucker that owed us money down onto the grill at this joint off of Rampart. The way the cooler rattled in its frame bringing me back to the hiss and pop of his flesh and the sweet smell of pork filling the small kitchen as his face cooked.

I smiled. That'd been a lesson he'd never forget. He'd see that shit every time he looked in the mirror.

Truth be told, I don't even remember what he owed us money for – drugs, more than likely. Maybe he got behind in the books? I didn't care. Ruth pointed; I did my thing. It'd worked; but now I was in the uncomfortable position of having to point and sit back – and I *hated* sitting back.

I picked up my phone, the good one, and scrolled through the numbers. I smiled in a bit of irony when I found hers… Justice was something I hoped never caught up to me, at least, not citizen justice. That wasn't real justice, though. Any man lived the life we did knew that. No, it wasn't justice, it was *control*. We made our own justice out here in the street and it was far more reliable, a hell of a lot quicker, and usually, a hell of a lot fairer.

I put the call through and waited as it rang. I hated talking. I wasn't much of a talker; but this wasn't something you sent in a text.

"Hey, you! Long time no talk. How have you been?" She sounded… better – more vivacious, brighter – and she *was* a sweet woman. Brave. Seen some shit and been through it but hadn't let it change her. Hadn't given into it. I had a lot of respect for that. Of course, it *had* been a while. How long, I didn't know. Time did funny things in my head.

"Doing good," I said roughly, and I took a sip of what was in my glass, appreciating the soothing burn going down.

"Oh, yeah?" Justice asked, a sly tone to her voice. She was sharp, and I had to think her own healing journey made her keen on wanting to fix everybody. Problem with that was there wasn't any fixing the kind of broken in my head. There just wasn't. Didn't mean I didn't appreciate her tryin' but the woman needed to learn that some things were just a lost cause.

"Yeah," I said and couldn't help but smile. "Actually, I need a favor from your man," I said. "Somethin' low key, just lookin' someone up for me like he does."

"Oh," she said and sounded a bit guarded now. "Nothing bad, is it?"

"No, not at all. I wouldn't call you for none of that," I said and it was true.

I took a deep breath and I partially lied to her.

"I met a girl, and I didn't have my phone on me. She wrote her number on my hand and before I could put it in, the last couple of numbers rubbed off. Was hoping your man could help so I could, uh, run into her again. You know?"

There was a long pause on the other end of the line and finally Justice said, "Aww, that's really sweet! Hang on, he's actually in his den. Gimme a second here."

I heard her get up and move across either a room or the house. She knocked lightly and I heard her man Radar's voice muffled and indistinct.

"It's La Croix," I heard her say faintly, a little distant as she held the phone out or down.

"Yeah?" Radar had come closer and I heard some static as something rubbed against the phone's mic as it was passed over. "La Croix! Man, what's up?" he asked.

"I need a small favor," I said. "A personal one. No club business."

"Oh yeah? What's up?"

"It's about a girl..." I said and let my breath out slow and even. Somehow a knot of tension between my shoulders, that I hadn't even known I'd carried, loosened as I thought back to my encounter with Alina Bouchard only minutes ago, out front of her building and the club's compound.

At the way her wide, silvery eyes had looked up into mine. How it'd been the first time I'd even been close enough to look into those eyes.

They were a cool gray, the outer iris ringed in darker smoke – like the mist off the Bayou in the early morning light, before the sun had even finished clearing the horizon out through the cypress trees.

Her eyes reminded me of my most favorite time of day. Out there, in the swamps I grew up in, when the rest o' the world was still silent and sleeping. When I felt the absolute most alone that I ever did, and I enjoyed the fuck out of my solitude.

"How can I help?" Radar asked in my ear and I closed my eyes and nodded slowly to myself.

Yeah. I wasn't ready to let little miss Alina outta my sight. Not completely anyway.

I gave Radar what I had and downed the rest of the bourbon in my glass while he clacked at some keys on the other end of the line.

I stayed on with him, getting rife with nervous energy I just had to walk off. I wandered out through the club, letting my ugly fuckin' mug stave off any unwanted attention by glowering something spectacular.

Outside, the heat and humidity were a slap in the face with a warm, dead fish. The smell of the river wafted faintly this direction and it wasn't great. Most people disliked it, but to me it just smelled like home.

I stared out the open gate to the compound at the empty spot at the curb where the moving van had been parked. It was long gone, though. I looked up to the empty window of her apartment. The lacy, sheer, and ruffled curtains that framed the portal into her world were gone too.

Fuck.

I didn't like that, and I didn't like the anxiousness that I'd not see her again that knotted me up between the shoulder blades.

I wandered to the curb and stepped down into the street, wandering across and up onto the corner while I waited.

"What was the last name again?" he asked after a moment. "The spelling, I mean."

"Bouchard. B-O-U-C-H-A-R-D," I told him, spelling it out.

"Oh, shit. That's why," he muttered and went on about being a dumbass for having had it spelled wrong for a moment.

"Looks like she's moved, or just moved. New address isn't out there yet."

"You got where she works?" I asked, scuffing the toe of my boot through the strip of dried brown grass between the sidewalk and the curb in front of her building. I wasn't lookin' for nothing in particular but I guess I found it anyway.

A glint of gold caught my eye, metallic against the golden twist and ruin of the desiccated grass under my feet. I bent at the waist, phone to my ear, and plucked the gold band from the weeds. It was bent, slightly, from having been stepped on, but the moment I brought it up where I could see it? I knew it was hers.

The delicate filigree, the simple elegance, and the small chip of gemstone in the setting screamed that it belonged to the woman with the freckles and the fiery red hair.

I wrapped my fist around it, feeling the bite of the metal into my palm and I swear, I could feel a tenuous connection to her, out there, somewhere in the city.

"Ah, here we go. She's got her bartender's license. Clean record on that, and she works at a bar down on Bourbon. Need her schedule? Pretty sure I can crack their shit in a jiff if you do."

"Nah, man. Just the name of the bar," I said.

"Sure thing. I got you."

I looked up into the blue sky above and listened as a cicada screamed and wondered which place it would be that she worked at. If it was one of the classier joints that I would stick out in, or if it was a dive where I'd fit right in.

Guess I'd find out.

CHAPTER THREE

*A*lina...
  Maya and I fell into a giggling, shrieking tangle of limbs as she tried to wrestle the remote control out of my hands. I was trying to change it from whatever high drama reality trash television show she wanted to watch to something, *anything*, different.

"No, no, no!" she cried as I went in for the cheater's attack she always used on me, tickling her ribs to make her let go of the remote.

We tussled, and finally, victory was mine! I got the remote and spilled off the couch onto my butt, howling with laughter even as the floor beneath me bounced a few times from the downstairs neighbor punching or hitting the ceiling in a bid to get *us* to be quiet.

"Oh, shit!" I said in an ominous whisper around my laughter.

"Aw, they'll get over it." Maya waved me off. "Not like we do this *every* night."

I rolled my eyes and said, "Not how I want to impress the new neighbors!"

She made a dismissive "Pfft!" noise and said, "They're used to my bullshit, though."

I smiled and stifled a laugh behind my hand.

I'd moved out of my apartment to move *in* with Maya. She had a place just off the French Quarter – which, *yeah,* high-dollar real estate, but her family had owned this place for like, *ever*, and she had just kicked her last roommate out for stealing from her. She was renting my room to me for an absolute *steal.*

I couldn't complain. I mean, I was walking distance from work, had a great view from here for the parades when it came to that, and honestly, I was hoping to bring a little bit of calm and balance to my best friend who honestly did the opposite for me – but in a good way. She sort of had this magic way of getting me out of my shell and, I don't know, charged my social batteries?

I mean, I could switch it on at a moment's notice at work, could extrovert all night long, but the second the bar shut down? Blargh. I was done and ready to go home… unless Maya was around. Then I could stay up a little bit later, like now. It was something like four in the morning and I was as jazzed as I ever was at work as we play fought over remotes and spilled popcorn all over my couch – which had been in better shape than Maya's.

We'd had so much fun redecorating and incorporating both of our wildly differing eclectic styles into something that looked so fantastic in here.

My earth tones and greenery, her shiny modern metals and squared off furniture. The perfect blend of natural and modern.

Things felt right. I was happy. She was happy. The world was our oyster and nothing could stop us!

"Yeah, still!" I protested. "I'm the one that's gonna have to see and deal with them when you're model-and-fashion famous, jet setting off to New York, Milan, and Paris."

I struck a few duck-lipped poses, and she crossed her eyes and fell out laughing in a fresh set of giggles.

"You know you could do it, too!" she said, and I rolled my eyes and shook my head.

"No way," I said. "Not tall enough and way too many freckles."

"Oh, stop it! Modeling's changed by leaps and bounds, you know. Plus, your freckles are to die for. I would kill to have them."

I shook my head and flipped through shows on our favorite streaming service, landing on something I knew we both liked.

"Oo! Oo! Oo! Yes, please!" she cried excitedly.

"Much better than that stupid family reality drama," I said. "Those people are so insipid. I don't even know how they got famous or why you bother watching them," I said.

She stuck out her tongue at me. "Neah!"

"What?"

"Don't yuck my yum," she complained. "It's a total guilty pleasure. They make my family seem tame by comparison."

I laughed and shook my head.

"Mm, your family's not that bad," I told her.

She twisted her lips back and forth and said, "Not as bad as yours, fine, sure, I'll give you that – but they still suck in their own way."

"I don't know," I said. "Your dad gave you the apartment..." I looked around us and she rolled her eyes at me again.

"Yeah, only to keep me out of his hair."

I snorted. "Your dad's bald."

It was her turn to roll her eyes at me. "You know what I mean." She let out an exasperated sigh.

"Yeah." I nodded in agreement. "I know."

I scraped my bottom lip between my teeth and twisted my fingers around the spot where my great-grandmother's ring was supposed to be on my finger. Only a thin tan line remained, and I was still pretty heartbroken about it. It was the only thing I had left of her.

Maya sighed and said, "I'm sure it'll turn up..." But it sounded halfhearted at best. I nodded and forced a smile.

"I'm sure you're right."

I'd lost it in the move, and honestly? I didn't have a hope or a prayer of seeing it again. I mean, I never took it off, and it'd slipped off my finger somehow. It could be anywhere. I didn't think it was in a box in storage and I'd torn through *everything* that'd come here. I thought it was gone, gone... and that hurt.

The only bright spot in my childhood had been going to visit Gramma Mimi – no, that wasn't her name, it was Sarah, but I couldn't call her Gramma Gramma when it had been my grandma that took me to visit in the first place.

I didn't have the happiest of origin stories. My mother had me when she was sixteen. She didn't want me, but my grandma wouldn't hear of her getting an abortion. At the same time, my grandmother didn't want me either but guess what? Mom abandoned ship as soon as she was able and I honestly only remember meeting her once.

I was seven.

She'd come to my grandmother's to ask for money and I'd heard the whole fight. I didn't know what "rape" was, but my mother had flung the word at my grandmother like some sort of ice javelin and had screamed how she'd never wanted me in the first place. Likewise, my grandmother – a deeply Christian woman for all she never went to church on Sundays – had screamed back some shit about it being God's will and had demanded of my mother, "You think I want her? You think I want to do this shit all over again? It was bad enough with you!"

Let me tell you, that scars a kid and kids *know*. At least, I did. I mean, I never wanted for food, clothes, or a roof over my head and my grandmother did that single mom thing. She was sixty something now, and let me tell you what – she took a chainsaw to those apron strings.

Like, as soon as I was eighteen! I got home with her and Gramma-Gramma from my graduation to a load of packed bags and a "good luck."

I was lucky I had the savings I did and my grandma grandma? I had *never* seen her swear or say a single unkind word or *anything* until that day. She lost it on my grandmother and had blasted her into next week.

I *wasn't* kicked out that night – but whew, that battle raged. I swore as soon as I could get out, I would be out, and *as soon as I could* was the very next week. I pulled up stakes and never looked back. Still, I think the whole thing broke my grandma grandma's heart. She went back to her assisted-living facility and a few weeks later, she had a stroke.

She didn't make it much longer past that. A little under a year?

Still, she did accomplish one thing. She had completely written both my grandmother and my mother out of her will and left what meager money and possessions she had left to me.

I got the ring and her books. That was it. My grandmother took everything else anyway, and I didn't know how to fight it at all, so I just let it go. The only reason I got the ring was because my great-grandma had given it to me on one of my last visits before she died. Unable to speak, just looking at me beseechingly to take it as she pressed it into my hands with her gnarled ones.

I'd not taken it off since.

It'd fit perfectly for the longest time until I'd gotten involved with Patrick. I swallowed hard. Just one more reason to hate him. He'd stressed me out so much with his lies and his gaslighting me, making me feel crazy when I knew, *I knew I wasn't*! I'd lost so much weight, the ring became loose and had slipped off.

The only person I hated more than Patrick for that was myself for *letting* him get to me that way.

"Hey." Maya broke me out of my reverie and I looked up and smiled at her.

"What?" I asked.

"Nuh-uh," she said, shaking her head resolutely. "Don't do that."

"Do what?" I asked innocently.

"Think about them," she said. "Don't you dare."

"Sorry," I murmured.

"I said *no*, Queen!" She pushed against my shoulder with her toes in their pink fluffy low socks that she wore around the apartment, using them to slide over the polished hardwood floors.

I smiled and shook my head. See what I mean? She was the best.

We'd become friends when I was nineteen and we waitressed at the same place. Her dad had cut her off, and she'd been on the struggle bus for a bit. But she hadn't cared and we'd become fast friends, bitching about the grabby-hands practical-pedophile of a manager we'd had to work under.

Yeah, Maya had gotten fired from that job and arrested for assault when she'd dumped a tray of drinks on the floor and started wailing on that manager with the tray when he was getting more than a little too up close and personal with a fifteen-year-old waitress, having backed her into a corner.

I'd kept my job, mostly because I'd stood there too shocked to say or do anything.

It was like Maya had been born with all the fire in her spirit and I'd just gotten it in my hair.

I'd started looking elsewhere for employment right away, and Maya's dad had bailed her out of jail. Unfortunately, it didn't do much for their relationship being as Maya's dad was a prominent city political figure. He didn't care why she did it. All he cared about were the *optics*.

Boy, did I feel that. I was raised the same way, only I didn't know who the hell my grandmother had been trying to impress. She wasn't prominent in any way unless you considered her for the position of reigning Southern Ice Queen. Then she took the title to town and there wasn't anyone more prominent in the city than her – or so she thought. The irony of her name being *Karen* wasn't lost on me.

Anyway, Maya and I stayed friends. The best of friends. I'd managed through hard work and determination, as well as selling some of my art on the side, to work my way up in the restaurant industry from waitress to hostess, ping-ponging back and forth until I was old enough to legally serve and then bartend – where the *real* tips were at if you asked me.

Maya had beaten me there by a few months and had passed me along all kinds of tips and tricks, which was great and had helped a lot.

Then, somehow, some way, she'd found something more suited to her wild nature. She'd started working at a strip club behind the bar, and while she wouldn't dance, she'd somehow gotten into the world of escorting and *whew*… the money she made. I wished, but I could *never!* I just wasn't built like Maya was. She was resilient, fierce, brave beyond your wildest dreams.

…but not me.

No, I had way too many hang-ups from my pseudo-southern Baptist and thoroughly weird upbringing.

I don't think I would ever come to grips or understand how my grandmother came from my sweet grandma grandma. I totally understand how my bio mom came about from my grandmother, though. Sheesh.

We watched the sword-swinging fantasy epic with the long, silver-haired hero and the snappy dialogue between him and his Bard friend, who was the type of hot that it might as well be criminal with how dopey he could be.

We crunched popcorn and binged several episodes until I couldn't stop yawning and with a smirk, and the glimmer of sunrise coming in around the ratan blinds over our windows and French doors, Maya nudged me with her foot and sent me to bed.

I smiled tiredly and clambered to my feet.

"G'night, girl," she called after me, turning off the television.

"G'morning," I said, waving over my shoulder. I went into my room and shut the door.

I mean, it was what it was, and what it was, was morning. I hated getting it wrong… it was just one of my things.

CHAPTER FOUR

*L*a Croix...

"Lenny, boy, c'mere and see if you can get this man his part. I can't figure what the hell he's sayin'."

I had just set my tool tray down and was only half through wiping my hands on the filthy red rag I'd found somewhere out there in the yard when Big Saul called me over. I went to the front counter and frowned. The old-timer in front of the desk was one of my people – that's to say, one of the swamp people.

He looked at me through watery blue eyes and held out what he was lookin' for and I asked him a few questions. He perked up at the Cajun comin' out of my mouth and fired back in rapid French-Creole that I could keep up with, but barely. Language was like a muscle. If it went unflexed long enough, you lost some tone or whatever.

Still, I worked out well enough from the busted shit he handed me what it was he needed. Nodding, I picked my tool tray up off the counter and jerked my head at the man to follow me out into the yard full of weed-choked and rusting hulks of boat motors and hulls.

I wiped the sweat from my brow and midway through pulling his part, I had to stop for my phone ringing in the back pocket of my coveralls.

"Yeah?" I asked by way of greeting.

"P. it's me, Hex."

"I know who you are, asshole." I scowled. I hated talking on the phone.

"Got a problem, brother. Bring your big ass in when you're done there," he said.

I grunted an assent, then returned the phone to my back pocket.

"Heh." The old man I was pulling the part for grinned at me and spit tobacco juice on the ground. With a few more turns of my socket, I had the starter for his outboard free and was handing it over.

I told him Big Saul would handle the rest up front.

I looked to the sky, through the shadows cast by the surrounding trees and the Spanish moss hanging from them, and nodded to myself.

The day was almost done.

Did I need to work here? No. Was it the smart thing to do? Yes. Always good to have a day job to cover what a man did at night. I didn't need the money, but the government didn't know that. Nor did they *need* to know that.

Big Saul got quite the cut to punch my timecard and to pay me regular. He also got my help more often than he didn't. I was here, I did my job, and I did a good one at that.

When I wasn't here, he kept my alibi above board on the odd occasion I had shit to do during the day.

It was the way shit worked. He covered my ass; I greased his palm.

Fuck, why did that sound dirtier than it needed to?

I shucked off my coveralls and hung them up on their peg in the back before I pulled down and shrugged into my cut. Next, I took my ass out front to my bike, waving over my shoulder at Big Saul. He was on the phone behind the counter, the buzz and flicker of the fluorescent lighting over his head distracting as he grunted, "Mm-hm," into the phone cradled against his big, bearded cheek.

Big Saul was *big*. Something like five foot six, but like four hundred pounds. He had an encyclopedic knowledge of any type of engine or boat motor, though. Folks from all over the state in and out of every parish knew that Big Saul was the one to call when they couldn't figure it out.

He gave me a pair of raised eyebrows and a chin lift, acknowledging I was leaving without so much as breaking stride in his listening or conversation on the phone as he henpecked with two fingers on the ancient keyboard the invoice for whatever part he was gonna need pulled.

He still had three other guys here and out back in the yard. He didn't need me; so, I wasn't worried about it.

I wasn't overly worried about whatever the hell Hex wanted, either. Whatever it was, it'd be handled in its own time. No reason to get my blood pressure up. All that tended to do was make my short-fused temper even shorter and nobody wanted that.

If Hex was calling me, though, it meant one thing and one thing only... someone was fixin' to bleed or even die. I was that guy and there weren't no bones about it.

I rode into the city, making for the club's compound, and I found a few of the guys smoking angrily just inside the gate.

"'Bout fuckin' time you got here," Hex grumbled as I killed the engine to my bike and I swung my dark gaze in his direction.

"Where's the fucking fire at?" I demanded.

Hex sighed, pinning his hands to his hips as he hung his head low and I frowned. He looked like he had the weight of the fuckin' world on his shoulders and it wasn't like him. He was pretty chill most of the time, even when things got hot. He was usually the guy who was cool under pressure. Except he wasn't cool at all right now and I saw it in the glint in his eye when he looked back up at me.

"The prospect," he said.

I swung a leg over my bike and stood up, crossing my arms over my chest, and demanding, "Spill it, it's not like you to beat around the bush."

Hex sighed. "He got himself stabbed. He's at the hospital an' he's gonna be okay, but—"

"Who, what, when, where, why, and how?" I demanded, my scowl deepening. He cut to the chase.

"Who would be his own kin, some kinda family squabble. What over, I don't know but I have to suspect it has to do with his mamma," he said.

I grunted, giving a nod, and waited for him to continue.

"Anyhow, he got himself stabbed about an hour or so ago, an' called me up to let me know they was taking him in the ambulance to the hospital there downtown."

"Alright," I drawled. "Where'd he get stabbed at?"

"Near as I can tell, his momma's house."

"Do we know why?"

"If I had to guess, drugs… money… she ain't much of a mother near as I can tell. You know the type to come to the life," he said, and I nodded. Most of the men in with the likes of me and Hex came from broken homes. Hell, I wasn't any exception to that rule. My momma'd died giving birth to my little sister, who didn't much make it past a day beyond our mother. My daddy didn't give two fucks about me and let me know every minute of every day what a pain-in-the-ass burden I was to him and his getting his drink on.

Some of that was on the mend now that I was an adult, but not really at the same time… The Voodoo Bastards was more family than a lot of us had ever known and I had to bet it was for Louie, our prospect. It was time to show him how we looked out for each other.

"His momma the one to stab him?" I asked.

Hex shook his head. "Her boyfriend, not quite Louie's stepfucker or anything. Ain't been around long enough for that. Guess she's only been seein' this one a few months or whatever."

"What was Louie doin' over there?" I asked.

"Bringin' his momma some groceries," Hex said and his tone was flat, nonplussed, and I couldn't tell if he was pissed at Louie or the situation, or what.

I raised an eyebrow.

"I didn't get a lot," Hex said. "They were working on him, or whatever. Still don't know how takin' your mother groceries ends up in you gettin' stabbed."

I sucked my teeth and made a tsking sound while I calculated some things and said, "Well, I'm fixin' to find out. Take Axeman with you out to the hospital and see what you can get. I'll take Saint with me an' go pay dear ol' mom a visit an' see what's what."

Hex raised an eyebrow at me and asked, "You sure?"

"You think I'm gon' let it stand?" I asked, and he gave me a slightly feral grin.

"Nah, it's as it always was and ever been, retribution sure and swift."

"Get back at me with the details as soon as you can," I muttered.

"Need to know how far to go on puttin' the hurt on?" he asked.

"No, I know how far to go with that," I said and Hex gave me a careful nod.

"You know you should just let Saint and some of the other boys handle it," he said, and I gave him a look.

He sighed and nodded, saying "Awright, go on an' do what it is you're gonna do."

I nodded. He knew me well enough, and I rarely went too far left of center or did anything out of character on something like this. It was all business as far as I was concerned. I didn't let much get personal.

"Saint!" I called and Saint came jogging up. "You're with me," I said, and he gave a nod.

"On it, boss. I'll follow your lead."

I nodded and got back on my bike while Saint jogged on over to his, exchanging a few words with some of the other guys lingering in the yard inside the fence line.

"You watch yourself," Hex said as a parting shot.

I called out to his back as he walked away, "That's what I'm bringing Saint for."

Hex waved over his shoulder and went for the knot of brothers standing around. I fired up my Harley, big and flat black with purple pinstripe detailing that faded into green flourishes. Sharp and lines crisp, my bike stood out as unique unto itself, but not so much as to be ostentatious. I wasn't into loud and obnoxious. That'd all been Ruth and had helped lead up to his downfall in a way.

Saint fell in beside me and we maneuvered out the gate and down the street on the way down to one of the poorest neighborhoods in the city. While the club itself was in the lower ninth ward which had the reputation for being one of the poorest and the roughest, I knew Louie's momma's place was somewhere over in the seventh. I didn't know the exact address, but I'd been out that way once and Louie had pointed it out to some of us as we'd ridden by.

That boy loved his momma dearly, worked at earning a love back that just wasn't there to be given. I knew it because I'd lived it with my daddy. At a certain point it broke something inside you but Louie wasn't to that point yet… I didn't know if he was now, but it didn't matter. He was on the cusp of earning his full patch with us and was already all but one of us, so this was the last time any shit like this was about to go down with him.

In fact, we needed to have a club vote on it sooner rather than later given we were going to these lengths for the kid.

We pulled up down the block from the dilapidated shotgun house that'd the kid had been so proud to point out to some of the rest of the boys that late afternoon sometime last year, and we killed the bikes.

There were still a couple cop cars outside the place, and a woman sat smoking on the front steps.

She might have been attractive once, but now she was wrinkled and entirely too thin. Her reddish hair a bad dye job and kinked and crackling around her head with a straw-like texture. She looked like someone had poked a drinking straw in her and sucked out just about every nutrient a healthy body needed. Even all the way from here, Saint and I could see the crusty scabbed sores down the side of her leg where it was probably being eaten by whatever drug she'd been shooting.

She smoked furiously and shook her head at something the female cop asked her as she sucked on her cigarette. From here, I could see her eyes were as hollow as her fuckin' cheeks – empty and devoid of any fuckin' soul.

"*That's* Louie's momma?" Saint asked, and I didn't even have to look to see the disgust on his face when I could plainly hear it in his voice. It was a derision I shared. I mean, Louie was a good kid, as far as kids went. Twenty something and an unfortunate Army washout; he could and would have done well in the military if not for this bitch. He'd come running home when she'd OD'd on whatever the fuck and he'd gotten word of it. Loyal to a fault to the woman that'd birthed him, he'd fucked up any ability to remain by bailing to come to her rescue, and the Army had kicked him to the curb.

He'd crossed paths with the lot of us on the city's underground-fighting circuit. He was a good fighter, had heart, and liked to ride. Things just sort of naturally progressed to what it was today.

Still, I stared at this woman and all I felt was a certain amount of anger at her mixed with my disgust. She'd yanked chance after chance out from in front of her boy with her selfishness, and it was time for that shit to stop.

"How you want to play this?" Saint asked.

"We got all fuckin' day," I replied. "We wait."

"Looks like we're gonna be waitin' a while, boss. I don't see any dude that looks like he could stick ol' Louie. Think he was arrested?"

"Probably. As for this," I said, thrusting my chin at the scene unfolding out in front of us, "we wait long enough for the pigs to fuck off, and we have a go at Louie's mom."

"You think Louie gon' be right with that?" Saint sucked his teeth, his keen gaze fixed on the cops and Louie's junky mom.

"Louie don't get a say no more," I declared. "The blood of the covenant is thicker 'n the water of the womb."

Saint gave a sage nod. "Too right," he agreed and leaned forward, bracing his forearms on his gas tank.

And so, we waited...

CHAPTER FIVE

*a*lina...

"Lina!" I whirled behind my bar and I could *feel* my face light up as Maya leaned way over it.

"Hey, you! What brings you around these parts?" I called over the thumping bass of the bar music.

"I got a gig!" she cried. "Modeling, this time!"

"Alright!" I cried, and I hugged her over the bar.

"Hey, watch out now!" Mike cried as I disengaged from Maya and nearly stepped on him as he passed behind me.

"Sorry!" I cried, and he waved me off, hitting up a guy further down the bar to see what he wanted.

I smiled and called out, "We gon' celebrate when I get home?"

"I can't," she called. "I have a date." She made a face, and I knew it was one of *those* dates. I didn't judge, though. She was an adult and could do what she wanted. To be honest, she made *really* good money, to the point that I just *wish* that I could do it... but I just couldn't. Not me. I made good tips behind the bar, but nothing like what Maya could make in just a couple of hours with one of her... eh-hem... *gentleman callers*, as I liked to call them.

"Okay, I love you!" I called out. "Be careful!"

"Aren't I always?" she called back with a shrewd grin and I had to grin back.

I rolled my eyes, my giggle swallowed by the loud music and the general bar noise as she blew me a kiss and melted into the crowd.

I set myself to working the bar and mixing up drinks for a group of ladies just out to have a good time.

It was a busy night, thick with tourists, and I swear it felt like it was over in a flash.

I was closing, when Mike sauntered up, counting out the night's cash tips out loud. He was a good guy – always fair and always made sure to be totally transparent.

"Whew! We done good tonight," he said, slapping the stack of bills against the edge of the bar.

"How good?" I asked curiously.

He grinned and said, "Three hundred."

"Not bad," I said.

"A piece." He arched a brow and handed me my cut. I nearly swallowed my tongue.

"Hot damn!" I cried, taking my share, folding it in half, and sticking it into my front pocket.

"Good work there, hot stuff," he said with a wink and wandered away.

I laughed a little and shook my head. Tomorrow night I'd be working with Dorian which would be nice. Dorian walked me home at night but alas, Mike lived the opposite way.

We finished closing and Mike locked up behind us. With a wave goodbye, we parted, walking in opposite directions up and down Bourbon while revelers crawled the streets in their drunken confusion, laughing and shouting. I kept my hands in my pockets and a death grip on my apartment keys as I walked briskly in the direction of home.

I had my pepper spray, and my wits, but still, I didn't have a three hundred and sixty degree visual. I could only focus on what was in front of me or off to my sides. How was I to know that a shadow had detached from one of the bar fronts and drifted along the sidewalk behind me?

CHAPTER SIX

*L*a Croix...

The front door of Louie's mamma's place folded like cheap origami under my boot, the doorframe shattering as she shrieked and sputtered coming up off the filthy living room couch. I backhanded her a good one, and she flew back onto it, her knees coming up to her chest as her hands went to her mouth.

I sat down on the coffee table across from her and leveled her with my gaze.

The first thought that struck me was that it was Louie's eyes starin' back into my own, showing too much white around 'em as the fear set in. Saint had my back, standing in the doorway, leaning nonchalantly against the frame, his back to me, facing out into the street.

"What do you want?" Mamma Louie demanded.

"Want to know where your man stays," I said.

"Here, he stays here," she said. "But he's in jail."

"For now," I told her and then I gave her a hard look. "But he don't stay here no more. You feel me?"

She was still, too still; a frightened little rabbit – and I could almost taste that fear riding the tainted and fetid air of her drug den house.

"Your boy, you even care what happen to him?"

"He was askin' fer it," she said and her voice was high and frightened. I smacked her again, and she started to cry. I didn't care.

"Wrong answer, woman."

"What do you want from me?" she wailed between tears and I told her.

"Your boy, you're dead to him, y'hear?" I demanded. She looked at me wide-eyed.

"You gonna kill me?" she asked, breathy.

"You ever take advantage of 'im again, I just might," I said.

"You can't do that," she said and I gave her a feral nasty grin.

"Bitch, I do what the fuck I want."

I shoved a business card against her chest, plain white, with just a single number printed on it. The number to my burner.

"That man o' yours shows back up here, you call this number. You don't, and I find out about it, I'll do more 'n smack your bitch ass around a little bit," I told her.

She stared at me, mutely, and when I understood that *she* understood, I got to my feet.

"Don't fuckin' test me," I told her over my shoulder. "I am not the one."

Saint and I departed and rode back to the club.

Hex had texted an hour or two ago with an update on our boy.

He'd had to be put in surgery. They'd saved his ass, but it was close. He'd been bleedin' like a stuck pig. That'd just served to piss me off even more.

Back at the club, I called a meetin' – everyone had turned up, which was good. We'd voted unanimous that ol' Louie be patched in and I'd given Hex the order. By the time Louie got out the hospital, his cut would be ready.

That ought to cheer the man up; if'n he could pass his final test.

Business concluded, my need for violence gone pretty much unsated, I stared up at the darkened window to little Alina's vacant apartment.

Came to be, I could look up there at her lacy embroidered curtains and could find a measure of peace even if she wasn't home, but those curtains were gone now and the place just felt empty inside, like me.

I got up and flicked my joint against the cracked asphalt and sighed.

"You leavin'?" I heard Saint call out. I glanced back and nodded, and he saluted me with his beer.

"Shiny side up, cher," he called, and I threw him some chin and went for my bike to do somethin' just for *me* for a change.

I took a leisurely ride, turning down this way and up that a way, wending my way the long way toward Bourbon Street, and where I knew that my little Alina would be.

I walked along the cracked sidewalk through partiers and revelers. The ones with enough common sense left parting before me like the red sea. The rest too stupid to move got shoulder checked or just plain shoved the fuck out of my way. Nobody was drunk enough or stupid enough to nut up on me.

I was slightly disappointed by that.

I stopped in line outside the bar that Radar had named as the one Alina had last worked a, and showed my ID to the bouncer, who looked from it to me a couple times before his eyes settled on my cut. He frowned, and I raised an eyebrow, daring him to tell me no colors inside the bar – but he didn't. He wasn't stupid, and I wasn't here to fight, just to have a beer and look at my girl.

I ended up at a corner table with a good view of the bar, and a waitress came and took my order.

I told her my favorite beer and was immediately transfixed by the redhead behind the bar. It took me a few seconds to realize the waitress hadn't budged and was waiting on something.

"What?"

"I said we don't have that. Would you like something else?" she called over the loud music.

"Oh, just bring me something like it, I don't care what," I said, waving her off.

She drawled, "Ooookayyy," and whisked herself off and out of my line of sight.

I watched Alina through the crowd, pleased that she drew my beer from the tap, and waited for it to come to me.

"Thanks," I told the waitress and peeled off a hundred. "Just keep it coming."

She gave a nod and wandered off and I was left to watch my girl. The sense of peace her beautiful face, lovely heart, and angelic soul brought me, settling over my shoulders like a mantle.

Last call came and went a few hours later, and I picked myself up, left a generous tip for the waitress on top of whatever else was left out of the Benjamin that I'd given her, and I headed out the door in the thick of the throng leaving the bar.

I took up some real estate against one of the posts holding up a balcony across the way and watched the bar's front door.

It took her a while, but eventually, she emerged and the anxiousness that'd been building in her absence faded back into the background again.

She waved at the other dude that'd been behind the bar, and I gritted my teeth, unhappy with him as they parted ways.

She went up the street, striding as though she was on a mission, and I detached myself from the post and kept pace with her from across the way.

CHAPTER SEVEN

*A*lina…
It happened in a flash. I didn't see him, but with speed that was near blinding, a hand was over my mouth and I was off my feet, hurtling sideways into the mouth of an alley.

I tried to scream, but his hand was over my nose and mouth and the back of my skull was smacking painfully into the brick wall, my back fetching up hard against it as my assailant spun me and shoved me into it.

He kept his hand over my mouth. His other hand he cupped between my legs over my jeans.

"You be nice and quiet now, y'hear?" he demanded, and I blinked, trying to see but there was light behind him, casting his face in shadow. He rubbed me suggestively through my jeans and said, "Aw, yeah… now that's nice. That's real nice."

I whimpered behind his hand and struggled, both of my hands wrapping around the wrist of the hand that covered my mouth like a band of iron.

The light behind him winked out for a second and he made a strangled noise. Something warm, wet, and smelling of copper pennies hit my face and chest, splashing over my hands.

He slipped to the ground choking, both his hands to his throat.

He was lanky, white, balding, and covered in jailhouse tattoos, and he was bleeding profusely from between his fingers around his own throat.

I felt nauseous, the world swimming, streaks of flashing black in front of my eyes. I gasped, and the taste of his blood flooded my mouth and I gagged, staggering. I couldn't get enough air. Try as I might, no matter how much I tried dragging any breath in through my nose, it was like soup.

"Easy," a low and deep voice rumbled from nearby me.

I choked, gagging, and a hand clamped down on my shoulder. I dragged in a breath to scream but all I could see, feel, and smell was my assailant's blood. There was so much blood! I staggered under that grip and there was a rushing in my ears. I grabbed onto something slick and in places rough, digging my fingers in as my vision went and the world narrowed down to a long, dark, black tunnel as I fell.

CHAPTER EIGHT

*L*a Croix…

He was so fixated on her, he never even noticed I was coming. I got up behind him, knife at the ready, and I grabbed him, forcing his head forward and his chin to his chest. At the same time, I drew the razor edge of my Balisong blade across his throat.

Most people would have grabbed him by his bald fuckin' head and ratcheted his head all the way back – but I knew better. That wasn't any way to cut a man's throat unless you wanted him to live.

No, if you wanted to perform maximum damage? You wanted the best chance at making that fucker bleed out fast? You pushed his head forward. It brought all the blood vessels and veins to the edge of the blade, let that steel kiss his throat like a lover, muscle and sinew parting in a liquid rush.

I dropped his ass to the dirty-ass alley floor and smirked as he choked on his own blood, thinking to myself – *That's what you get for touching what's mine.*

Alina staggered on her feet, making a strangled noise before it terminated in an awful retching noise.

"Easy." I tried to steady her on her feet, but she staggered, her freckled face pale in the light from over my shoulder, from the mouth of the alley.

She grabbed onto my cut, her clear gray eyes stark and terrified as she looked up at me, but I knew she didn't see me. Lightning quick, I folded the Balisong and shoved it into my pocket.

"I've got you," I murmured, but she was already sagging in my grip. I dipped, grunting as I came up with her in my arms.

I kicked out at the man wheezing at our feet and waited for a spate of passerby to go by on the sidewalk outside the alleyway.

I stopped at the mouth of the alley and stepped out into a lull between throngs of tourists and strode up the sidewalk… just taking my drunk girlfriend back to her place.

It's what I projected with every stride – that this was normal. All of this was perfectly normal, even as the thrill of the kill was overtaken by a total rush of another sort. The rush of having my little Alina in my arms.

I made it to her apartment building and hit random buzzers until someone buzzed back. I lucked out, but at the same time made a note of the apartment – because they buzzed open the front door to the lobby without even coming over the intercom to find out who it was entering. So, in effect, I was lucky for the purpose I needed but at the same time, I didn't like the fact that my woman could so easily be gotten to. Something about that would have to change.

I dismissed it for now, taking the stairs in even steady strides up to her floor and stopped at her door.

I set her down carefully on her feet, leaning her up against the wall, trapping her body with mine as I went through her pockets and came out with her keys. She had a seafoam green mace canister attached to her keys, but she'd never even had the chance with it. Hadn't thought to actually use it.

I worried for her, walking home alone in the wee hours of the morning like that with no one to watch her back. I mean… if I hadn't been there…

I tamped down my hatred at the thought. I'd already killed the bastard once and there wasn't any doing it again. Hell, I doubted it would even make the news. If it did, it would only be because it was either a slow news day or the fact that it'd happened right off of tourist-rich Bourbon.

I keyed us into her apartment, tossed her keys into the bowl on the table just inside the door, and jockeyed her into position in my arms, lifting her again.

I knew her room the moment I saw it.

Earthy and organic, the furniture a tasteful mishmash of things that could almost be antique but definitely wasn't in the antique price range. Probably, a good portion of it, had been rescued off the street, waiting for the trash pickup. Stuff that she'd lovingly restored by her own hand in the interest of thrift and economy.

I knew about the dresser. Had seen her in the courtyard on the side of her old building redoing it. The results up close were nice. Very nice, but her... *fuck*.

I turned on the bedside lamp. A sturdy metal and glass base, bronze, and a crackle effect amber glass. Something out of the seventies, probably. Something she'd made look older, from a bygone era, with a hand-stitched paneled lampshade. The kind with the beading and the fringe – a wire frame paneled in tulip fluted decadence and lovingly crafted in peach, pink, and cream hues. The material satin and lace, the fringe satiny and held at the apex of points and swoops with beads.

Again, I saw her hand in it, and I was proud. She made such beautiful things.

The light was muted, and I appreciated that. The golden glow shimmered in her fiery copper locks that were like silk against my fingers as I lowered her head to the cream pillow beneath it.

I winced at the swelling lump on the back of her head and I worried. She'd been out for a while, and I knew that could be cause for concern. Usually, a motherfucker got knocked out in my presence, I didn't have to worry about it so much, seeing as I was usually the one to render them unconscious... but she was a different story.

She was covered in arterial spray, along her graceful neck, a wide swath of it across her mouth and chin. It was dried and flaking by now, and I hated it. Worried for her, and about what diseases that junky drunkard dipshit could have had coursing through his veins before I'd emptied them out on the stinking alley floor.

I couldn't leave her like this. I needed to clean her up. She couldn't stay marred like this.

I went to her dresser, opened a drawer, and found lacy underthings. That pleased me. She had a lot of matching sets. A lot of satin, silk, and soft lace. I liked that. I closed the drawer without touching and went to the next.

In one of the bottom right drawers, I found a slick pile of satin and silk; and just what I was looking for. I laid the long nightgown out on the corner of the foot of her bed and with a lingering look at her angelic sleeping face, I went from the room to find the supplies I would need.

I found the washcloth and soap in the bathroom, and a big metal bowl in the kitchen. I filled it with warm, gently steaming water, and I returned to her.

I cleaned her up carefully and as gently as I could. I wasn't used to being gentle, but it was… nice.

Her skin was soft, her soap fragrant and delicate, lightly perfuming her skin. I knew I was obsessed and that there wasn't any cure for it. I also knew it was unhinged being here, doing what I was doing, but hey, I'd come to grips with that part of myself a long-ass fucking time ago.

I washed and wrung the cloth countless times and worked carefully at slipping her out of her denim jacket and the bar tee she wore beneath it. Every bit of her clothing went into a pile on the hardwood of her apartment floor, off her bedroom's area rug.

I would take them with me. Burn them. I didn't want any evidence of what'd happened anywhere near her.

I vaguely over worried for a moment about her hair, about the wall behind her, but she was pure. Radar had said she had no record, not even a parking or a traffic ticket. She was too good. Certainly, too good for the likes of me… although now, after being so close to her, after washing and dressing her and laying her back down softly in her bed, I didn't think I could handle anyone else being near her. I certainly couldn't handle the thought of another man touching her like I just had.

Still, it would be best if I kept this as a thing from afar, for her sake more than mine.

I sat at her hip and watched her facial expression twist.

She would wake soon, and I didn't want her to see me. I didn't want to have to answer questions or watch the fear flash in her eyes.

I'd already seen that once when I'd helped her with her couch. That flash of alarm was still a fresh wound even a month and more later.

I swallowed and touched lightly the dented ring on its black cord around my neck. The piece of her I held close to my heart…

I wanted her to have a piece of me.

Was compelled somehow…

I thought about it, and finally, I looked down at my cut.

There were several patches on the front that were gifted or earned, but only one of them was starting to peel. The iron-on adhesive starting to give way. I'd needed to sew it on for a while, I just hadn't gotten around to it.

It read one of my life mottos – *Silence is better than bullshit.*

Once upon a time, it'd been gifted to me by Ruthless. It was a reminder to me, to stay in my lane and to do better than he had because toward the end there? Only thing to come out of his mouth had been a diatribe of bullshit.

Still, he was my friend, and if ever there was anything close to a regret for a kill I'd done, his was the one which weighed heaviest.

I pulled the patch from my cut and tucked it into her curled fingers at her side.

She whimpered and turned her head slightly and I stood carefully. I didn't want to move too hard or too quick. I didn't need her to wake prematurely. I bent carefully and put my lips to her forehead. She sighed out softly and relaxed again.

I straightened, letting my hand slip from hers which was a peculiar sort of exquisite agony.

Then, I gathered her bloody things and left her. I stopped at her door to go through her pockets and put anything I found along with her keys in the wooden bowl by the door and then with a hard sigh did the hard thing. I went out the door, twisted the lock at the knob and shut it behind me, securing her alone inside.

CHAPTER NINE

*A*lina...

I woke to sunlight streaming between the slats of the wooden venetian blinds over my bedroom window. The light and gauzy curtains to either side hadn't been drawn the night before to diffuse the hard light that managed to creep around the edges and between the slats of the blinds and that made me frown.

I never forgot to do that... why did I?

I sat up and put a hand to the throbbing ache in the back of my head, wincing at the bruised sensation radiating through the back of my scalp and at the knot that took up residence in my stomach as I gently palpated the goose egg I found there.

I gasped; the very breath stolen out of my lungs when I saw what I was wearing. I clenched my fist at my hip and blinked at the rough fabric sensation that was in it. I brought my hand up off the top of my covers which remained undisturbed beneath me and read the rough black patch with white writing on it.

Silence is better than bullshit.

I frowned in confusion and looked around and down at myself again. I was in a nightgown that I had thrifted once upon a time. The cream satin hugging what I had that passed for curves, and the lace trim elegant. It was only something I wore on special occasions. You know, for like a partner or if I was feeling blue and just needed to pick myself up and feel a little pretty for a change.

It was one of my very favorite things. Something I cherished; and so, it was something I didn't wear often.

So why was I wearing it now?

I couldn't remember... I mean, the last thing I *did* remember was leaving the bar and setting out for home. I didn't know how I got here, or what happened, but clearly, I'd taken some kind of a knock to my head because *ow.*

I got out of bed slowly and went to Maya's room and stared at her empty made bed, perplexed.

I knew she had a... a... a *date* – for lack of a better term – last night; for lack of a better term; but she *never* stayed out overnight. She *always* came home. That was part of the deal.

I worried and went looking for my clothes from the night before but I couldn't find them. What I *did* find were my things – like my keys, phone, wallet, all the stuff from my purse, gathered in the bowl we used for our keys and loose change. The cash from my tips from last night was all there, too. I counted it. Three hundred and three dollars. All there. But my purse and my clothes – all gone and I do mean *gone*, nowhere to be found in the entire apartment! I looked.

I'd found one of our popcorn bowls in the kitchen sink and when I shuffled into the bathroom, I found one of the decorative washcloths missing off the towel rack. My confusion only mounted as I discovered my soap had somehow relocated to the bathroom countertop as well. I put it back in the shower and I felt sick, worried, afraid, and uncertain. *Just what had happened last night?*

I thrust the feelings aside as the worry for Maya surged anew. I swallowed hard, and with my phone in my hand from where I'd found it with the rest of my things on the entry table, I padded back into my room with it. It was dead. I needed to plug it in. I did, and I sat on the edge of the bed, barely able to breathe, as I held my breath, waiting for the screen to indicate it had enough charge to turn it on.

"Yes!" I cried, and some of the tension leaked out of me before returning as I anxiously waited for the screen to turn on.

I swallowed hard and when the phone had cycled through all of its startup bullshit, I held my breath again for precious seconds as I waited for a text, a voicemail, something; *anything* to let me know Maya was okay to come through...

Except there was nothing.

"Shit," I muttered with feeling.

I tried to call her but it went straight to voicemail.

"This is Maya!" her voice sang out cheerily. *"You know what to do..."*

The tone sounded, and I spoke, "Yeah, hi, Maya, it's Lina. Where are you? Call me as soon as you can. The strangest thing has happened and I need to know you're okay. Love you, girl. Bye."

I ended the call and let out a breath and looked up and around. Nothing else seemed to be out of place in the apartment, other than the things I'd already noted.

I didn't know what to do. I mean, calling the police seemed stupid. I wasn't harmed except for the bump on my head. Yes, things had been stolen... but like, nothing of *value*. My keys, phone, cards, identification, and even cash was all accounted for.

Besides, what would they do? Likely just take a report and leave. I didn't like it, but what else could and would be done?

I checked the front door. It was locked at the knob already and I threw the deadbolt just to feel a little bit more secure. With nothing left to do, I waffled between more sleep and a shower.

With the amount of anxiousness and worry I was feeling, I opted for the shower first. Then once out, I called Dorian.

"Hey, what's up?" he asked sleepily and I scraped my bottom lip between my teeth.

"I don't know," I said, and I heard him sit up.

"Lina, what's wrong?" he asked, and I sniffed.

"Uh, something really weird is happening. Maya had a date, and she's not home and I don't know... I'm, I'm scared."

"I'm coming over," he said, and relief flooded me. He took the phone away from his mouth and I heard him say, "Marcus, wake up. Something's up over at Lina and Maya's. We gotta go."

He came back onto the line and told me to hang tight and that he would be here in fifteen. All I could do was warble a broken "thank you" into the phone. I didn't know what was happening. All I knew was that any sense of security I had lay shattered around me and it was some kind of special agonizing that I didn't know *why*.

CHAPTER TEN

*L*a Croix...

"What the hell you get up to last night?" Hex asked. "You look like you ain't slept."

"I didn't," I told him, adding, "And never you mind what I got up to."

He raised an eyebrow at me and fixed me with a hard look. "You wanna come again?" he asked coolly and I had to give it to him – he was right. We'd agreed no secrets, but then again, every man had his secrets and my little Alina was mine. She was something that I kept closely guarded. The one thing I allowed myself. The one thing I called my own and would not share.

I grunted. "It's nothin' to do with the club," I told him. "It's personal."

His other eyebrow joined the first, rocketing into his hairline.

"Personal? Outta you?" he spit. "Well, I'll be damned."

"I miss something important?" I demanded.

"Naw, not overly so. Saint filled me in about your trip to Mamma Louie's."

I grunted and nodded. "She ain't called yet."

"You think she's gonna?" he demanded, and I lifted a shoulder in a shrug.

"She don't, it's gon' be a case of play stupid games win stupid prizes. I won't let the insult to Louie or the club stand. Somebody's gon' pay. If it's not her man, it'll be her."

Hex eyed me, his gaze guarded and neutral.

"You ain't think Louie's gonna have some feelin's about that?" he asked carefully.

"We're gon' find out," I said, and I jerked my head in the direction of the bikes.

"Visiting hour upon us?" he asked.

"I do believe it is," I said, and he nodded.

"Awright, now. Let's do it."

We rode out to the hospital and took ourselves up to Louie's room. Collier was sittin' with him. When we walked through the door, Collier looked up tiredly from where he sat in the chair by the bed and got up for me, moving aside so I could sit with our boy.

"Hey, boss," Louie said, and he sounded so tired.

He was deathly pale, and his expression pinched. I asked, "You hurtin' boy?"

"Not too bad, just tired mostly. You need me t' git outta here?"

"Naw." I shook my head and looked him over.

His face crumpled a little bit and he said, "Don't suppose you'll spare my momma?"

I kept my gaze steady and even on his light green eyes and said, "It's up to your momma if she gon' spare herself."

His face crumbled further, and I told Collier, "Give us the room."

Collier went out without another word and Hex closed the door and leaned up against it.

"You go 'head and let whatever you got inside out. No judgment here," I said and Louie broke, his face crushed under the weight of his sorrow. He wept, and I couldn't say I blamed him for it. He was still young. Barely twenty, shit – not even old enough to fuckin' drink by citizen standards… and all the boy wanted was his fuckin' momma. But what he wanted and what she was didn't exist in the same woman.

"You gotta let this go, son," Hex said, but not unkindly. "She ain't do you a single goddamn favor. Not once... and it's a fuckin' shame, too."

I agreed wholeheartedly.

"She revoked her privilege of callin' you family," I said. "She don't deserve you, brother."

Louie looked at me astonished and asked, voice trembling, "Does... does that mean...?"

I looked back over my shoulder at Hex who pulled Louie's fresh cut out from behind his back where he'd had it tucked up under his.

"Almost," I said, taking it from Hex and putting it in his lap. "You gotta heal first before you get your colors. You gotta heal, and you gotta handle this business with your momma's man. I gave her an ultimatum last night. She calls me when he gets hisself out, or we come for her and you know I keep my promises."

Louie paled and nodded, unfolding the cut in his lap, his fingers, with the IV leading into the back of his hand, running over the name flash on the front of the leather vest that read *Loup Garou*. It's why we called him Louie for short. His drunk ass told some stupid story one night about how he seen one in a park at the edge of Lake Pontchartrain. Even stone cold sober, he swore by that shit, and so the name stuck.

"I don't wanna hurt her," he said sadly. "She's still my momma."

"Somebody ought t' tell *her* that," Hex muttered and fresh pain lanced through behind Louie's eyes. I could be sympathetic, but that wasn't going to help Louie become strong, nor would it put his true loyalties to the rigorous test that being a part of this club required.

"You got your choice, man. The club, or her," I said, and I put hands to my knees and pushed my tired ass back up onto my booted feet.

"Heal first. Tackle the rest later," Hex advised and Louie nodded absently, his eyes fixed on the fully flashed-out cut, the only thing missing? The big patch with the club's purple, gold, and green, the Baron Samedi with his top hat bustin' out the fleur-de-lis on the back.

Hex opened the door, and we joined Collier out in the hallway.

"Go on home," Hex said to Col. "I'll stick around with him until another brother can come 'round."

I nodded and jerked my head at Collier to walk with me.

He fell into step beside me and heaved a big sigh in the elevator once the doors shushed shut.

"How's he doin'?" I asked him and he nodded.

"He'll be alright," Collier said.

"You hear any o' what was said?" I asked.

"Wasn't listenin' at key holes, boss."

I fixed him with a look and he colored faintly.

"I heard what you told him," he finally admitted.

"Think he'll pass the test?" I asked, when what I really wanted to know was *"do you think I'm asking too much?"* but I was the president. I couldn't appear weak. That was something that wouldn't end well for any man under the banner of the Voodoo Bastards' name.

Collier nodded. "He might hesitate a minute – I don't know a man who wouldn't. Not when it's their momma…"

I nodded, and the elevator stopped. The doors opened and without looking at Collier, I told him the cold hard truth, "I wouldn't."

He swallowed audibly and said, "An' that's why you're the boss man."

I nodded slowly as we stepped out into the hospital's lobby to traverse it on over to the parking garage's bank of elevators.

"Not something any of you boys should forget, neither," I told him.

"No worries there, boss. I don't think any of us could."

"Good deal," I said.

We stopped at the bikes in the garage and Collier looked up at me and said, "Louie's been good to us. Time for us to be good to him. We don't let a brother fail. We don't let a brother fall. He'll do what needs doin', boss. We're his family now."

I nodded slowly, keeping my face devoid of emotion when all I wanted to do was grin like a fool with pride.

"That's the right answer, C. Just what I wanted to hear," I told him and climbed onto my bike.

"Silence is better than bullshit," he said and I looked over at him. "You lost your patch, boss."

I did quirk a smile then and said, "I didn't lose it. I know right where it is, and it's right where I want it to be."

Collier gave me a dubious look and said, "Whatever you say, boss."

He fired up his bike, and I started up mine. We rode back to the club. Once I saw my tired brother through the gate, I split off and headed on out of the city, pointing myself toward the swamp I and my blood family had called home for generations.

I killed the bike out back of the ol' family homestead – the house I grew up in, way up on its stilts.

"Where the fuck you been?" my daddy demanded, coming down the bank to the old dock as I unwound the line, tying my old boat in place.

"Places," I muttered in consternation.

"Oh yeah? Doin' what?" he demanded, spitting. I looked up at him as he eyed me with his light blue and watery eyes – the complete opposite of my own. I'd gotten my mother's eyes.

"Things," I answered shortly.

He huffed a laugh that was a mix of disgust with a shot of derision.

"The fuck you want from me?" I demanded.

"Some goddamn respect might be nice," he shot at me.

I looked up at him and ripped on the cord, starting up my boat motor.

"Should have thought of that a long while back when you was whoopin' my skinny ass as a kid," I told him curtly and motored my way away from the dock, his angry fuckin' scowl burning twin holes in my back.

I couldn't wait for his fuckin' cancer to take him, but the bitter old fuck was too spiteful to let it take him down easy.

He always was a prick. Cancer honestly just seemed to make his ass meaner.

Just meant I had to be meaner than that.

I closed my eyes, the sun lighting the world on fire with the blood coursing through my eyelids as I turned my face up into the punishing warmth.

The same copper fire of her hair that'd felt like silk between my fingers, a sensation that'd chased the rage and pain away for a time and made me damn near calm.

I'd never met anyone or anything like my little Alina Bouchard... I didn't think anything other than a long ride by myself would ever work to make me calm.

I always figured I would be a lonely soul. That it was probably all that I deserved... but she made me want more.

I just didn't know how to go about it.

CHAPTER ELEVEN

*A*lina...

I sat on our living room couch and fretted over my missing friend. Dorian and Marcus were here, Dorian pacing back and forth in front of the television while Marcus, who was one of the sweetest, most compassionate men I'd ever met, sat beside me on the couch, rubbing comforting circles on my back through my thin, oversized tee.

"Well fine! She's been missing for twenty-four hours, then!" Dorian cried into his phone.

He made an exasperated noise and swiped a hand over his face.

He shook his head, and I felt crestfallen, a creeping tendril of dread seizing around my heart and squeezing.

"Yeah, well, thanks for nothing, then."

He hung up and gripped his phone in such a way, shaking it as though he was ready to throw it. He looked over at me and his boyfriend and sighed.

"No dice," he said.

"I gathered that," I said glumly.

"What do we do now?" Marcus asked.

"According to the police? We wait," Dorian said and didn't look at all happy about it.

I had told them everything I could remember, and now that Dorian was off worrying about Maya, which we could apparently do nothing about for the time being, he focused his energy onto me.

"I think you should come stay with us for a night or two. Call off work tonight. I can hustle and maybe call in Jonathan if he'll come in."

I was already shaking my head.

"No," I said. "No, no, no. I can't sit, cooped up somewhere with nothing to do – I'll just go crazy. And like I said, nothing but the clothes I was wearing last night is missing. Which is creepy, and weird, I know," I said, holding up a hand to stave off his protests. "But I don't *feel* like I'm in any trouble or danger and—"

"Okay, now is not the time to go all crystals and astrology witchy woo-woo, girl," Marcus protested before Dorian could.

I couldn't help it. I snarked a bit of a laugh at that and shook my head.

"I'm not – really," I protested, then thought about it. I was biting my bottom lip again and I let it go to say, "Okay, maybe I am, but for real. I don't think I'm in any danger here. Quite the opposite. I feel safe as can be. I'm far more worried about *Maya*."

"Well, we're worried about the *both of you*," Dorian countered and I nodded.

"I get that, but I'm here and I'm fine. We should really be focusing on Maya."

"Right, but where do we even start?" Marcus asked, and I sighed.

"That's the million-dollar question right there," I said.

"Where's her computer?" Dorian asked. "Doesn't she book all of this online or whatever?"

I nodded. "Her laptop is in her room but I think she uses her phone for most of it."

"Well, let's see what we can do," Dorian argued, and I nodded. I got up, Marcus following suit, and we went into Maya's modern-esque room. I sat at her desk which was simple and minimalist and keyed the laptop screen to life by pressing "enter" several times.

We were immediately greeted by a lock screen asking for a personal identification number.

"Any ideas?" Marcus asked.

I tried the last four digits of her phone number. Nope. I tried the last four digits of *my* phone number – no again. I sighed in frustration and Dorian asked, "You know her PIN for her bank card or whatever?"

I tried it – and bingo.

I rolled my eyes and said, "I should have thought of that first."

I went through her email and found the one that listed the hotel, date, time, and the name of the guy she was supposed to meet. First name only, no other identifying information. That was upsetting to me.

She'd always said she had everything. Name, work, all that stuff and that she was as safe as safe could be.

"God, Maya... *why?*" I muttered under my breath.

"Call the hotel," Dorian said evenly. Marcus was already on his phone, looking up the number and dialing.

They wouldn't tell us anything... but of course, I wouldn't honestly expect them to.

I hated this. I hated it so much.

"Has she ever done this before?" Dorian asked, hopeful. I knew he was grasping at straws; hoping that I would say yes and that he could ratchet his anxiety down a notch. That Maya would walk through the door any minute with a "sorry!"

I wanted that more than anything – for us to just be mad at her for a while, and that would be that... but... I just couldn't lose this sense of just absolute *dread* I carried in the center of my chest. The weight of it undeniable, the sense that last night at the bar was going to be the last time that I saw my friend and how things had just so quickly gone sideways – turned upside down in a friggin' heartbeat.

"I mean, it is Maya..." Marcus hedged and the three of us all looked at each other, apprehension on our faces, the worry manifesting as an almost physical shimmer between us.

"Exactly," I murmured. "It's *Maya.*" I turned back to the glowing screen of her computer. "And to answer your question, *no*, she's *always* come home. *Always.*"

She was the wild child of the four of us, for sure; but she wasn't stupid. She was a little crazy in a manic pixie-girl kind of a way, but she didn't ever go *this* far… never… something had to have happened.

"She would have called by now," I said, certain. "Or answered her phone."

"I don't know what else to do," Dorian said and Marcus sighed.

"I guess the only thing we *can* do," Marcus said, and I looked up at him. "We wait," he clarified, and I felt my shoulders sag.

"The police won't do anything until she's been missing twenty-four to forty-eight hours," Dorian said unhappily, and I shook my head.

"Anything could happen in that amount of time," I argued.

"*So much* could happen in that amount of time," Marcus added.

We three looked at each other and the helplessness dragged at all of us.

"What else can we do?" Dorian asked.

It was another million-dollar question.

CHAPTER TWELVE

*L*a Croix...
    Louie's momma didn't call. It was days and days later and he was out the hospital and had come back to us at the club. Still, we waited three *more* days past that. We knew the son of a bitch that'd stuck him was out. We could use a fuckin' computer. He'd been bonded out by somebody the morning after it'd happened. Not sure who'd posted his bail; maybe a boss or whatever. Poor son of a bitch that done it wouldn't be seeing that money ever again.

    Louie didn't look none too happy as we rolled up on his momma's house. It was me, Louie, Collier, and Saint. Retribution was imminent, and I had to say, I was a little bit skeptical that Louie'd have it in him to deal with his mother accordingly. That was alright, though. He didn't need to really. His brothers had his back in dealing with the snatch that'd bore him. She certainly wasn't no mother – that title was one she ain't earned.

    "I don't think I can do this," he confessed, and the conflict was clear in his green eyes as he stared down the block at his momma's house.

    We'd ridden in, him and me, while Collier and Saint followed us up in the van. They'd parked it right out front.

"You want that patch bad enough, you will. They done disrespected you, son. Retribution must be swift and the toll must be paid. Blood for blood, kid. That's the only way this goes down."

"I don't care about *him*," he said, rolling his eyes in my direction.

I nodded, hanging my head, and looked over at him. He eyed me and I said, "That thing in there ain't your momma, boy. She ain't been your momma in a long-ass time."

He pursed his lips, and he nodded. He knew. I think he'd known a long time, but he was a good kid, like I'd said. Loyal to a fault. We just needed to ensure that his loyalty was in the right place and there weren't no test bigger than this.

"I always just kind of hoped she'd come back, you know? Be like she was when I was a little kid. Be proud of me."

"The drugs done took your momma a long time ago, and as far gone as she is… there ain't no comin' back," I said. It hurt to say it because the same could be said for my daddy and his drinkin'. Shit, it was a competition at this point on what'd kill him first – his boozin' ways or the cancer.

Louie sniffed, and looked away, and I told him, "You go on an' mourn. It's the right thing to do… but she gone." I flapped my hand in an upward motion, signifying she'd flown high long before now – which she had.

"How you know?" he asked me. "Who left you?"

"My daddy," I told him. "His body still walkin' around in the Bayou back home, haunting the fuckin' house I grew up in… but he gone, too. The drink took him a long time ago. I think I realized it when I was a little younger than you are now, about seventeen. He tried to kill me, an' I put him in the hospital. Went to prison for a while for it. First time I think I ever stood up to 'im."

"Really?" he asked.

I nodded. "Yeah, buddy. Tried as an adult. Spent two years inside."

"He lived though," he said, and I nodded.

I told him the truth, "If'n you can call it that. He's got the cancer now. Only a matter of time before his body follows his soul to the pits of fuckin' Hell. I imagine your momma's got some shit to answer for on account of how she's treated you."

"Nah," he said and hung his head. "I ain't been the easiest kid to deal with."

I raised an eyebrow at that and nodded slowly. "Gonna have to agree to disagree on that," I said. "You a lot of things, Louie – but you ain't no pain in the ass. You're one of the biggest assets this club could ask for. I don't know what that cunt put in your head but you're one of the easiest guys we ever git along with. Bitch is crazy thanks to those drugs." I sucked my teeth, and he stared at me and looked like he was gon' cry.

"You keep lookin' at me like that, I'm liable to think you wanna suck my dick," I told him and he snorted and laughed.

"Yeah, sorry, boss. You ain't my type, even if you do got the biggest titties I ever seen."

It was my turn to laugh, then – which I didn't do too often. I was jacked and built like a brick shithouse. I guess my pecs were in fine fuckin' form for the kid to say that.

I shook my head and said, "It's a hard thing you about to do, Louie. Don't think any of us 'ould ask this of you lightly. This club ain't nothin' without loyalty. You understand that, don't 'cha?"

I turned my head and looked at him. The resolve in his eyes as he met mine was impressive.

He nodded. "Y'all been there for me more 'n she ever has," he said simply and I nodded slowly. He got it. He understood. This life wasn't pretty, and I was hoping against hope for his sake that this would be the ugliest thing he ever had to do for us. It was a *big* ask, and I knew that.

"You ready then?" I asked him.

"No," he answered honestly. "But let's do it." He grunted as he got off his bike and I followed suit.

He wouldn't have to scrap with nobody. That's what we was for – but he would have to be the one to pull the fuckin' trigger.

That was on him.

We met up with Collier and Saint outside the house. I stayed with Louie and jerked my head that the other two needed to go 'round back.

They pulled their black ski masks down over their faces and I nodded to Louie that he should follow suit, lowering mine down, too.

He brought it down, and I pulled my hand cannon out of the back of my waistband and checked my weapon. Louie was a good kid, and he did what I did – checked the semi-automatic pistol he had on him for readiness.

"Remember to police your brass, kid. Don't lose your head – an' don't forget, we got you."

He nodded grimly, and we quietly went up the front steps and took to either side of the front door.

He looked at me, and I looked at him. I cocked my head ever so slightly to indicate that he was the one callin' the shots, now. His shoulders lowered as he let out a pent-up breath and when he was steady – galvanized and ready for what may come, he gave me a nod.

I gave a nod back and silently counted to three, bobbing my head slightly with each count since he couldn't see my lips, covered as they were by the mask.

On three, I squared up on the shabbily repaired door and blew the remainder of the frame apart, the door flying into the house as Momma Louie shrieked on the couch and half climbed up the back of it. A fresh goddamn needle hung out of her arm. I was impressed the bitch could even find a fuckin' vein.

There was a shout from the back, an echoing crash, but we had to focus on what was in front of us. I trusted Col and Saint to have whatever was happenin' in the back in line.

"You sons a bitches! I just fixed that door!" she shrieked, even as Louie leveled his gun in the shell of a woman's face.

He hung his head, hesitating, and I started to raise my gun. He said to her, "I'm sorry, Momma." His voice broke on the honorific the bitch didn't deserve. Her eyes went wide, her mouth dropped open, but before she could speak, he painted the wall behind her head with her fuckin' brains – putting her broken body riddled with the drugs that ravaged it to rest.

"C'mon," I urged at the cursing and heavy blows comin' from the back. Louie looked to me and nodded. We piled down the long narrow hallway and ended up just inside the back door where Saint and Collier were in a spirited brawl with the guy that stabbed the fuck outta Louie – I hoped.

"That him?" I demanded, and Louie nodded, his eyes a little wide and showing just a little bit too much white around 'em through the eyeholes in his mask. I nodded, handed him my gun, which he took automatically, and waded into the fray to make quick work of him.

A few heavy blows to the back of his head and he went down and out.

"Git him in the van," I ordered, holding out my hand for the gun I'd passed off to Louie. He handed it to me and handed me his, then waded in to grab the fucker's legs without hesitation.

"You ain't supposed to be liftin' nothin'!" Saint scolded.

"We got this," Col affirmed.

Louie backed off an' Col and Saint took the fucker out the back and down the steps to go down around the house. I clapped Louie on the back of the shoulder and said to 'im, "C'mon, brother. You did what needed doin' – it's time to go home."

He nodded a little too quickly, and jerked in my grasp but I resisted him, steering him out the back after Saint and Col with their burden.

"You ain't gotta go back an' see dat," I told him. "Ain't no good here."

"My brass," he said. "You told me to remember to police my brass."

I nodded.

"I got it. You go on around the outside."

He nodded and did as he was told. I went out front to the living room and found his shell casing, and with one last lingering look at his momma's ruined face and the dripping gore down the yellowed wall behind her head, all I could do was shake my own.

"We'll do right by him," I promised her. "Better 'n you ever could."

I walked my ass out the wrecked front door and down the steps. The van was already gone but Louie? Loyal fuckin' Louie still waited, his bike runnin' and ready to go. I tossed him the shell casing, and he pocketed the damn thing and then we was out of there.

Back at the club, Louie was given a rowdy hero's welcome and his colors were waiting. Well, sort of. The bourbon and whiskey flowed and all too soon, the rest of the guys had the prospect face down on one of the pool tables, wriggling under his cut as they ironed on his colors patch as he was wearing the damn thing.

Hex wandered over as I tossed back the rest of what was in my glass. He eyed me.

"He did the deed then?" he asked, and I nodded.

"Told his momma sorry and blew her eyes out the back of her head," I said dryly.

He pitched a low whistle. "Ain't that some shit?" he asked, staring out into the crowd. "What about the one that stuck him?"

"I'm about to head out and take care of him," I said. "Saint and Col are on their way back."

"You ain't goin' by yerself," Hex declared, and I looked over at him.

"I'd planned on it."

"I ain't askin'," he said. "I'm tellin' ya, you ain't goin' by yerself. You the president now, my friend – and the president ain't go nowhere without his entourage."

I snorted and spit on the floor. "Fuck all that shit," I said. "I'm perfectly capable of handlin' myself."

"Oh, I know it," he agreed. "But need I remind you just what you signed up for when you accepted the position you're in?"

"No," I grunted. "You ain't gotta."

"Missin' the good ol' days?" he asked.

"Ain't nothin' good about any of my days," I told him and he huffed a laugh.

"Hmph! There you go, always a bowl of fuckin' roses," he said with dry humor.

I just grunted non-committedly in return and watched the general fuckery in front of us.

"Take Axeman or Cypress with you," Hex said judiciously.

"I see Axe all the time, man. It's been a minute since I been around Cy."

Hex looked over and up at me and nodded slow. "Now you're gettin' it," he said, and I frowned at him.

Sometimes he had a way of thinkin' he was the smartest man in here. One of these days, it was gonna lead him into makin' a serious mistake, underestimatin' another man at the wrong time and in the wrong way. I wasn't no dummy, but I sure as shit didn't see things the same way he did. Still, this time around, him actin' smarter 'n me rankled me a bit.

"Cypress!" I called out, and he looked over. I jerked my head in my direction and he passed off his beer and headed my way.

"How drunk are ya?" I asked, and he shook his head the same time he shrugged.

"I'm not," he declared.

"Good." I gave him a sage nod, once up, once down, and turned to leave.

I heard Hex bark a laugh behind me and he told Cy, "Why you been voluntold there, good buddy. I wouldn't leave the man waitin' if I were you."

Cy pulled up even with me just before we got to the door.

"Where we goin'?" he asked, and I slid my gaze up to him, the bastard a head taller 'n me for which I was damn jealous.

I said, "That's for me to know an' you to find out."

He grinned sheepishly and shook his head but didn't ask anymore dumb questions.

We rode out to the edge of the swamp, and took a deep-woods track on in from the main road. It was dangerous, riding along it, so we only went as far as to keep the bikes hidden from the main road and walked in the rest of the way.

What we called the Smokehouse wasn't much to look at. A shack, really, just up the bank at the edge of the water. Hidden. On private property that belonged to a shell company. Untraceable, which is exactly what we needed it to be.

"We comin' out here for a reason, boss?" Cy asked nervously, stopping just inside sight of the bikes.

"We got some business to finish with the man that stuck Louie," I said and Cypress visibly relaxed.

"Oh, hey… good, that's good," he said, and I eyed him.

"Guilty conscience?" I asked, and he practically blanched.

"No way! Why would you ask that?" he demanded.

"Lookin' nervous is all," I said evenly.

"Can y' blame me?" he asked with a hint of consternation. I searched his face in the dappled moonlight, the trees shifting in the light breeze, causing the shadows to shift across his face.

Cy was a good-lookin' dude. Full country, his neck was as thick as the tree he was named after which is consequently *how* he'd gotten his road name. He was born and bred out in these swamps like I'd been. Grew up huntin' and fishin' – learnin' the family trade of gator huntin' which he still practiced today with his daddy.

"Cy," I said. "Outta all the bastards we ride with, if it ever came down to it? I'd trust you the most," I told him, and I meant it.

He frowned, perplexed.

"Even over Hex?" he asked.

"You ever voice it aloud, I'll deny I ever said it – but yeah. Even over Hex," I said, which was only partially true. He scowled; his confusion compounding.

"I don't get it," he said, and I shook my head.

"Ain't meant for you to get," I said, putting us back into motion where we needed to be.

"This one of those 'the enemy of my enemy' or whatever?" he asked.

"You ain't as stupid as you look," I told him with a savage grin and he grinned back.

"Man, fuck you," he said and I laughed, the tension dissipating between us.

We made it to the shack in silence. That's one of the things I appreciated about Cy the most – the tall bastard didn't feel the need to talk my ear off. I didn't like idle chatter or conversation just for the sake of fillin' up the night with a bunch of fuckin' noise.

We found our captive quarry chained up, a gag stuffed in his mouth and duct tape wrapped around his head to keep it in. He had some more duct tape wrapped around his eyes, and I chuckled to myself. That shit would hurt like a bitch comin' off and would probably take his fuckin' eyebrows with it.

Not that he'd really need 'em where he was going.

"Unwrap his ass," I ordered Cy. I stood in front of the bastard while he did it, my feet shoulder width apart, my arms barely crossing over my chest from how musclebound I'd gotten.

Cy wasn't gentle about it, the dude in our crosshairs screamin' around the gag. Had to hand it to the old cuss; as soon as his eyes adjusted, he couldn't and wouldn't quit glarin' daggers at me.

"That's good enough," I told Cy before he could get started on the gag. "I don't need 'im to talk – just listen."

I leveled my gaze on the man. It wouldn't be the first time I'd killed someone without ever knowing their name.

"You fuck with one of us, you fuck with us all," I told him, and it was true. "There's a certain strength in numbers," I said, and I looked him up and down shrewdly. "Pretty certain, you wouldn't know nothin' about that though, am I right?"

His watery brown eyes were downshifting from hatred to wary uncertainty.

"Pretty fuckin' sure you never saw yourself going out this way, either. Am I right?"

His nostrils flared and his eyes showed a little too much white around them.

"I figured," I said, and I reached into my back pocket and flicked my Balisong open, back and forth, the steel flashing in the glint of the camp lantern, the only illumination in here. The Smokehouse didn't have any electricity or facilities, but that wasn't what we needed out here. Just a private place to deal with assholes like this, far enough away, no one would hear the screaming.

"Beautiful, innit?" I asked, flashing the light on and off the blade into his eyes. "The way the light shines off her, the way she clicks and clacks when you open her up? Like excited chatter. Like she knows she's about to taste flesh and lick the blood from bone. I know it gets *me* excited." I gripped my boner and bounced it up and down through my jeans once to draw his eye away from my face.

"Jesus Christ," I heard Cypress mutter. He'd stood himself way back in the corner, leanin' up against the wall with his arms crossed over his chest like a shield to defend himself from the uncomfortable display goin' on in front of him.

I didn't pay him no never mind.

I was focused on the man about to kiss my blade. About to fuckin' bleed for me. That warm, wet, wash of crimson that made my own fuckin' blood sing.

There was only one thing that thrilled me more than the rush of killing a man, of watching the light die in his eyes… and that was getting to touch my little Alina.

Though the thrills were both extreme in the regard that they made me *feel something*, they were as different as dark was to light, as heads were to tails – both present, both strong, two very different sides of the very same coin.

"Heard a boy from another club say, *'you fuck us, we fuck you back ten times harder,'* and I don't know, it stuck with me," I said, circling the guy.

He jerked from the chains that held him suspended on his knees from the ceiling, the metal rattling as I disappeared around his back.

"You stabbed our boy, what? Three times?" I asked.

He shouted from behind his gag.

I rammed my blade home, into his right kidney, and I went on and on, counting each one out.

One, two, three, four, five, six, seven, eight, nine, ten, eleven, twelve, thirteen, fourteen, fifteen, sixteen, seventeen, eighteen, nineteen, twenty, twenty-one, twenty-two, twenty-three, twenty-four, twenty-five, twenty-six, twenty-seven, twenty-eight, twenty-nine, thirty!

I'm pretty sure I rendered his kidney and maybe a couple more of his major fuckin' organs into hamburger. By the time I was done; he'd stopped screaming from behind his gag. Instead, his head hung back, some of his blood vivid against the silver tape over his mouth as his eyes leaked tears down his temples and he swallowed hard. His gaze was fixed and unfocused as he slid into shock, I think. I didn't particularly care.

"Ain't so tough now, are yah?" I demanded. I wiped my blade off on the top of the thigh of his dirty jeans.

He whimpered some, and I looked to Cy.

"Let's load him on the boat and feed him to the gators."

Cy looked back at me with no emotion and gave a nod before letting his arms fall to his sides and taking a step forward.

"I got this," he said. "Why don't you head on over to the pump house and get yourself cleaned up.

I looked down, my arms flecked with blood, my right hand slicked with it almost to the elbow, and nodded.

"Yeah," I said after I heaved a few breaths.

I wondered briefly what my little Alina was doing.

CHAPTER THIRTEEN

Alina...
I'd gone to the police station to try and get them to listen, or to at least take a report, but no dice. With nothing else to do, I had gone to work. Dorian looked up from behind the bar, lifting his chin in that way that was asking, without blurting out our business across the whole-ass bar.

I sighed, and knew I looked both tired and crestfallen as I shook my head.

His face dropped along with his shoulders and he looked just as frustrated as I felt. Days and days had passed, and I just couldn't seem to get anyone to fucking *listen to me.*

The night was a busy one, which was something, considering how hot and humid it was out there.

The extreme heat of the day had carried over into the night and that was never a good thing on Bourbon. It was like the gods had seen fit to anoint the street with crazy when it was like this. The lights of the bars could sometimes wind up muted by the strobing lights of emergency vehicles. The music drowned out by sirens. If we were lucky? It'd be medical emergencies rather than violent felonies.

I didn't know what the rest of the city looked like on a night like this, but I had to imagine it wasn't nearly as awful as Bourbon could get. Mostly because it felt like the whole city was *here*, leaving no people to commit crime, or have a seizure, or to pass out from dehydration or with a case of alcohol poisoning.

We had a patron go down by mid-shift, but Clyde, our manager, took it, leaving me and Dor to mind the bar.

I was grateful for it. I still had a massive headache and both Dorian and I were running off fumes from lack of good sleep, worrying about Maya who was missing over a week by this point.

By the time the night was over, we were both dog tired.

"How were tips?" I asked and Dorian made a face, curling his lip in disgust.

"Looks like one-eighty a piece."

"Not so bad," I said.

"Not so good if you pulled in over two-fifty last night," he said. I nodded.

"Feels like we were twice as fuckin' busy," I muttered.

"When? Last night or tonight?" he asked.

"Tonight," I said.

"Oh, gross."

Yeah, that about summed it up.

We closed, and Dorian walked me home.

"Thanks," I said.

"You want me to come up?" he asked.

I shook my head. "No, you go home. I bet Marcus is waiting."

"Yeah, but he can wait a few extra minutes if you need me," he said, rolling his eyes like I was being ridiculous.

I rolled my eyes at *him* for that and wrapped him in a hug.

"I'll be fine," I said.

"Think she's up there?" he asked, peering up the outside of our building at where the windows to mine and Maya's apartment were. They were dark except for a subtle golden glow around the blinds of one of them from the lamp I always left on before I left, for when I came home.

I shook my head.

"I don't think so," I said.

"Fuck," he muttered. "Where *is* she?"

"I don't know," I said and I tried not to despair.

"Okay, well try to get some good sleep," he said, and he put a hand to my shoulder, rubbing a thumb across it. I nodded.

"You, too," I said. He waited until I had keyed my way into the lobby and the door was shut behind me before he smiled through the glass and turned to go on his way.

I turned and looked up the wooden stairway and sighed. It was going to be a long march up to my floor.

Anticipation that I tried to curb like my enthusiasm was buzzing in my chest as I keyed open the lock to our front door.

I let myself into the apartment. I failed at being a realist and went right back to my go-to optimism by calling out, "Maya? Are you here?"

Of course, I was met by nothing – just a ringing, resounding silence.

Shit.

I set my second favorite purse aside; the first having gone missing the same night as my best friend, and I tossed my keys into the bowl.

Sighing, I went into my room and toed off my shoes, moaning in relief as my feet made contact with the cooler hardwood of the apartment floor.

I went in to shower, to wash the bar off my skin and try to send some of the tension in my body down the drain.

Unfortunately, the shower was where my tired mind felt most at home, enough to worry and gnaw at the problem in front of me.

Where was my best friend?

Where was my roommate?

Where had Maya gone?

The police weren't interested in helping, at all. I had even called the non-emergency line at precisely the twenty-four-hour mark on my break and had all but begged them to at least take a report! They wouldn't send an officer, and they wouldn't take the report over the phone. It was maddening. They just wanted me to go into the department the next morning and to file in person.

I swear to God, if I had her father's phone number, I would call him. I had a feeling they might move on it if they knew she was the daughter of a sitting city councilman. Then again, he might not care so much... according to Maya, he didn't – but I was confused on the subject.

I mean, if he didn't care, why did he let her stay here? She argued it was just to keep an eye on her and to make sure she stayed out of trouble but I don't know.

I shut the water off when I was done and stepped out, wrapping myself in a towel.

I took a seat at the vanity we kept in here and stared at myself in the mirror.

On top of the mystery of Maya missing, I still couldn't recollect what'd happened to *me* that night. How I'd gotten home or how I'd changed... where my stuff went. Any of it. Still, the only thing I could remember was leaving the bar, then waking up in my own bed.

I picked up the patch from the vanity where I'd set it when I'd stepped in to shower.

I hadn't let it out of my sight since I'd woken with it in my hand.

Silence is better than bullshit.

Was it a threat? I wondered.

Silence... but silent over *what?* Maya?

I didn't know, but the creeping dread ticking up my spine like spider's legs took hold and nested at the base of my skull. I swallowed hard and set the patch down, picking up my brush to run it through my long hair.

I sprayed my leave-in conditioner on and brushed it some more. I liked having my hair brushed, and I would often sit and think, brushing through my hair in long even strokes until it dried.

I didn't have anything else to do tonight but fret, and so that's what I did. I sat in the air-conditioned hush of our apartment, staring blankly at my reflection in the mirror, as I thought myself in exhausting circles while I brushed my hair dry.

THE NEXT MORNING, far too early, I rose and dressed in jeans, a sturdy pair of walking boots, and a clean white fitted tank top under a fitted country-green-and-white plaid shirt. I pulled my long, straight, copper hair into a high ponytail and I did my makeup natural and subtle. I stood in front of the mirror on the back of my bedroom door and took stock of myself.

I sighed and couldn't help but worry that due to my petite stature, I would be dismissed like an errant child again; only now I would not be ignored. Even if I had to raise a ruckus.

I pulled on a light windbreaker and took an umbrella in case it rained. Slinging my purse over my chest, I took my leave and to the street.

The walk wasn't an insignificant one, and it was in the mid-nineties today, the humidity ridiculously high. Thunderstorms were predicted, hence the umbrella, and I hoped against hope for one to roll on through because they tended to cool things down significantly.

I marched into the nearest precinct, my heart sinking when I caught sight of the same desk sergeant as the last time I'd been.

"You again," he said by way of greeting and he sounded annoyed.

Seriously?

"Me again," I affirmed, and if I'd been a cat, my ears would have been plastered flat to my skull. Firmly, I said, "And I'm not leaving until somebody *talks to me.*"

I raised my eyebrows and planted my feet shoulder width apart to indicate I wouldn't be budging. With an amused look that downright infuriated me, the man behind the counter fished a clipboard somewhere out from beneath the desk. He turned to the row of filing cabinets at the back wall, and opened one, running one of his blunt fingertips over the tabs and stopping at one to pull a stapled stack of papers out. He sighed an exasperated sound, and put the papers on the clipboard.

"Have a seat over there, fill this here out, and I'll see if anybody in the back has the time to talk to you today," he said. He shooed me off with the clipboard and the papers without handing me a pen. That was alright. I had one of my own.

I dropped into the seat he'd indicated and looked over the form and stewed in my rage. My best friend had been missing for *over a week!* You would think they'd maybe want to do some of that serving, seeing as it was way past time for them to do any protecting, dammit!

I filled the paperwork out to the best of my ability, which all things considered was pretty damn good. Maya and I were *best friends.* We knew everything there was to know about each other and then some.

The first bit was straight forward enough – *age, sex, height, weight, eye and hair color, skin color* – that sort of thing.

The next was a bit trickier – what she was last wearing? I didn't know. I know what she was last *seen* wearing at the bar but I assumed she went home to get ready for her date, which meant she had changed.

If she even made it home, Alina...

It was a sobering thought. One I dismissed.

I sighed and wrote down what I'd last seen her wearing and added that she could have changed and that her last known location could have possibly been the Ritz – which I knew from the email on her computer but I didn't share that part; not yet.

I felt sick lining out what she did for work etc., knowing that she would be judged, but I would rather the judgment and condemnation of strangers and that she be found safe than the alternative of never knowing. I wanted her here and mad at me more than anything.

"You the one lookin' to file a missin' person's report?" a voice asked me. I looked up at a woman who in a word, looked... bored.

"Yes, my friend Maya, she's missing."

"You finish that yet?" she asked, thrusting her pointed chin at the clipboard in my hands.

"No, not yet," I answered.

"'Kay, good. It'll give me enough time to get a cup of coffee. I'm Detective Lydia Baumgartner. You are?"

"Alina, Alina Bouchard," I said, and I held out my hand. "Nice to meet you."

Her blue eyes flicked from my hand to my face and she tucked a tendril of her blonde hair back behind her ear and said, "Right. I'll be back in a few minutes. You finish that up and we'll talk." She inclined her head and took a step back and I dropped my unshaken hand.

Rude, I thought to myself as I watched her walk away.

I put my mind to finishing the report in my hands and managed to not only finish but to double-check my work and make sure I didn't miss anything before she returned.

"That done?" she asked.

"Yes!" I handed it to her, and she glanced over it, flipping the pages awkwardly, her cup of coffee in her other hand.

"Okay," she said with a gusty sigh. "Go ahead and give Pritchard back his clipboard and you can go. We'll be in touch."

"What?" I asked, completely gobsmacked.

"You heard me," she said. "We'll be in touch. Try to have a good day."

She turned to walk away from me and my temper snapped.

"Don't you walk away from me!" I snarled, and she turned.

"I beg your pardon?"

"Yes. Exactly. What the actual fuck is wrong with you people?" I demanded. "It says on the side of your fucking cars you 'serve and protect' but I haven't seen either of those things out of you! *Maya Bashaw*! She's *Councilman Bashaw's daughter* and she's *missing*! Maybe *now* you'll want to care about her," I said, and the tears stung my eyes. I was so fucking *angry*... and I felt so fucking *helpless* and I *hated it* with a passion.

"Look," the detective said sharply. "We'll look into it. City Councilman's daughter or not – she'll get the same treatment as everyone else. Now I suggest you go home and *we'll be in touch*."

She turned testily and marched away from me, the desk sergeant buzzing her through the door and into the back.

I went back to the desk and tossed his clipboard onto it.

"Thanks," he said.

"Fuck you," I snarled at him. He just shook his head, chuckling; fucking *laughing at me.*

"Assholes," I muttered to myself as I stalked up the street and wondered to myself, *now what was I going to do?*

"Damnit, Alina," I grumbled to myself. "You shouldn't have lost your cool." I sighed and tried not to lose all sense of hope.

CHAPTER FOURTEEN

*L*a Croix...

She looked stressed.

I sat in a curved corner booth with some of my guys and watched her move behind the bar.

Sure, she'd smile real nice when she was talking to a paying customer – but the minute they turned away or she did; automatically going through the motions of making a drink? Her lips lost that easy smile. Besides that, I noticed that even when they tipped up at the corners, that smile of hers just didn't reach her eyes. Not like when it was genuine.

Something was wrong, and it damaged my calm in a way that was unsettling. I didn't like it, but I didn't know what needed to be done to fix it – and so I did what I always did. I sat back and watched.

Our waitress was leggy and blonde and did abso-fucking-lutely nothing for me, though Cypress and Bennie certainly appreciated the view.

"Alright," Axe declared. "I don't know why the fuck you picked a place like this – but I'm out. It's just a little too mainstream and touristy for me."

Hex laughed and got up too. "I'm with you, man. Y'all fellas have a good one now, y'hear?" He winked at me, knowing damn well why I'd picked this place.

"Night, bro." Bennie fist bumped each of their fists and Cypress threw 'em some chin.

"Night, boss," Hex said and threw me a wink. I nodded.

He was just bein' fuckin' cagey with the rest of our boys. He saw all and remembered all, and again; he knew *exactly* why I was here… though I appreciated him not diming me out to the rest of the guys about it. Them pokin' fun was sure to set me in a bad mood.

My little Alina, and all that surrounded her, meant too much to me. I don't think I could or would be a good sport about any ribbing. You know?

The waitress came back by and I glared at her for stepping between me and my view of Alina. She took our empty glasses and asked if we wanted anything else. I gave a nod, fixing gazes and intentionally creeping her to make her go the fuck away.

Cy and Bennie ordered more beer, and she fucked off back in the direction of the bar. The next thing I knew, Alina was coming around, picking up our waitress's tray, and heading our direction.

I straightened up a little and cracked my neck which was suddenly rife with tension. She stopped at our table and set the beers out for us.

"Alright, fellas, here you go!" she said with a chipper demeanor, and I knew it for the lie that it was.

"Thanks, darlin'," Bennie said and Cypress, catching the look on my face, shut his trap from saying anything flirtatious and simply gave the girl a nod of respect.

"Thank you," I said and she cocked her head.

"I know you…" she murmured, and I blinked, long and slow.

Shit.

I hadn't expected that.

Had I given myself away?

"Yeah, no… you helped me out a few weeks back," she said, pointing at me and shaking her finger absently as she placed just where she knew me from.

"I'm the girl, with the couch. You helped me lift it into the back of the van when I moved out of my old apartment," she said and I nodded.

"I remember," I said.

"Alina, Alina Bouchard," she said and held out her hand to me. "I didn't get your name."

"La Croix," I said, and I stared at her mystified before slowly bringing up my hand to hers.

Was this really happening or was I dreaming?

She shook my hand lightly and her skin was soft.

"Thanks for that," she said. "I think you saved my life. I was fixing to be crushed to death under the weight of that thing." She laughed and Bennie and Cy were looking at me like they'd never seen me before.

"You're welcome," I said.

She tipped up her tray and said, "I'll be back around to check on you guys in a bit. I'm taking over for Sandra, your other waitress, alright?"

"Sounds good," I said with a nod and I felt something very akin to electricity flow through me, energizing me and filling me with… I don't know what.

"Boss," Bennie said, and I turned my head slowly in his direction, my eyes fixed on my little Alina's back as she made her way back to the bar.

"Boss?" Bennie asked again, and I turned to look at my men.

"What?" I demanded.

"You mind telling us what that was all about?" Cy asked.

I shook my head and turned it to look back at Alina who was back working her bar.

"No," I said, and I got up. "Gonna take a piss. Don't follow me."

I left them both sitting there, shrugging, and giving each other mirrored looks of confusion.

I took a piss, washed my fuckin' hands, and splashed some cold water on my face.

I didn't understand how one look from her could unravel my resolve so much. How those cool gray eyes left me stuttering and a fuckin' speechless mess, saying stupid shit and short circuiting my fuckin' brain.

I tore some paper towels from the dispenser and mopped the water from my face. After a few deep and even breaths, staring into the blackened pits of my own eyes in the flaking and rusting mirror over the sink, I felt like I had my shit together enough to go out there and face her.

I was halfway back through the crush of people around the bar to my booth with the boys when she crashed into me.

"Oh, God!" she cried as two empty glasses fell from her tray and shattered against the concrete floor. "I'm so—" her voice cut off before she could say sorry and I was keenly aware of her hand on my cut at my side, bracing herself from pressing full against me as people milled around us.

She took her hand away slowly, and I looked down on the crown of her copper hair and waited her out.

She slowly raised her head, her eyes tracking a little bit slowly, and the confusion in her eyes was telegraphed clearly as she looked up at me.

Her voice was lost to the crowd and the pounding music, but I could read her lips easily enough.

"It's you... it was you..."

I didn't give anything away, keeping my face neutral and devoid of any emotion. I simply stared at her for as long as she stared at me.

Finally, as though waking up from a spell, she sidestepped me and was gone amid the crowd.

I looked back at Bennie and Cy who were openly staring at me through the shifting bodies between us, and with a scowl, I went back to the table.

"What'd you do?" I demanded.

"Nothing, man," Bennie said, his voice a little tight with fear as he raised his voice above the crowd and music.

"We just finished our beers," Cy added.

I dropped into my seat and shifted back so I could see all the angles and soon, my little Alina had returned. She set down Bennie and Cy's beers and then tossed down the patch I'd left with her onto the table before me and the boys, arching her elegant eyebrow at me. Her mouth was set in a stern and stubborn line and I felt one of my eyebrows arch in return.

I turned my head to Cy and Bennie and in a tone that would brook no argument, I told them both, "Fuck off."

Wordlessly, they got up and left us, going to chat up some girls in the opposite corner.

Alina took Bennie's seat nearest me.

"Who are you?" she demanded.

"I told you, La Croix."

"That's a seltzer water that tastes like despair. Who are you really, and how did the patch that goes there, wind up in my hand in my apartment?" she demanded, pointing to the empty spot on my cut that still had the glue residue in the shape of my patch.

"I wanted you to remember me," I said.

"Well, I don't," she said curtly, and she turned her head, tears brimming on her lower lashes.

"Don't do that," I said quickly.

"Do what?" she demanded.

"Cry."

"Well, it's kind of hard not to!" she snapped. "So, are you the reason? Is this some kind of threat?" she demanded.

I scowled hard at that. *Someone was threatening her?* Or she thought someone would? I wanted to know why, on that; but first things first...

"The reason what?" I demanded.

"The reason she's missing?" she shot back stubbornly.

Again, my eyebrows rose, this time from my scowl into an expression of wondering, as in – *just what the hell was she talking about?*

When I didn't say anything, her shoulders slumped.

"My roommate, my best friend... she's been missing a while now and no one will do anything. I'm scared," she said and her expression was glum, bordering on desperate. If it was one thing I learned from Baby Ruth, it was that in desperation, there was opportunity.

"I ain't got anything to do with your friend goin' missing," I told her and she looked back up at me.

"I don't remember anything from that night," she confessed. "The last thing I remember was leaving here, then waking up at home."

"That's a good thing," I told her. "You don't want to remember."

She frowned, troubled, and looked up at me.

"You were in our apartment?" she asked.

"I was," I confessed. "Your friend wasn't."

"*Shit*," she swore softly. I couldn't hear it, but I definitely saw it and the feeling behind it on her expressive face.

"The police won't help me," she said, and she shook her head. "I've tried so many times, but they just won't take me seriously."

"Fuck the police," I answered, and then I leveled her with my gaze, throwing the offer right on out there. "I could find her."

She raised her chin, defiance in her eyes that muted and disappeared altogether as she caught that I was dead fucking serious.

"Everything has its price, though, little Alina," I warned her.

"How much money would you want?" she asked.

I shook my head slowly.

"Not money," I answered.

"No? Then what?" she asked, and I seized the opportunity it presented.

"*You.*"

Her eyes widened in shock.

"What?" she asked.

"You heard me," I told her.

She chewed her bottom lip in apprehension and looked both troubled and thoughtful.

I slipped a card out of my cut, one of my plain ones with my burner number on it, and I held it out to her.

"Take all the time you need to decide," I told her. "Just remember, your friend is out there somewhere, and I'm probably, more than likely, your best bet at finding out what happened to her."

She took the card from my hand and took a deep, fortifying breath.

"I don't think I need to take any time," she said, but she didn't sound sure. "I want Maya found. I want her home." Now, *that*, she did sound certain of and I felt pretty confident that I'd be hearing from her.

I nodded slowly and said, "Call me. We'll negotiate the details somewhere else when you're not at work," I said, and it was as though she woke from a dream. She startled and looked around us and stood up quickly.

"I'll call you tonight, after I'm off," she said evenly, and I nodded, thinking that I could wait and maybe we could have that conversation in person.

She rushed off back to her bar, and I settled back to watch her once more.

I would be lying if I said that it didn't please me that her eyes tracked back my direction every time she had a moment to spare a thought.

CHAPTER FIFTEEN

*A*lina...

He stayed, and I kept stealing glances in his direction.

I didn't understand him. His fearsome appearance was hard, his tattoos the stuff of nightmares, and those eyes... they were horrifying, the inky blackness butting right up against the deep dark brown of his irises that were so damn dark that in certain light, like the dim lighting of the bar – well, they might as well just be black, too.

His card was burning a hole in my pocket and I wanted to finish our conversation even though that single little word had seared its way into my mind and made my heart quail...

You.

He wanted *me*... as currency; as a trade to find Maya. It should have frightened me way more than it did and I think that almost frightened me more – that it wasn't as scary as it should have been. But I was *desperate* by this point.

I knew in my heart, if it was *me* who was missing, that Maya would be spread eagle and waving him and his whole club in to bring it on.

But I wasn't Maya. I wasn't half so bold or unafraid, and I was certainly confused about La Croix.

I needed time to think, but Maya didn't *have* time, which just made things worse when it came to the jumbled confusion of thought and emotion in my head.

The bar closed, and La Croix seemed to move like a shadow. One minute he was there, and the next? He was gone. I hadn't seen him leave, and I was sort of hoping he wouldn't, that I would get the chance to talk to him more tonight. To tell him my decision before I could talk myself out of it.

I didn't know what to make of him, but there had been nothing but surety in the set of his body, in his dark gaze, when he'd said he could find my best friend.

I didn't believe he was trying to take me for a ride on that.

Well, he *was*, but not of the scammy variety.

Shit.

"Hey," I looked up at Sandra across from me.

"Yeah?"

"The creeper," she said. "He left this for you."

I frowned and she handed over the patch...

Silence is better than bullshit...

...and it clicked.

No. I didn't think a man who would permanently glue that patch to his vest was much for spewing bullshit. I mean, it would be a little hypocritical, don't you think?

The Voodoo Bastards were known for many things around the city and the local parish; hypocrisy wasn't really one of them.

"Thanks," I said and I stuffed the patch into my pocket. I sighed and finished out my closing. I guess he really was gone then, and I'd be forced to call him.

Damn.

My anxiety about the whole thing only served to ramp up another notch, and I began to question and talk circles around the whole notion silently in my head.

I'd been wrong about one thing – he hadn't gone, because when I left, he was waiting outside.

"Hi," I said lamely, rocking back on my heels. He raised his chin in a sort of salute, I guess.

"Figured I'd walk you home," he said. "The one you were bartending with tonight is a fuckin' pussy and don't do it."

I blinked and looked up the street in the direction Jonathan had gone.

"I mean, it's not like it's his *job*. He's off work just the same as me."

La Croix just stared at me, silent.

"Where are your friends?" I asked, curious.

"Told 'em to fuck off again," he answered with a one-shouldered casual shrug.

"And they always do what you say?" I asked.

"They fuckin' better," he answered.

"Or what?" I asked.

"That's for us to know. Club business."

I raised my chin some and said, "And what? Club business is man business? Not for us little women to know?"

His lips curled ever so slightly and he said, "Safer that way."

"For who?" I asked.

"For you."

"I see..." I trailed off, but to be perfectly honest, I didn't. I couldn't even begin to understand how that whole world worked. I was keenly aware that while his world and my world coexisted side by side, they were *not* the same world.

"If you're waiting for *me* to fuck off so you can walk home – I think I've already proven I know where you live," he said.

I blinked and stuttered out, "N-n-no, I wasn't... but... uh... just how *do* you know where I live?"

"I know a lot of shit," he said, again, with that one-shouldered and casual shrug.

I slowly started up the sidewalk in the direction of home and he fell into step beside me.

"Just what happened that night?" I tried asking him and he shook his head.

"If you don't remember, it's best that you don't. Believe me."

I swallowed hard and asked the real burning question, "Do you think you can really find her?"

"I know I can," he said, and it was flat, deadpan, and completely certain.

"Do you already know where she is?" I asked curiously, having thought before that could be the case, but wanting to press it, to make absolutely sure before I fell for some kind of a trick or something. He stopped and I stopped to, turning to face him.

"I don't know where your friend is. No bullshit. You want me to find her, I'll find her... or I'll at least find out what happened to her if it comes to that. I wasn't lying when I named my price, either – no matter the outcome."

I swallowed hard and said, "You mean, like, sex?"

"No, not just sex," he answered. "I want *you*."

"I don't think I get it," I said. "Like, what? You want me to be your girlfriend?"

He nodded.

"I want to spend time with you. Learn about you. I want you to be with me. Go for rides, and yes – I want us to fuck," he clarified.

I think my face went beet red, and I was grateful for the cover of darkness and the splash of neon lights, hoping it would disguise my discomfort.

"I'm not a whore," I said, and it came out sharp. At the same time, I immediately felt guilty for saying it like that. I mean, I would *never* judge Maya for her decisions but me? I wasn't, I couldn't... *God,* I resisted the urge to hide my face behind my hands.

What was even happening, right now?

"I never said that," he answered without hesitation.

"But you want me to pay you for your services with sex," I pointed out.

"Yes," he answered evenly. "But it's not like *that*," he added.

"But doesn't that, by definition, make me some kind of a whore?" I asked.

He touched my shoulder, gripped it firmly, but not painfully, and I jerked my eyes up to meet his.

"*It's not going to be like that,*" he insisted and he was dead serious.

"I mean, it sounds like it's going to be exactly like that," I said incredulously. His lips twitched in a slightly victorious little smile before he could look away and sigh.

He shook his head.

"It's not," he insisted.

He was completely mollifying, and we were just going back and forth at this point in a weird little deadlock. I raked my bottom lip between my teeth, thinking.

"I won't hear you talk about yourself like that," he said, finally, his voice gentle. "We clear?" He dropped his hand from my shoulder and I swallowed hard and nodded mutely, not trusting myself to speak. I mean... Shit. He just sounded like Maya just then. Like something she would say to me when I was being down on myself because of how I was raised. I swallowed hard, the tears threatening at the corners of my eyes.

I turned back up the sidewalk, and we continued walking in silence for a time.

"When can you start?" I asked softly, my mind stolidly made up, and he stopped and looked at me.

"You saying you agree? Because there ain't no you gettin' cold feet after I start," he said.

"No – no, I'm not," I said. "I mean, I understand."

"You're sure?" he asked, and I nodded.

"I have to find her," I said and didn't even bother to hide the desperation in my voice.

"You agree to the terms?" he asked again. "I look for your friend, and you agree to be mine – no matter what the outcome?"

"If you look for my friend, and you don't stop until you find her or what happened to her, then I'll be yours," I said, affirming things for him. "Starting now," I added, which is what he sounded like he wanted to hear.

He nodded slowly, and said, "Then the terms of our agreement begin now, my little Alina."

The way he said my name, it was almost as if he'd spoken some kind of magic spell into existence. Something tangible and binding, and who knows? Maybe the Voodoo Bastards really were into voodoo magic of some kind.

"So mote it be," I murmured, because it just seemed like the right thing to do, that a spell really had just been cast and that it needed my binding final word as well.

"Go inside, cher," he said, and I looked to my left and blinked. We were standing at the entrance to my apartment building.

I turned back to look at him and he looked down at me.

"When will you start?" I asked him, standing up straighter, my heart hammering in my throat.

"Right now," he answered, and I nodded.

"What do you need from me?" I asked.

"Right this minute? Nothing," he said. "If I need anything, I'll be in touch."

I nodded and he raised his eyebrows, like he needed to hear it.

"Alright," I said, lingering on the sidewalk with him for whatever reason... I didn't know why.

I got out my keys and keyed my way into the lobby. He pulled the door shut behind me and stood on the other side of the oval of glass set into its sturdy and thick wood frame of the door with all its old and fancy brass trim.

I stared at him through the thick glass for several moments and realized – I was intrigued by him, more than I was afraid.

Wasn't that some food for thought? Or maybe it was just the Goddesses' will...

I didn't know, but it felt right, so for now? I would go with it.

CHAPTER SIXTEEN

*L*a Croix...

She lingered on the other side of the glass and I stood, committing every line, every swoop and sweeping curve, every constellation of freckle that peeked through her worn makeup, to memory.

She was so beautiful, it made the heart ache and long... much like a deep longing for someplace called *home*, even when you'd never much had one.

I waited until I could no longer see her as she ascended the stairs before I pulled my phone from my cut.

I called Hex.

"Yeah," he grumbled into the line, his voice thick and heavy with sleep.

"I've never asked anything of you or this club," I said to him. "I've towed the fuckin' line since day one. Been the sword you've wielded against friend and foe alike."

"Man, La Croix, you okay? What's going on? You drunk?"

"I'm not drunk, but I am in need, my brother. Can I count on you?" I asked.

Silence metered out over the line, like the collective universe held its breath while the gravity of my words sank in to Hex.

"What do you need?" he asked. He was awake now. Alert. The wheels turning.

"Meet me at the club," I said.

Without hesitation, he said, "Alright. Be there in a few." The tone sounded in my ear that he'd ended the call.

I rode straight for it, and when I pulled in, Hex was waiting. I tended to forget how close the fucker lived to the clubhouse.

I got off my bike, and he pushed off from the doorway, turning sideways in it, to let me by and following me back to my office.

I took a seat at my desk and he dropped into the seat across from it.

"So, where's the fire at?" he asked and let out a gusty sigh.

"She's home. I walked her there."

"She? She who?" he asked, his eyes flashing and the calculations beginning to tick behind his eyes.

I told him everything – about Alina, about the promise I'd made and what I'd asked for in exchange and he listened.

"Shit howdy, that's a lot," he said and huffed a bit of an incredulous laugh. Then his eyes flicked back to mine and he said, "I'm proud of you, brother. It's not our usual thing and I don't suppose we could really ask the rest of the brothers to pitch in over much, seein' as they get no benefit really, but yeah, you can count on me. I'll help. The rest of 'em, we gotta leave it up to them – you know? We don't need no echoes of Ruth around here. That was all around a bad situation."

I nodded, listening to his council, pausing, considering it, and finally, I nodded again.

He was right. It was shit like I was asking that'd made the things go down like they had – selfish, but mildly so at first, devolving into a tyrannical regime. Treating the lot of us like we was at his beck and call, and we couldn't and wouldn't stand for that. Thus brothers smarter than Ruth – namely Hex and yeah, even myself, had started to plot against him. This life was about bein' free of a tyrannical system, not about trading one for another.

That's what'd got Ruth in the end. The club had divided, and heads had needed to roll. He'd been adding brothers left right and center for a while, boasting big damn numbers, even numbers, which had gone against the fuckin' bylaws. Throwin' the rules and any sense of caution to the wind; and why?

Because Ruth had dipped into the party favors just a little too fuckin' much and had lost his way. Couldn't be reasoned with to put the fuckin' nose candy down. Had found his self in a perpetual cycle of relying on uppers, then downers, then uppers again until he'd lost his fuckin' mind and there weren't no ability to reason with the fucker.

I'd felt some guilt over that. Over lettin' the man lose his way so thoroughly. I think we'd all fallen into the trap of belivin' Ruth's bullshit that he was fine and had shit in hand. By the time it was obvious he didn't? Well, shit was just too late an' several other brothers were addicted too, yo the point they took Ruth's side and had cozied up to the wrong fuckin' bear.

We were twenty-three, and me and Saint had taken us down to eight with Hex's careful and precise guidance. It'd been a bloody and fucked-up civil war. One we'd kept private for the most part; and it'd scarred every last one of us that'd wound up left and loyal to the colors over the individual men that'd wore 'em.

I'd had to kill friends and brothers; people I'd liked, all in a bid to protect the sanctity of the club. There were no loyalties tested to these colors like mine had been, and I'd always and forever remained true to the Voodoo Bastards. Now that I sat at the head of its table – It took that loyalty and deference to a whole new level and I felt like this was some kind of moment of truth, you know? That it was time to find out if these colors were going to be loyal back to me or not.

I knew what I was asking here was a *big* ask... just as I knew it could be something that was *too big*, but there was only one way to find that out, and closed mouths didn't get fed.

Hex cocked his head and said, "Y'know, the only reason I say this even needs to be put to a vote is the way I see it... too long have decisions been made by leadership and leadership alone in this club. Which is how we arrived in the situation we did with Ruth and his power-hungry bullshit in the first place." He sighed and put his boot heels up on the edge of the desk.

"I thought then, and I still think now, that we was lookin' at things all wrong, or that Ruth certainly was. I wanna make sure you an' I don't get set in the ways of before... that we don't fall into the same patterns for the sake of familiarity or make the same damn mistakes. Change came fast, but it ain't come easy," he said. "Let's call church and put it to a vote. Even if the rest of the boys say nay, you know you got me."

I nodded. It was the best idea, but it was also a little frightening. I mean, I guess there wasn't any way faster to find out if your brothers liked you or not.

"Let's do that," I agreed, even though a knot of uneasy dread took up residence in my chest.

Could I do what my little Alina asked on my own?

Yes.

Would it be much faster and a fuckload easier if my brothers were involved, and likelier with a better outcome?

Absolutely yes…

"You look spooked," Hex said, eyeing me critically. "I ain't never seen you look spooked before in my life. Just what you feel like you got ridin' on this?" he demanded.

I leveled my brother with my gaze and told him the fuckin' stark truth of it.

"Feels like everything," I said.

"I didn't realize you were in so deep over that girl," he said. "What's it about her?"

"I don't know," I answered honestly. "I know I certainly don't deserve something as pure or sweet – but now I've got my chance and failure just doesn't feel like an option."

He nodded and looked contemplative.

"You don't think you got a shot with the rest of the boys?" he asked, but he kept his face neutral. I knew the look. It was the same one he got when his curiosity was piqued and he felt like gathering information to solve some kind of a puzzle.

I looked off to the side, distant.

"Feels like I'm cashin' in all my chips on this," I said, and it was true.

"How's that?" he asked.

I shook my head. I didn't want to say it out loud. Just how much I fuckin' wanted this for myself. Just how much I wanted *her*. Just how much I felt out of my depth and how fuckin' vulnerable and alien that feeling was.

Silence is better than bullshit, I thought, and it was far too tempting to bullshit to hide my honest answer and true feelings which I wasn't about to share.

Hex cleared his throat, knowing when not to press, and dropped his boots to the concrete floor.

"First thing's first. We call the boys in. Find out how much help they willin' to put in on this. Second thing, you an' me? We figure out the girl and how to magic make this work. Awright?"

I looked to Hex and nodded slowly. He shot back a look that was nothing short of ride or die, and it put me at a little bit of ease. No matter what, I could see plain as day he had my back on this thing.

"Thank you," I said, and he nodded.

"Brother, we're in this together. We made that decision together a long time ago and I mean to honor it."

I nodded again; glad we were on the same page. I had a lot of trouble trusting anything out of anyone. Had never been given a whole lot of reason to believe anything anyone said. I watched what they did, instead. Hex had ever been even keel and steady with me; and yet, even with him, I had trouble truly believing.

"I want to call them in now," I said, and he laughed a bit.

"I don't think that'd help your cause much, bringin' 'em in at the ass crack of dawn like that."

I felt my lips quirk up in a rare smile. "I said I *wanted to*. Don't think I'm stupid enough to do it. I want this, I want *her*, more than I've wanted anything in my life." I let the confession out.

"I'd ask if she had a magic pussy or something, but I know you ain't hit it," he said. At the look on my face, he cocked his head to one side and searched my expression with an expression on his own face of open curiosity.

"Interesting," he said, and I didn't say nothin'. I think my face said it all. I didn't like the way he talked about my little Alina like that. I didn't like it one bit... and no, you couldn't ask me why. I didn't have an answer for you.

Still, that was good enough for him, and seemed to tell him all that he wanted or needed to know.

CHAPTER SEVENTEEN

Alina...

My phone rang with a number I didn't recognize and I frowned at it. I usually didn't answer, but it could finally be the police or something, so I did.

"Alina?"

His voice was deep and sent a shiver down my spine despite how warm it was in my room. I'd turned the air conditioning to something warmer since I didn't know what was going to happen. I mean, I certainly couldn't afford it on my own...

"Yes," I said softly then, "Wait – how did you get my number?"

"One of the same ways I'm gonna use to help find out what happened to your friend," he said, and I sat up.

"You need something from me?" I asked.

"If you're up to it. I need you to let me in."

"You're here?" I asked, getting up out of my bed and going to my front door.

"I am. Downstairs," he said.

"Did you buzz?" I asked.

"No, I called you," he said and I could hear his smirk over the line

– which I could almost visualize but I couldn't remember. I hadn't seen him smirk, ever, *had I?*

"Gotcha," I murmured out loud for his benefit, and I hit the buzzer by the door to pop the door downstairs. I heard the buzzing through the line and the latch of the door disengage.

"Save this number," he told me before ending the call.

I saved his number while I stood there, waiting for him to reach my front door. I still jumped when he knocked twice, even though he didn't do it very hard.

I opened the door to see him standing there with two other men and I swallowed hard. Both of them were imposing in their own way and only one of them was one of the men he'd been with at the bar the night before, the one with the neck so thick it almost made his head seem too small for his body. I wasn't saying that to be mean, it was just true.

"Um, hi," I said faintly and stood aside, letting them in. All three walked into mine and Maya's apartment and the open, high-ceilinged space, suddenly seemed much smaller for their presence.

"I just woke up," I said, and La Croix turned his head to follow my movement as I shut and leaned up against the inside of the door.

"This is Cypress," he said, leaning his head over to indicate the taller man with the neck as thick as a damn tree trunk. I nodded carefully in Cypress's direction and he nodded back. His hair was close cropped and brown, as though his head had been shaved and was in that phase of growing back, where it was just about to tip into the point of being a head of hair. Still too short to grab onto while he went down on you, but long enough it was there.

I tried not to let myself blush at the errant last thought that I'd had... I mean, hadn't I just given myself lock and stock to La Croix? Technically, I didn't get to think that way anymore about anyone else, *did I?*

I didn't know how any of this was supposed to work, and considering the one person to ask was Maya, and that I was doing this specifically to find her? Yeah... yikes... *complicated.*

"An' this here is Saint," he said. Saint was slightly taller than La

Croix but not as tall as Cypress. His long dark hair was pulled into a ponytail, and his dark beard was trimmed neatly along a strong jaw.

All three of them were ridiculously muscular, all three practically wearing the same thing – sturdy black boots, roughly worked in and stained jeans, and those black leather vests with the patches all over them. Cypress wore a gray sleeveless shirt up under a black wifebeater. Saint had on a clean white tee with the sleeves rolled up shorter, but La Croix? La Croix wore only the ink under his skin.

"It's nice to meet you," I said and kept my back pressed to the door.

Intimidation radiated from the three men like an oven and I didn't know what to do. I was both scared and intrigued and the conflicting emotions were at war with one another to the point that I didn't know which would win over the other.

I did have to say, I had *so many questions* for La Croix and I was more than slightly disappointed that the other two men accompanied him. I mean, I wasn't comfortable asking them in front of anyone else.

"So, um, what did you need from me?" I asked when the silence stretched between us post-introduction.

"Your friend got a laptop or anything?" Saint asked.

"Oh, yeah, in here," I said, and I led the way into her bedroom. Saint took a seat at her desk and woke the machine up.

"Lemme call our guy. See if he can get this opened up," he muttered, reaching for his phone. I reached past him and keyed in her PIN and the screen flowed from the lock screen to her open email which was the last screen I'd had the machine on, the morning after she'd disappeared.

Saint looked up at me. "Thanks," he said. "Mind writing that down for me?"

"Sure." I pulled a pen from the cup on the corner of her desk and jotted it down on the notepad for him.

"Thanks," he said. "You can leave me to it."

"Sure," I said. "Um, I know it's the afternoon, but coffee anyone?"

"We'd like that, cher," La Croix said and I swallowed hard, not sure what to make of the term of endearment.

"Okay."

I went into the kitchen. Cypress stayed, standing behind Saint while he got someone on the phone and worked at Maya's laptop. La Croix followed me to the kitchen.

I went to the coffee pot and threw the old down the sink, turning on the tap to wash the pot before fixing new.

La Croix leaned back up against the counter a little closer than was comfortable, his dark eyes wandering over me.

"You sleep like that?" he asked me, cocking his head.

"Usually," I replied softly.

His expression was unreadable, but certainly didn't telegraph pleasure. I looked down at the army-green tank top and the blue and white vertically barred men's boxers I had on.

"I liked the nightgown better," he said.

I blushed furiously, caught off guard and said, my voice clipped, "I only wear that on special occasions."

"You deserve to wear beautiful things no matter what the occasion," he said, and I whipped my head around to look at him. There was no cruel joke to his expression, nothing but that strange and unnerving placid stoicism. His arms crossed a bit awkwardly over his chest due to his size.

"I tend to save my favorite things," I said as I filled the back of the coffee pot with water.

I discarded the old filter and grounds and lined the basket with a new one.

"You should enjoy your favorite things," he said, lifting one shoulder in a shrug. "Every chance you get. Life's too short."

I paused, opening the cupboard and considered his words. I suppose, for a man like him, that made sense. I suppose, thinking about it a little more deeply, that it made sense for anyone, really.

In that regard, instead of reaching for the cheap stuff, I brought down my favorite coffee blend and scooped a generous amount into the waiting filter and basket.

I started the coffeemaker and shoved it back into its spot on the counter.

"What... what happened that night?" I asked again, because it was high key driving me nuts not knowing.

"There was some trouble an' I took care of it. You took a knock to the back of your head and fainted, so I took care of the rest after that, too," he said and I scraped my bottom lip between my teeth thoughtfully.

"The only time I've ever fainted in my life is at the sight of blood," I said and then I returned my eyes to his as the pieces fell into place... *had my missing clothes been taken because they'd been covered in blood? And if so, whose blood?*

"The less you know, the better," he said, and I nodded, my mouth suddenly gone dry, and in that moment, I chose to believe him, dropping the subject completely, except for...

"Whatever happened," I said. "Thank you for getting me home safely."

He nodded but didn't say a word else on the matter.

I opened my mouth to ask a question, hesitated, looking back through Maya's bedroom doorway at Cypress standing there, and closed my mouth, unwilling to ask.

Instead, I asked quietly, "Did you have to bring them?"

His head didn't move, but his eyes slid in the direction of Maya's doorway.

"To find your friend? Yes. They're here to help. Why? You want some alone time?" he asked.

"I would like to ask some questions," I said quietly. "About... things... um, regarding our..." I cleared my throat. "Arrangement."

His gaze had settled back on me as I pulled down four mugs from the cupboard.

"Plenty of time for that later," he said with a one-shouldered shrug. "When's your next night off?" he asked.

"Um, tonight," I said.

"Yeah?" he asked.

"Mm-hm."

There was an uncomfortable lull in our conversation and he pushed off the counter, dropping his arms to his side. I didn't mean to, but I think I flinched.

He stilled and his voice pitched low so that only I could really hear, he said, "Lemme take you for a ride tonight, then. We can get somethin' to eat maybe, an' that way you can ask your questions."

I pursed my lips, rubbing them together, and finally nodded. I didn't have any other plans.

My phone vibrated on the counter where I'd set it and he leaned back against the counter again on the other side of the sink from me, his arms returning to their intimidating posture over his chest as I snatched it up and looked.

It was Dorian, asking about Maya.

I told him, *nothing yet*, and I knew he was just as frustrated as me. I'd gone to the police *again* three days ago… and nothing. I didn't even think they were looking. It was like screaming into the void, I swear to God.

Well, I would never quit.

I swallowed hard.

"Your boyfriend?" La Croix asked, his voice careful and measured.

"What? Oh, no. I don't have one, anymore. That was my friend Dorian. The guy that helped me move. He lives with *his* boyfriend, Marcus, just down the way. He was asking about Maya." I spoke quickly, and I didn't know why I'd just told him all of that other than maybe fear… and I meant that as in fear for Dorian.

La Croix relaxed marginally, and I ventured with a question of my own.

"What about you?" I asked softly. "Wife or girlfriend?" His eyes locked with mine as though he was willing me to understand something and the silence stretched between us.

"Just you," he said finally, and I believed him. But holy shit, what a way to say it.

I nodded, crossing and uncrossing my own arms, my body jangling with nerves as the coffee maker gurgled, filling the silence between us. Saint's voice slipped between the noises the coffee maker made every once in a while. He was still talking on the phone.

"Why?" La Croix asked finally, and it took me a second to realize he was asking why I was asking if he was single. I shrugged without looking.

"Reputation, maybe? I mean, I guess..." I murmured, unwilling to look him in the eyes.

"Reputation?" he asked.

"Bikers," I said softly.

I think he cracked his first smile at me. I mean, I heard it with the rush of air he let out that sounded like it was on the edge of being a laugh.

"Womanizers, you mean?" he asked.

I blushed, embarrassed. Good Lord, I sounded like an asshole when he put it that way. *Way to stereotype, Alina...* although with our arrangement, I guess it wasn't too far off the mark.

"No," he said to curb the uncomfortable silence. "That's fair. Some of us, but not all of us. I guess that's just like any other man, though," he said. "I mean to say, I think it's less about 'biker' and more about bein' male, if you get me."

I nodded but didn't look at him. I couldn't. He was being gracious which sort of made my humiliation complete.

"Does anyone want cream or sugar?" I called out, and the chair to Maya's desk creaked as Saint looked around and out this way.

"Two of each, please?" he called.

"Just a sugar," Cypress called. I looked to La Croix.

"Black," he said evenly.

"Of course," I murmured.

I fixed everyone's coffee, took them around, and La Croix and I sat across from each other in silence in the living room, drinking ours.

My coffee finished, I asked, "Would it be impolite if I took a shower and things?"

"Impolite?" he asked, and I had to smile. Okay, maybe that *was* a little weird of me to phrase it that way, but he reassured me and said, "No."

"Alright, thank you," I murmured. I got up, collected everyone's coffee cup who was through drinking, refilled whoever asked for it, and stowed the used cups in the top rack of the dishwasher.

La Croix watched me from the couch, his eyes following my every movement and though his eyes unnerved me, with the ink in the sclera like it was, I don't know… I didn't feel threatened or scared – at least not as much as before. I don't know how I felt, to be honest. Just that I could eliminate those off the list.

I went into my room to gather some clothes and things to take with me to the bathroom and he appeared in my doorway. I jumped. He'd moved so quietly, I hadn't even heard him.

He watched me as I went to my dresser to look through things and said, "Dress for the slide, not for the ride."

"I'm sorry?" I asked, perking up.

"It means dress for protection, not for something like comfort with the heat," he replied.

"So, what? Like, jeans and boots?"

"To start," he affirmed.

"Okay, what else?"

"A tee shirt, or even tank top is fine. A leather jacket would be good, but if you can't have that, a denim one'll do. I'll get you some gear. I either need your sizes or for you to come with me to the store to pick some things out."

"You don't have to spend money on me," I said quickly.

He cocked his head. "Perk of the deal," he said.

"How so?"

"I have you now," he told me, and it didn't sound creepy or overbearing, just a statement of fact. "There's a certain responsibility in that, cher. I find your friend, I get you in the bargain, sure, but that means I take care of you."

I swallowed hard. "I don't know what to say to that," I said.

"You don't say nothin'. Just go with it for now, okay?"

"O-o-okay," I stammered.

He nodded, and I put a pair of jeans out on the foot of my bed, found a pair of good sturdy boots, and put those out too. I settled on a white tank, a brown belt to match the boots, and a light, lace, rust-colored kimono to go over it.

Some gold hoop earrings, and some gold charms on a long chain made the outfit complete, but I didn't have the type of coat or jacket he requested.

I chewed my bottom lip and decided I would check Maya's closet for one when I got out of the shower. I knew she wouldn't mind. We borrowed each other's clothes all the time. Thrifting and fashion were personal favorite passions for the both of us.

I took my things into the bathroom with me and shut the door. Once secluded, I felt myself marginally relax.

I didn't know how to do this. I didn't know how to feel, or what to think, or even what to do… but I would do *anything* to have my best friend, who I loved so much, back here with me.

CHAPTER EIGHTEEN

*L*a Croix...
    She shut herself into her bathroom with an armload of clothes and I stared long and hard at the door for a minute.

I turned my head and caught Cypress and Saint both looking at me, both grinning like a couple of fools. I scowled and Cy looked down at Saint and Saint looked up at Cy, both of them giggling like a couple of damn ninnies before Saint leaned back and took back up with her housemate's computer.

I took the time offered to me to do some reconnaissance, wandering her and her friend's place, inspecting their bookshelves and finally getting to learn all that she was reading when I'd spy her through her window back when she lived across from the club's compound.

She had a collection of the classics, from Jane Austen to Mary Shelley, the Brontë sisters, and Dickens. She even had some Lewis Carroll and J.M. Barrie. Some of this shit I had a vague knowledge of, the rest, fucked if I knew. But she liked to read and that was something I could maybe work with.

There were other books, more modern shit. Shit like astrology and numerology. Looked like witch shit, which was *also* something I could work with.

One small nook in the place held a small table and an old-ass sewing machine. I couldn't tell if that was my little Alina's or if it was her friend, Maya's.

I went back into my girl's room, letting my eyes wander her things. She liked candles, and rocks. She had all kinds of crystals and things, mostly small ones, all around her candles and on shelves.

Her desk was neat and orderly, but she didn't have a computer like her friend. Instead, she had paper and pens. The paper rough and lookin' handmade. I wondered if she did it herself. There was a basket on the corner of her desk and it held a thick waxed thread, big sewing needles, and some other things I had no name for.

The shower cut off, and I didn't pay it no mind. Her bed was unmade; just a triangle of covers thrown back, not rumpled with the sheets and blankets twisted together like mine. She made it every day I'd bet, but she hadn't had the chance today. Me and the boys had gotten here first.

In the corner by a window, back out in the main area of her place, there was an easel and a pad of paper on it. A light sketch of what was down below on the street had been half water colored and I saw the touch of my girl's delicate hand in the strokes.

Everything about the friend's room said she didn't have the quiet soul or the patience, so it had to be my little Alina.

The bathroom door opened, a billow of steam rising toward the ceiling through the open portal and my girl stepped through.

"Hey," she said. Her hair was pulled back, braided over her shoulder. She hadn't wet it. It would have been darker if she had, and I hadn't heard a dryer.

"You good?" I asked her.

"Yes, better… thank you."

I nodded and heard Saint groan as he got to his feet.

He and Cypress came out.

"Go on and leave that computer on for us, would yah?" Saint asked. "We got a guy in there workin', tryin' to find some things out."

Alina nodded carefully out of the corner of my eye and I looked back to her from the boys.

"Y'all 're free to go about your business," I told 'em.

"You sure, boss?" Cypress asked, and I turned from Alina to just look at him.

He raised his hands in surrender and Saint knew better than to argue with a look like that.

"Thanks for the coffee, Miss Lina," he said and Alina smiled and nodded.

"You're welcome," she said. Saint gave me an imperceptible signal he wanted to talk.

"I'm gon' walk these two down," I told her. "Come on down when you're ready."

She nodded. "I will."

I went out with the boys. Once out on the street, I asked, "What you got?"

"Radar is in, lookin' around," he said. "Lookin' through her email, looks like she was some kind of high-class hooker."

"Angle worth lookin' into," I mused aloud. "She an independent, or she with one of them places?" I asked.

"That's not the kicker," Saint said, scratching his cheek with the back of his middle fingernail, not really answering my question. With the look he was giving me, there was a better theory rattling around in his skull, one he didn't look all that comfortable sayin' out loud. Like it'd bring the wrath of the voodoo queen herself down on our heads.

"Spill it," I said in the face of his reluctance.

"She's a Bashaw," he said shortly and winced.

"Name supposed to mean somethin'?" I asked. The name *was* some kind of familiar to me, tickling the back of my brain, but for some reason, I couldn't place it.

"City Councilman Nathan Bashaw ring a bell?" he asked.

"A sitting city councilman's daughter?" I asked, scowling.

"Ah yup," Saint declared.

"Shit," I muttered. Well, that *did* put a bit of a different spin on things, now didn't it?

"What's a girl like that, with all her daddy's money, hookin' on the side for?" Cypress wondered aloud.

"Probably daddy issues," Saint said. "Most girls doin' somethin' like that with a daddy that rich and powerful are lookin' for some kind of revenge," he said.

Yeah, *but revenge for what,* was the honest question.

I nodded slowly and said, "Keep diggin' for me. See what rocks you can get turned over and what comes a crawlin' out."

Saint nodded and Cy said, "You got it, boss."

"Keep the dirty side down, boys," I told 'em.

"You keep the shiny side up," Saint said, shooting a finger gun at me. I nodded and watched them mount up and ride off.

The door to Alina's building opened behind me and I turned to see her emerge. She had a pleather jacket on that was more fashion than function and big on her. Had to be her roomie's. I couldn't keep the scowl off my face.

"What's wrong?" she asked and leaned away from me.

"First thing's first. We gon' get you a proper jacket. That ain't no good. I doubt it's even real leather."

"It's not, but it's the best I could find," she said and she continued to quail a bit. I didn't like it, but I couldn't say as I blamed her.

"You ever ride afore?" I asked.

She shook her head.

"Awright, c'mere…" she drew nearer reluctantly, and I got on the bike.

"Get on behind me," I told her. "Step here."

She did, and I told her, "Make sure you keep your feet on these pegs or you're liable to melt the soles off them boots."

"Okay," she agreed.

I handed her a helmet. I'd brought extra, just in case, and she put it on while I brought mine off the handlebars. No fuckin' way was I gon' let any pig have an excuse to pull my ass over. That was another thing I had to get her, a proper helmet that fit her good. One with a facemask maybe. Better safe than sorry with a pretty face like she got.

"Hold on to me, lean with the bike and not against when we turn, and you should be fine!" I shouted over the roar of the engine once I'd started up the bike.

She snugged herself up close to my back and put her arms around me.

I checked traffic and pulled us smoothly out and away from the curb.

The city traffic was slow enough to get her used to the bike, and we weren't goin' all that far – just over to the big Harley-Davidson right there over in Metairie. There was a Harley store just around the corner from her on Decatur, but that place was fuckin' useless. Just tee shirts and shit. No bikes, and certainly no real riding gear.

No, you wanted the good stuff? Boots and chaps, leather and helmets? You went to the big Harley store and dealership over in Metairie.

I kept us on the surface streets. It made for a longer ride, but the speeds were slower. I checked and rechecked at stop signs and cross streets and felt like the woman behind me was made of fuckin' glass.

It was weird for me. I didn't worry about a thing, usually... but I was a cursed bastard. Felt like most days if I didn't have bad luck, I wouldn't have no luck at all, and I didn't want that on her.

Once there, we parked and got off my bike. I took her inside and was pretty much immediately assailed by a fuckin' salesman.

"Welcome to Harley-Davidson, how can I help you?" He came up to us and he was a dumb shit. He thought he was some kind of shark, smellin' blood in the water, but in reality, I was a bigger shark than he could ever be.

"Need someone to help her find the right fit. Helmet, good boots, and a jacket," I said, and the guy wilted a little.

"Sure, no problem," he said and was all too happy to pass us off to somebody else for the smaller commission.

I didn't care. I just wanted my little Alina taken care of. Cost was no object.

We walked out an hour later, over her innumerable protests with her delicate herbal scent crushed under the smell of new leather.

She was good, that was all that mattered to me.

The sun was starting to dip when we hit the highway out of the city. She held on for dear life when I punched through the bullshit city traffic and sent us screaming out in the direction of the country.

There was a place with some down-home Louisiana cooking that I liked on the way out to my place. Figured we could have our talk. She could ask her questions, and we could maybe come to an understanding more 'n we already had.

By that, I meant, I could take her temperature on how squeamish she was and set a pace accordingly.

I had to say, the feel of her pressed to my back was mighty fine. Better than even the last time I'd had the occasion to fuck; and all because it was *her*.

It was dark by the time I pulled off into the parking lot of the place I'd picked.

Alina shuddered against me as I stopped the bike and heeled the kickstand down to park it. She got off and went for the catch on her new helmet and pulled it off.

"You awright?" I asked her, eyeing her carefully, and she nodded.

"That is both terrifying and exhilarating and I can't decide which it's more of," she said.

I nodded, and said, "For me, it's the last one."

She gave a wry twist of her lips and said, "Understandable, else why else would you do it?"

I lifted a shoulder in a shrug and said, "I'm not a pussy."

She cracked a smile and laughed at that, but I wasn't tryin' to be funny. I was just telling the truth.

We went inside, and I got us a booth. It was dark, most of the light comin' from all the neon beer signs behind the bar and on the walls up around the ceiling. There was a light out the wall at each table, but it was just one of them candle-looking glass bulbs further muted by a miniature lampshade.

Alina tipped the menu into the sparse light and squinted at the print. I didn't need to look. I knew what was good.

Our drinks were brought and Alina finally came back up out of the menu.

"Y'all know what you're havin'?" the waitress asked.

I let Alina go first. She ordered some kind of salad.

"And for you, honey?"

"Fried alligator," I said, and she smiled.

"Alright now, that'll be right out."

The waitress left, and it was suddenly me and Alina alone... no menu for my girl to hide behind.

"You said you had questions," I said, when the silence had stretched just a little too long.

"Um, I do," she said, inclining her head just a little.

"Ask away," I told her and her blush was unmistakable, even in the low light.

"I don't know where to start," she confessed.

"Start with what you want to know the most, cher."

Her eyes lifted to meet mine, and they widened slightly. She was beautiful, and it struck me just how much – those lips of hers slightly parted, her eyes wide and full of silver light...

I burned this moment into my mind, knowing that the best was yet to come, my cock already hard in my jeans, making me shift in my seat.

"I guess... I guess, how do you want to do this? Um, I don't know. I never imagined in a million years I would do anything like this. I... I'm... I don't know." Her stammering was adorable.

"You're off tonight. Let's see where it takes us, yeah?" I said steadily.

She nodded and said, "Okay."

"Tell me..." she said after some quiet. "What do you, like, *do*?"

"I run my club," I answered her absently, transfixed by those smoky, misty, silver eyes of hers fixed on mine.

"Right, but for like, work?"

Ah...

"I work in a junkyard," I answered. "Pullin' parts and fixin' old boat motors."

"Really?" she asked and her clear eyes conveyed surprise.

"What'd you think I did?" I asked.

She shrugged and looked away. "I don't know, which is why I asked."

I felt my lips twitch and nodded slowly.

"Now that you do know, what do you think?" I asked carefully.

"I think that it's surprisingly… normal."

"Yeah?"

"Yeah."

"Well, I guess that's alright," I said and felt somehow a little bit lighter. Her smile sent me up on cloud nine.

CHAPTER NINETEEN

Alina...

We talked... well, *I* talked, asking a million questions, and yes – I was beating around the bush. I wanted to ask about what he *liked*, as in the bedroom, but I was afraid of the answer.

I didn't know what to make of him, honestly. He was impossible to read, and so very intense it was scary... but he was honest. Like, *brutally* honest. Raw in a way I had never encountered before.

We ate our meal in silence, and it was really good food. The salad was real greens and not iceberg lettuce like most restaurants served. The dressing was fresh and made in-house. The meat was grilled to perfection and the flavors all married wonderfully. I'd learned things about this man that I suddenly found myself bound to who I didn't know anything at all about. Normal things that made him seem a little less frightening in some ways.

"Don't you want to know anything about me?" I asked at one point.

"I already know things," he said.

"Like what?" I asked, curiously.

"You love books," he said. "Used to sit outside and smoke, watching you read."

"When I lived at the other apartment?" I asked.

"Mm-hm," he hummed around a mouthful of fried gator.

"There was a window seat there," I said. "It was my favorite place to sit while I read. One of my favorite features of that apartment period, really." I braced my elbow on the table and my chin on my hand as I regarded him. He didn't say anything, and I put my arm and my head down, going back to my food.

"Mine too," he said, and I looked up sharply from where my attention had been refocused on spearing more salad onto my fork. He wasn't looking at me, but rather his plate as if he hadn't just said something that was at once incredibly sweet, but also incredibly unnerving.

"Saw a man fuck you on that same window seat," he said a minute later.

"Oh my God!" I said, my fork clacking sharply against the edge of my salad bowl as it fell from my nerveless fingers. He looked up from his plate at me. In place of the cruel smirk I had almost expected, there was a heat, a serious look in his eyes, on his face, that almost felt a little too intense while I sat there feeling like every ounce of color had drained out of my face with embarrassment.

"That's something I wanna know," he said.

"What?" I asked, dabbing my mouth with my napkin, trying to hide the creeping blush.

"Why aren't you with that guy anymore?"

I glanced back down at my plate, putting my napkin back in my lap and took up my fork again. I said unhappily, "He cheated on me. I found out and it hurt. I ended it." I sighed, and when I looked up, he was staring at me, the intensity of his eyes more, not less, and he'd literally stopped mid-chew.

"What's his name?" he demanded, and I blinked once, long and slow, taken aback. He'd asked so calm and quiet, in such a way that left me totally perturbed.

"Does it matter?" I asked softly.

"It does to me," he said.

"What?" I asked. "Would you hurt him?"

He remained silent, and I waited him out… but then I realized –

silence is better than bullshit, and La Croix had no intention whatsoever of bullshitting me, so he simply wouldn't answer me.

I swallowed hard and said, "Anyway, I was crying about it on Maya's couch and she said she'd had it with her roommate. She asked me if she could get her out, if I would come live with her. You know, sort of a fresh start. The beginning of a new chapter. I guess I was a little desperate for change by then so I agreed."

"She a good friend to you?" he asked and his tone had hushed.

"The best," I said with a wan smile. "We hexed the shit out of my ex while drunk my first night after I moved in." I couldn't help my little laugh at the memory that wasn't all too long ago. "I just want to find her," I finished.

He nodded evenly. "Got the whole club lookin'," he said, and I cocked my head.

"How many of you are there?"

"Nine," he said. "Now that the prospect's patched in."

"Patched in?" I asked.

"Earned the big colored patch in the middle," he said, jerking a thumb over his back.

"Ah." I nodded and resumed eating.

We lapsed into silence for a while again while I thought about his demand for my ex's name. I had half a mind to give it to him, but not without knowing the precise consequence of that action, no way... Did I want his dick to rot off from whatever disease he picked up from one of his side hos? Yes. Did I want him to die, or be crippled forever, or something like that? No, no I didn't think I did. I didn't think anything needed to go *that* far. I mean, he'd cheated... he hadn't murdered the pope or whatever.

When dinner was through, La Croix paid, and with a wave over his shoulder at the restaurant staff, we departed the bar and grill for the sultry Louisiana night and the ride... well, I don't know where he was taking me. We hadn't discussed it, and he didn't turn back the way we'd come from.

"Where are you taking me?" I shouted above the wind.

He shouted back at me, "Home!"

I supposed he meant *his* home because he certainly didn't mean mine... I mean, we weren't going anywhere near that direction.

We were out in the swamps, and I wasn't exactly keen on that. I mean, I was a city girl through and through and the only time I had ever been to the swamps and bayous had been on field trips as a child during the day; to the gator farms and such. You know, one of those trips with the science teacher that was supposed to be educational; and it was, but it was also more on the side of the fantastical for the kids. You know what I mean?

We pulled into a long driveway down a dirt and gravel track and I held on to La Croix nervously, breathing just a little easier when a house with a light in the window loomed into view.

"Is this your place?" I asked when he killed the motor and I'd dismounted the back of his bike.

"No, we got a way to go, yet," he said, and that made me silently gulp.

He held out a hand and waved me forward. I let him lead me to an old but still serviceable dock to the side and into the back of the house.

"I don't know about this," I said apprehensively, scrubbing my sweating palms along the tops of my jeans-clad thighs.

"Just a short boat ride, cher."

He stepped down into the aluminum flat-bottomed boat and held out a hand to me.

I swallowed hard and thought to myself I must be crazy. This was probably it. I wouldn't have to worry if I would ever see Maya again; because surely, I was about to die.

I took his hand and stepped down into the boat and took a seat on the low bench, shivering. It wasn't from the cold; I'll tell you that much. With it being the height of summer, it had to be in the seventies and eighties even at night. Add the humidity and it felt more like the eighties and nineties. So no, I wasn't shivering from cold at all.

My shaking only got worse the deeper into the swamp we went.

"You live in the swamp?" I asked as he steered the boat from the back, his hand on the handle to the outboard motor.

He simply nodded, and his silence just served to unnerve me all the more.

He pointed a light, and I shuddered at the points of light just above the waterline that blinked and then submerged – the eye shine of alligators. Points of light smaller than those surrounded us, along with raucous frog song joined by the evening scream of cicadas and the muted ratcheting tones of crickets – the symphony of the swamp.

I might have found it soothing, a far cry from the noise and flash of the city, but not knowing where I was headed, or what was going to happen to me? It put quite the damper on the experience.

We traveled for around twenty minutes, maybe a half an hour in reality – but it felt like a small eternity of turning this way and that through waterways that appeared random to me. I watched him steer us, and he seemed completely relaxed and at ease. I found myself wishing that some of that energy would rub off on me, but it seemed that the more at ease he seemed, the more anxious I became.

There was a light out there in the swamp. A manmade one, electric and shining steady. The closer we got, I realized that it was a porch light. The house was like a small, but regular-sized house, two-story and ramshackle by all appearances on the outside but sturdily built. It wasn't until we were almost right up on it that I realized it was built on a big ol' *barge*. Just sitting there, out in the middle of the Bayou. Nothing around for miles...

"How…?" the word escaped my lips before I could stop it.

"How's the light workin'?" he asked.

"Among other things," I said.

"Solar," he answered. "The water comes from rain catch barrels. Got me a sophisticated filtration system to make it potable."

My fear dissipated in the face of my curiosity. He pulled the little boat up alongside the barge and stopped the motor. There was a little ladder to step up out of it and onto the floating platform. He went up first, reaching down a hand to help me up. I slipped, and he lifted me as though I weighed nothing onto the barge deck beside him.

"Oh, wow." I took my hand back quickly and he asked, "You awright?"

"Yes." I nodded. "Thank you."

I looked around. Nearly half the barge, on the side of the house with only one narrow window with frosted and pebbled privacy glass, was a bank of solar panels. After a narrow walkway between the panels and the home, up snug against the side of the house, there were these big ginormous white tanks, the downspouts off the eaves of the house running into them. The roof of the home was pitched steep and was metal, the siding these shake tiles. Where there wasn't any of the shake weathered silvery by the elements, there was corrugated tin that was rusting in places, tacked in a strange patchwork to the outside walls – as though the outside of the home was only half finished and he'd run out of materials.

The building looked shabby and poor, like almost anything out in swamp country and I was a little nervous about what it would be like inside.

He put his hand to my back and guided me to the front door of the small home that once we were near it, seemed to be about the size of mine and Maya's apartment – which given that it was two stories tall meant that in all actuality, it was probably *bigger.*

Inside was *much* different from the outside – tidy and neat. Some of the furniture was certainly older and well-worn, but still well maintained. The kitchen was beautiful with dark tile countertops that gleamed softly under the muted light of the copper hood above the stove.

Inside the front door, there was a stairwell leading up to the second-floor loft, which took up half of the floor plan of the entire space and appeared to be the master bedroom. There was an office down here that didn't look much used, and what I thought was one bathroom for the whole place that was a door beyond the stairwell. I didn't see too much, because the front door was being shut behind me, and La Croix's hands were over my shoulders, taking my coat.

I let him have it, lifting my purse off from over my head to allow him to.

"Hang that right here, cher," he said, and I handed him my purse, which he hung with my jacket on a row of pegs along a board by the front door.

"How long have you lived out here like this?" I asked, as he turned back to me.

"Goin' on two an' a half years, now," he said.

"Does anyone know it's out here?"

"Hex, and Cy," he said. "Some of the other boys in the club."

I looked at my cellphone and no surprise – there was no signal. None, whatsoever. The fear crept back in.

"Wanna keep that charged?" he asked.

"Yes, please," I said. He took the useless phone from me and plugged it in at the end table at one end of the couch.

"What if something happens?" I asked, and he looked at me. "You know, like an emergency or something…"

"House has internet, satellite linkup. I got a sat phone… but ain't nobody to call, cher. The police?" He huffed a derisive laugh. "Anybody comes up in here that don't belong, the people out here, me included, handle that ourself."

I nodded, a bit wide-eyed and said, "I mean, I meant more like a medical emergency. Like what if one of us has a heart attack, or like a stroke?"

He smiled a slow curl of his lips and said, "It's my time, it's my time…"

I nodded mutely. That honestly scared me more, not less. I mean, how would I get out of here without him?

"You want the tour?" he asked.

I nodded again.

He led me around the bottom floor of the house first. There was a guest room, the office that I'd glimpsed, and the kitchen with a dining table enough for six in it. The living room took up the lion's share of the bottom floor, and then there was the bathroom which was nothing short of majestic – its ceiling and the one wall slanted and following the sharp incline of the stairs on the inside of the house, but it was also slanted *outside*. That being the part of the house with the corrugated metal as the siding, which made so much more sense when you saw this space on the *inside*.

The walls of the shower were stone, and the bathtub was a completely separate entity; claw footed, and deep – a majestic, hammered copper. I think I made an audible noise of longing at the sight of it.

"You like?" he asked, and I nodded.

"It's beautiful."

He nodded and I turned to look at the vanity, which was equally gorgeous – a stone backsplash and counter to match the shower, the sink basins also copper, the walls a warm golden, vertical shiplap. The floor was a deep gray slate tiling reminiscent of flagstone and the woven bathmats completed things nicely – the space masculine, but not overtly so, and ever so lovely.

"Just finished it in the last month or so," he said.

"You did this yourself?" I asked.

He shrugged one of his massive boulders of a shoulder and said, "I had help."

He jerked his head, and I followed him out and around to the bottom of the stairs. We went up, and I found us in his bedroom – which admittedly, wasn't much.

A bed, only one broken bedside table, and an old dresser that wasn't nearly right or big enough for the space. Probably something from his boyhood home.

There was another bathroom up here. I was surprised to find it, but not nearly as nice as the one below it. Just a shower, a sink, and a toilet and just like every apartment bathroom I'd ever been in with its cheap plastic shower wrap and basin. The vanity a Formica countertop around a plain sink.

"Doin' this one next," he said quietly at my back and I jumped.

"A bit anti-climactic after the other one," I murmured with a bit of a forced smile, keenly aware that we stood near his bed with its black sheets and rumpled covers and that the buck stopped here.

The first, of what would probably be many payments, was due.

He stepped in closer to me and said, his voice low, "Let down your hair."

I swallowed hard and reached up, pulling the hair tie off the end of my braid, separating the rope by combing my fingers through it.

His breath caught, and he pushed my light lace kimono off my shoulders. I kept my eyes off his face, the fear thrilling through me as I didn't know what to expect, and the garment fell to his floor.

"Look at me," he ordered softly, and I did… my gaze flicking to his, my mouth going dry, making it difficult to swallow.

I swear, he stared right down to the bottom of my soul.

"Please," I begged, hanging on the moment. "Just don't hurt me."

I hated how my voice trembled, but I couldn't help it.

He reached up, his fingertips lightly grazing my cheek, wrapping around the back of my neck, burying in the back of my hair. His thumb stroked along my jaw and I squeezed my eyes shut, hot tears leaking out of them as he stepped forward, closing the space between us.

I gasped as his lips touched my forehead lightly and a shudder ran through me from the crown of my head to the soles of my feet. I sobbed lightly, and his arms closed around me. Without knowing what else to do, I put mine around him and held on tight.

CHAPTER TWENTY

La Croix...
Hurt her?
Shit...

I guess I couldn't say I blamed her for thinkin' that was my thing just by lookin' at me; but no. I didn't derive pleasure out of inflicting pain on a woman unless that was her thing. Even then, I couldn't say it quite sat right with me.

I held her tight, my arm around her back, the other pressing her face to my chest, as her fear stained my cut with her tears.

"Shhh," I soothed, and I wouldn't let go.

She didn't pull away. She simply stayed, holding to me. I didn't understand how she could be so terrified of me and simultaneously seek comfort from my big dumb ass. I mean, it was confusing as much as it was thrilling.

Did I want her? More than anything. Did I want her to be willing?

Wasn't she already?

She'd agreed to the terms, knowing full well what that meant, what it all entailed, and she was here with me – that's all that I'd really asked.

The rest?

Shit. I didn't know. I trusted though, that I would either figure it out or I wouldn't.

Her weeping settled to the odd sniffle and finally she drew back from me and said, "I'm sorry. I'm just scared. I-I've never done anything like this and it's just... it's just a lot, I guess."

"It's alright," I told her, and I tried at a bit of levity. "I ain't bite 'cha unless you're into that sort of thing."

She laughed, dashing at the moisture under her eyes.

"Look at me," I told her. She resisted at first but finally did. I tipped her chin up a little more with the crook of my finger and she inhaled sharply, her eyes widening.

I lowered my lips to hers, slowly, carefully, and kissed her softly.

She didn't pull away, didn't resist, but neither at first did she return it. She stood wooden before me, her hands finding my waist, warm over my cut, and then she softened under my touch and carefully kissed me back.

I didn't think I'd ever gotten so hard so fast in my whole life. Not even when I was a boy with hormones raging right along with my temper.

I was better about the latter as a man, but this? This was testing the furthest reaches of my self-control.

She whimpered against my lips as I moved them softly against hers and it was a small, pleading noise that set me on fire. I stepped into her just a little bit more, both hands now cradling her face as I flicked my tongue against her bottom lip.

She gasped, her lips parting and I thrust my tongue past her lips, past her teeth, and stroked it against hers, pulling her body up against me. My hands relocated from her face to her hips and I drew her body up against mine as tight as it could go without trying to break her and force her inside me or some shit. We stood just a foot or two from my bed and kissed like we was on fire, and *holy gee – God almighty,* did I want her.

I fucking *burned* for her. I had for a long while now, but shit, this was an inferno as opposed to a candle flame.

I tore my mouth from hers and with a small sound of protest at my taking my lips from her, I lifted her tank over her head. She lifted her arms, and I pulled it off her, letting it hit my bedroom floor along with her wrap.

She stepped back into me immediately and lifted her lips to mine. I returned to kissing her, reveling in her taste and her soft skin.

My hands played along her ribs, and I tore my mouth from hers to look at them, my hands with their darker tattooed skin against her pale flawless white body was a sight. Her chest heaved, breathless from my kisses and I looked up from my hands to catch her watching me, warily, her eyes wide.

I cocked my head, and she swallowed hard, her hands at her side as I touched her.

She was a dream come true, a fantasy I'd had more times 'n I could count made real, standing right in front of me.

"Take it all off," I uttered, and I took off my cut, hanging it off the hook by my bed that I had there for it.

She bent and untied the laces on her boots, toeing them off and then straightened.

Her hands shaking, she went for her belt. I watched her every movement as she had her jeans join her rust-colored jacket thing and tank on the floor. I didn't even fully remember the thing falling from her slender shoulders, didn't remember taking it from her. That was alright, though.

She wore a matching bra and panty set, and it was nice. A neutral beige, lacy and sheer; the deep rose of her nipples peeking through.

While I didn't think she'd counted on getting fucked tonight, she'd prepared for it anyway, and I was alright with that.

"I like this," I murmured, reaching for her, grasping her by the hips and pulling her closer. "It's nice."

She swallowed audibly, and she was a bit stiff under my hands, leaning back just a bit in my grasp, her resistance subtle but there. She was still afraid, and I had to see what I could do about that.

I wasn't used to easing a person's fears be they man or woman. I was used to leveraging that shit to my advantage; so, I found myself at a severe *disadvantage* with this, but that was alright. Nothin' easy tasted as sweet or was ever much worth havin' and my little Alina? She was quite the prize.

"You're alright now," I whispered, and she came to me, her reluctance ebbing like the waters around these parts afore a monster storm.

She closed her eyes and yielded under my hands and that was good, that was real good. I put my lips to hers again, even softer, even easier than before. She opened like a flower reaching for the sun, the tension leaving her body, her lips parting, the kiss deepening, and her arms twining reluctantly 'round my neck.

I pulled her tight up against my body and she moaned into my mouth, the sound as sweet as candy.

Her hands settled lightly on my hips, half against my skin which tingled, and half on my belt and the waistband of my jeans.

I delved my tongue deep into her mouth, tasting her, sucking on hers, nipping her lips lightly. I tore my mouth from hers once again, and nipped along her jaw, seeking out the sweet spot on the side of her neck, stopping to breathe along her skin and to nibble her earlobe along the way.

She whimpered, a soft little sound of helplessness and music to my ears. It lanced through me, went straight from my ears to my dick, making my cock jump where it tented the front of my pants.

I ravaged the side of her neck with my kisses and she wilted, no, *melted* into my embrace.

"I got you, baby," I murmured into her ear and she sucked in a sharp breath as I lifted her by her hips, spun her in place, and threw her down onto the bed. She let out a sharp yelp, bouncing once, and put her hands down. I moved lightning quick, faster 'n a striking water moccasin, and hooked fingers into the waistband of her panties.

She sucked in a sharp breath as I swiftly pulled them down off her legs and dropped them to the floor with the rest of her things.

I got over the top of her and returned my mouth to hers. She kissed me, making a strangled noise as I parted her knees with one o' mine.

Her hands went to my face, holding it firmly, keeping my mouth to hers and I liked that. She was getting excited. I could smell her, lightly perfuming the air with her desire, and I wanted to taste her so bad.

I kissed her fiercely, with passion, and worked my way down. She cried out, gripping the sheets at her hips as I pulled down the cup of her bra and latched on to one of her nipples, sucking, gripping it lightly between my teeth, teasing the hard little nub with the tip of my tongue.

Her chest heaved, and she writhed. I glanced up. Those gray eyes of hers that held me captivated every time I looked into them stared down at me, heavy-lidded with passion, as I worked first one of her perfect tits and then the next.

Eventually, I abandoned them to work my way lower, kissing, licking, and nipping all the way down her stomach, delving my hands down between her hips and the bed. I gripped her perfect ass in my hands and raised her up to my mouth, sucking on her clit and listening to the whining, panting, cry, she let out. She'd silently begged me for more with her eyes the whole way down here, and I aimed to deliver.

God, she tasted divine – sweet, clean, vaguely salty with a hint of musk. She tasted so polished, so pure, like the personification of a good hard rain that washed the world clean.

She certainly cleansed some of the sin from my soul, just by her taste alone. As though by pleasing her, I took some of her innate goodness into myself. I was one dark, greedy, son of a bitch. I would take all that she had to give me.

She writhed under me, her fingers gripping the bottom sheet, her hips bucking unbidden like my attentions were too much. I had to disagree; they weren't *nearly* enough. I put an arm across her hips, pinning her down, holding her still, and slipped a thick finger up inside her and *oh, damn...* she was wet. So very wet, her cunt honey slicking my way as I teased around up inside of her to find that spot.

She shrieked in surprise and writhed again, her voice punctuating every one of her panting breaths as I worked her and I liked that. I liked that a lot – how vocal she was.

I worked her up, played her like a fiddle, and when she came apart for me, unraveling like a satin ribbon in my arms, she did it screaming – screaming her pleasure to the very gods who I damn know listened to their angel.

Hmm, yeah...

CHAPTER TWENTY-ONE

Alina...

I stared up at the ceiling with its lazily turning fan overhead and panted, my knees quaking, my thighs trembling, and I just *couldn't...* I couldn't do anything. I couldn't move, my limbs just feeling like they were weighted with lead.

"Mm." He sat up slow, sucking his fingers, and something about that was just... *wow. So hot.*

"How you feel, cher?" he asked me, going for his belt and I whimpered, so thoroughly ravished by his lips, hand, and tongue, I couldn't form coherent speech.

He undid his belt, the leather giving a little sigh of relief as it gave way, and he unfastened the button and unzipped.

My eyes went a little wide as his cock sprang free of his jeans. There was a slightly dark spot in the denim off to one side of his fly from where he leaked precum from the swollen, absolutely engorged head.

He was long and thick, almost frighteningly so. I mean, I had never taken anything quite so big. It was definitely one of those moments where I had to wonder if he would all fit. I mean, I wasn't exactly anything but petite and there wasn't anything about him at all that could be considered small. Certainly not his penis.

Oh, my God...

He kicked his boots off behind him and stood up off the bed, shucking his jeans down his legs.

"You want I should put a condom on?" he asked, and I nodded. I mean, I was on birth control; an implant in my arm, but you never could be too careful.

He pulled one out of a basket beside his bed and tore the gold foil packet open. His dark eyes watched me as I watched him make himself ready for me. I didn't remember doing it, but I found myself writhing on the bed in anticipation, my fingers between my legs, teasing myself for those demonic eyes of his which heated with the fire of lust at watching me. I found myself *wanting* him, *badly*... I don't know how I could go from crying, and being so afraid and ashamed of what I was about to do to *this*... to *wanting him* inside me so bad I could cry for a very *different* reason.

He got up on the bed, his condom-covered cock bobbing thickly between his legs, and he delved his hands beneath me, reaching up past the globes of my ass, his chest on my stomach, as his hands found the back of my bra and he blindly worked the hooks free.

He took it from me, and I let him. Just like that, we were both completely nude and in each other's arms.

He kissed my stomach, worked his way up my chest, and bit into my breast enticingly – not painfully at all. I closed my eyes and gave myself over to the sensation of his warm wet mouth on me. He met my lips with his and I kissed him. I could still vaguely smell myself on his skin, but I didn't care. I found it further arousing.

He dry-humped me a bit, rubbing his hard, hot, thick length up and down my pussy, the lips parting, as I writhed against him. Our bodies danced, erotic, slow, and teasing; and he changed the angle of his hips subtly. His cock got closer and closer to its goal and I jumped when it lined up to my entrance and partially slipped in.

He stilled immediately and tore his mouth from mine to rear back, to look at me.

It was strange staring into those alien eyes of his as he sank into me; so very strange, and so very tender... he cared, and that caring was etched into every line of his face. It showed in the careful control with which he introduced himself to my body. How when I panted, he slowed, misunderstanding me, afraid he was hurting me, when no... no, *not at all*.

The smile that touched his lips was a thing of exquisite beauty when I put a hand to his ass to keep him from pulling back. When I actually *pulled him in*, to the best of my ability – but he would take this at his own pace. A pace that I was finding to be maddeningly slow.

"Please," I begged, breathy with need. "Please, I need you to fill me."

He groaned as though he had just heard the sweetest music, and relented a little, easing into me all the way, giving a tiny thrust to make certain he was fully seated inside of me.

"Oh!" I cried, breathless, letting my head fall back, my back arch, and my body writhe a little to feel what it was like to have him *move*. The way his cock pressed out against my walls, the sensation of him slipping against them, and the feel of him touching deeper than anything I'd ever felt, rubbing places I swore had never been touched.

It was enough to turn me into a wild, feral thing in his arms.

He wrapped an arm around me, beneath me, locking it behind my lower back and making me arch a little more, pulling me down on top of him, going impossibly deep; lying against me, practically crushing me to the bed before he started to thrust. And oh, did he thrust with a slow, careful, measured rolling of his hips that made him touch *all* the right places. He sat up in just a way that he could get his other hand between our bodies so that he could work me from the outside as well as in. The same way he'd worked me with his fingers and his mouth, only this?

This was so much better.

"Oh, God!" He wrung the cry from my throat, and I dug my nails into his arms, trying to writhe, trying to work my hips up and down in counterpoint to his even thrusting.

He felt so good!

Better than anything I had ever felt before in my life, and I suddenly had no regrets striking such a bargain with this man.

Not if he did this.

Not if he *continued* to do this... which was the part that remained yet to be seen.

"Mm!" I caught the cry behind my lips as he picked up pace, working me so good, so deep, so well, I very nearly started weeping again with a sort of relief.

"You gonna come for me, cher? Think you can get there like this?" he asked, grunting like it was taking effort to hold back. He bowed his head and turned it, his eyes slipping shut as he lost himself in the feel of my body as much as I was lost in the feeling of his.

"Mm, yeah," I said breathy.

"Yeah?" he asked.

"Deeper for me?" I asked, and he pulled his other arm from beneath me, hooking it behind my knee so that he could fold my leg up and back and *oh,* how it wrenched a cry out of me...

"Ah! Yeah!"

He kept at it, deep, even, arduous strokes, as my breathing ramped up, breaths coming deeper and faster, my voice escaping me in feral little cries, punctuating each stroke as he kept on relentlessly, working me so patiently and beautifully, his face going from red to purple, the tendons in his neck standing out as he fought to restrain himself.

"Oh! Close! So, close!" I warned him breathlessly. "I'm so close!"

The sensation had been subtle at first, as though something in my pussy inflated and swelled, like a rapidly filling balloon. The sensation grew and grew, getting bigger and bigger, tightening my nipples, silvering my blood, a glow filling me steadily. Growing, growing, growing; until arching, screaming, I came. My pussy squeezed down and rippled out, dragging him in deeper still with its contractions as he shouted out hoarsely and collapsed over me, pressing in deep, pulling me against him tight. We lost ourselves each in the other, to the point there was no telling where one of us ended and the other began.

I came back to myself slowly, La Croix's ear pressed between my breasts, listening to the thundering of my heart. I found my arms wrapped tight around him, my hand against his back and both of us slick with sweat.

He panted and didn't seem in any hurry to move off of me, and that was nice. I liked the close contact, the warmth of his body against mine in the cool currents of air coming down over the top of us from the fan turning overhead.

"Hmm," he hummed in what sounded like satisfaction and smoothed a hand down my side from my breast to my hip, turning his head to kiss the skin over my thunderously beating heart, between my breasts.

He glanced up at me, locking his gaze with mine, and in that voice that was deep and blackened velvet asked me, "Did I hurt you?"

"No," I whispered, touching the side of his face. He closed his eyes and turned his lips into my palm and placed a kiss there.

"Good," he murmured, his voice husky with something akin to relief. I simply stared in muted wonder.

I didn't know what else to say or to do.

"Don't move, cher," he whispered, and he leveraged himself up too soon as far as I was concerned. I made a small noise of protestation and he stopped to look at me.

"I wasn't ready," I said shyly and his lips curved into another one of those rare smiles.

"Gotta get us cleaned up," he said. "But I mean it. Don't you move, now."

I held up my hands in surrender and he got up, pulling the condom off his cock as he went down the stairs.

I closed my eyes and shivered lightly. The air against my sweat-soaked skin almost too cool to stand it. I missed his warmth at the same time my mind was left reeling over all that'd been done in the last – well, however long since we got naked.

I never in a million years would have guessed he was capable of such gentleness... but not only had he *not* hurt me, he'd left me absolutely speechless. I'd never felt so coveted, so cherished... so appreciated and worshipped. I didn't think I knew what to do with the feelings all of those things evoked.

I heard him moving around downstairs and closed my eyes, just listening, perking up when I heard water start to run in the gorgeous copper tub down below. He came back up and asked, "You walk?"

I grinned, biting my bottom lip, and sat up, reaching out a hand. He reached down and took it and hauled me to my feet. Off balance not expecting such a strong tug, I crashed into him laughing. He laughed too, and dipped, making me gasp as he came up with me in his arms. I put my arms around his neck and he grunted, hoisting me up a little better and he fucking *princess carried me* down the stairs.

"You're surprising," I murmured, looking up at him.

"Good," he said, and I cocked my head curiously.

"Why do you say that?" I asked.

"Predictable is how you wind up dead," he said.

I thought about that, but the thought was quickly lost.

"Oh!" I said in surprise, my jaw positively dropping. Candles burned all around the bathroom – all kinds in varying thicknesses and heights, casting the whole room in a wonderous golden glow.

"You like candles," he said, and it wasn't a question.

"I do," I said softly.

"So, I lit some for you," he said, setting me carefully on my feet by the tub.

"Thank you," I said. He got in first, plugging the drain and held out a hand to me. I took it and stepped over the high edge. He got down and pulled me down gently between his powerful thighs, wrapping his large, muscular arms around me and pulling me back against his chest.

I closed my eyes and relaxed. He smoothed his hands up my arms as the tub filled, gathering my hair, and twisting it around and around, up off my shoulders, tying it in on itself into a secure knot at the top of my head.

"Where did you learn how to do that?" I asked softly as he dipped his hands into the water filling the deep copper clawfoot.

The water gently steamed around us and he was silent a while before he made a sound.

"Mm?" he asked, as though he'd been transfixed and not paying attention, then saying "Watching you," when his mind finally caught up to what I'd asked.

"H-how long?" I asked.

"How long, what?" he asked, pressing along my neck and out over my shoulders with his slick hands, massaging the remaining tension in me away.

"How long and how much have you watched me?" I asked carefully.

"All the time you lived across the club. Some since you moved," he answered honestly.

"Why?" I asked.

"Guess I'm obsessed," he answered.

I covered my face with my hands, running warm water over it, my mind reeling.

None of this was normal. The whole thing was unreal. The feelings I was having a riot of confusion… I mean, I was sitting in a bathtub with someone openly admitting they were *stalking* me.

Like, holy shit; it struck me. I had just let my *stalker* fuck me in his bed, and all in a bid to save my missing best friend. This wasn't real, this *couldn't be real*… but it was, and I felt like laughing. I felt like laughing until I cried from the wild absurdity of it all. The most absurd thing of all that left me questioning my sanity?

Just how much I fucking *liked it*…

"I don't know what to think of all of this," I confessed as he continued to rub my back, digging his thumbs into trigger points of knotted muscle along my spine and along my neck.

"You ain't gotta worry about a thing, cher. We'll find her. You're mine now, and you ain't gotta worry about a thing."

I closed my eyes and breathed in slowly through my nose and out through my mouth.

"I don't know anything about you," I said. "How is that anything to base a relationship on – which is totally crazy! Like, this is not how these things are supposed to work."

He pulled me back again, his arms over my chest and kissed my temple. It was like it was completely natural for him. Like he was perfectly relaxed and, no pun intended, at home.

I didn't know what bothered me more – the circumstances of my being here, or the fact that his touch was so good, so soothing, that by this point – even knowing that I shouldn't, I felt totally at ease.

… I was *glad*.

Who in their right mind found themselves *grateful* for striking a deal with their stalker? For agreeing to be his in exchange for finding their best friend?

I felt like I should feel all wrong, and it worried me that I didn't. I felt like I was maybe crazy.

I mean, only a crazy person would actually *like* being here, right? I had to be insane for feeling safe and good, for this feeling so *right* when I knew that the man who held me in his arms so gently was dangerous and clearly batshit fucking crazy to begin with for stalking me. I had to be some kind of batshit insane myself, for knowing that I cuddled with someone that was both capable of being as sweet as he'd been when we were alone together, as well as incredibly… well… violent.

Was he, though? a little voice in the back of my head questioned.

I mean, I had to imagine that he was. the Voodoo Bastards were notorious, and he wasn't just one of them, he was their *leader*. That *had* to mean he was capable of great violence even though I hadn't witnessed it personally.

Hadn't I? I mean, I couldn't remember… and hadn't he hinted that I didn't want to?

Something had happened to me, with him, the night that Maya had disappeared…

"What happened the night I don't remember?" I asked again, and his arms tightened around me.

He was silent, and I leaned my head back. I let myself be vulnerable for a moment, knowing that it was likely to hurt me, because it always had…

"It scares me not knowing," I said gently.

"I—"

He stopped and his voice when it came again was just as raw and honest as I'd ever heard it. "I'm afraid it'd scare you more knowing," he said. "I'm something to be feared, my little Alina, something to be feared always. But I don't want *you* to fear me."

"That might take more time," I said gently, genuinely wishing not to hurt his feelings after he'd shown me such kindness tonight. He kissed my shoulder.

"I know," he said. "And I can be a patient man."

"I believe you," I told him because I think I could. I mean, how long had he waited? How long had he bided his time before he could trap me? I shuddered, and he held me close, shutting off the tap with his foot now that the water was high enough.

I sighed out and tried my best to get my anxiety to settle and my guilt to calm. The anxiety for all the aforementioned reasons... my guilt because Maya was still missing, even if La Croix's club was looking for her. I had to ask myself, *should I really be enjoying myself in this beautiful bathroom?* Soaking in this beautiful tub after the best sex of my life and feeling this good, all while my best friend was still missing?

God, everything was happening at the speed of light, everything spiraling so far out of my control, spinning out *so hard,* and my life turning upside down and inside out. So much so and so fast, that I didn't know what to do, or what I should be doing differently. But what I did know is that no matter what I did? At this point, I felt wrong for doing it. Something that Maya would surely laugh at, roll her eyes, and with a shrug ask me why.

Why? She was always and forever making me face the absurdity of some of my feelings which had been ingrained and conditioned in me since childhood – especially feelings of guilt and shame. Feelings of inadequacy borne of too much time spent trying to reach unattainable sets of rules and moral principals no one could honestly be expected to reach.

Thanks, Grandma, I thought bitterly to myself.

"Don't," he said, and I sniffed and looked up into his stoic tattooed eyes.

"Don't what?" I asked softly, and he reached up, unlacing his fingers from mine and thumbed a tear out from under my eye.

"Don't cry," he said. "You're safe here, even though it might not feel like it. As for your friend? My boys are working on it as we speak. Some of the smartest men there are, are on it like a dog with a bone. We'll find something. I always follow through on my end of the deal."

"Somehow, I get that about you," I said softly, and he rested his chin on top of my head.

"Yeah?" he asked.

"Yeah," I answered.

"What else you know?" he asked.

"Not much beyond that, but I suppose I'll be learning. I'll hold up my end of the bargain too. I just need to figure out what that looks like."

"For now, your life ain't changed much," he said, and I perked up a bit. "You go to work, you come home. I'll see you when you got time off, come to your place some days when you're off work but gotta work the next, bring you for a ride or out here when you ain't."

I relaxed some and nodded. "Thank you," I murmured.

"For what?" he asked.

"For not rushing things," I said. "Well, for not rushing things, *much*," I immediately amended.

He chuckled, the bass rumble through his chest vibrating my spine in a way that made me smile in reflex.

"I take care of what's mine, cher. Never forget it."

"I'll try not to," I promised and closed my eyes and sighed.

It was early as far as my nights went, but I was tired, sated physically, but just mentally and emotionally exhausted.

"You just rest now," he said, and I turned my head and nodded.

"Okay."

CHAPTER TWENTY-TWO

*L*a Croix...

Alina was draped over me, her head on my chest and the rest of her lithe body snug against my side. It felt damn good to have her there.

I'd slept some, but I was one of those guys that didn't need much of it. Certainly not as much as she did. Three or four hours a night to every two nights was good enough for me. Still, I was content to just lie here under her and listen to her gentle breathing.

The sun was streaming through the windows and the single skylight I had up here and it shone like fire through her copper hair. I liked how long she kept it. Was surprised it had good texture; that it was shiny and soft. Most gingers I knew, their hair was a little rough and real thick. Hers *was* thick, a beautiful mane that complimented her skin and those beautiful luminous eyes of hers, but it felt shiny and soft, too. A treat for the senses, you know?

There was a whine coming from outside, a familiar one. I lifted my head from the pillow and Alina jerked against my side.

"What?" she asked sleepily but alarmed. "What is it?"

"Boat motor," I said, and she pushed off me, sitting up.

"Should we be alarmed?" she asked, already alarmed if you asked me. I didn't smile, though I wanted to. She was cute how she could get wound up over some of the littlest things sometimes.

I told her, "Don't know, cher." I sat up and pulled a gun from the bedside table, popped the magazine, and checked it was loaded out of habit more'n anything. Satisfied it was good to go, I rammed it back home.

I got up out of bed and went down the stairs to my front door. I glanced up to check on her, my girl looking around and pulling something up off floor by the side of the bed but my attention was pulled right back to the possible threat out there when the whine of the motor sounded close and then wound down. Which meant whoever it was, they was approaching my barge and lookin' to dock outside my door.

I went out the front door, gun at the ready, and lowered it when I saw Cypress and Hex headin' my way. Cy was drivin' the boat while Hex? Hex looked none too happy about bein' in it. He wasn't a fan of the swamp.

"Ho!" Hex called. "You wanna put some damn pants on?"

I turned from my door and glanced up. Alina stood in one of my tee shirts, the sleeves ripped out all down the sides. She was covered, but ho boy, just something' about her wearin' my shirt was enough to get my cock to standin' at attention.

"Who is it?" she asked nervously.

"Some of the boys," I said. "Why don't you go on an' get dressed, cher."

She nodded and set about gathering her things.

"Jesus Christ, he's got a fuckin' boner to boot," I heard Hex grumble. I turned to give the boys a view of my ass instead, headin' right on up the stairs and pulling on the first pair of shorts I could find. I left the door open for the boys, while Lina shut herself in the half bath up here to dress.

Tuckin' my firearm in the back of my waistband, Cy and Hex made their way inside, shutting the front door behind them.

"Got any coffee?" Hex asked.

"Not yet," I said, comin' back down. "You just woke us up."

"Yeah, we figured y'all was here when you don't answer your phone," Cypress said.

"Confirmed it when we found your bike at yo' daddies," Hex added.

"Make yourself at home, brothers," I told them. Cy went over to the couch and dropped onto it. Hex followed me to the kitchen and leaned a shoulder up against the wall while I set to making coffee.

"So, how'd it go?" he asked with a wolfish grin. I glanced up toward the ceiling and then back to him and gave a nod. His grin widened, and he nodded enthusiastically. "Well, alright now! I'm glad to hear it."

He hushed his tone halfway through when the bathroom door upstairs opened and Alina's light tread could be heard on the stairs.

She came down with a gusty sigh. She stood a little away and gave a nod to Cy who she knew and turned to me an' Hex, who she hadn't had the pleasure of meetin' just yet.

"Alina, Hex. Hex, this is Alina." I made the introduction as I went through the motions of loading up the coffeemaker.

"Hello," she said hesitantly.

"Well, hiya," Hex said with a nod and a smile.

Her silvery eyes turned on me.

"Where did you get this?" she asked. In her hands was the fine gold ring, the black cord I'd hung it on dangling from it.

"Oh, thanks." I went to her and tried to take it.

"No," she said, pulling it away from my grasp, and I turned a look on her. She quailed at first and then she puffed up and stood her ground despite her shaking.

"I asked you a question. Where did you get this?" Her voice was stronger than she looked and before she could blink or even think to keep it out of my grasp a second time, I snatched the ring from her by its dangling cord; and I do mean lightning quick. She gasped and took a step back. Calmly, I put it on over my head.

"That's my great-grandmother's ring," she said, and she was visibly upset.

"Finder's keeper's, baby," I told her. "Found it in the patch o' dead grass outside your old place after you'd gone. The day you moved out."

"It was my great-grandmother's ring," she repeated, shifting from foot to foot as if that alone would get me to change my mind and just hand it over. "It's all I have left of her aside from some books." I hated doing it, but this was a lesson she'd need to learn about how things needed to be different in front of my boys.

What I said had to go in front of the club but it didn't mean we couldn't revisit it when we were alone. She just needed to know, there was a time and a place for everything.

"I said, finder's keepers." My tone was final and I wouldn't have any argument. I gave her another stern look that should have conveyed it was the end of the conversation for now, and she calmed, but didn't look none too happy. That was fine. She could be unhappy. What she couldn't do was make me look bad in front of my boys with any disrespect. This little bit right now? It was alright because things were still new, but I would have to talk with her about how things needed to go, and soon.

When she didn't look like she was gonna fight me on it anymore, I changed the subject.

"What'd you boys find out?" I asked, cutting the bullshit and getting right to the point. I hadn't anticipated my girl being such an anxious little thing, and I wasn't keen on dragging things out and feeding that anxiousness any more than was necessary. The ring aside, I wanted to get her the answers she wanted and fulfill my end of the bargain and ensure she kept hers.

"You all know about this?" Hex asked. He pulled a sheaf of computer papers printed off a printer and slapped it against my shoulder. I jerked my head at my girl, indicating he should give 'em to her, seein' as I was still busy. I went back to fillin' the coffee pot with water to get it goin'.

He held them out to Alina who came forward and took them from him, but the look of betrayal she was givin' me? *Boy howdy.*

She opened them up and started to read. I was relieved to have those wounded eyes off me.

"Councilman Bashaw has designs on running for governor," she mused aloud, reading through what was on the top sheet.

"That he does," Hex agreed.

"I don't understand," Alina said. "You would think this would be a *terrible* time for Maya to disappear."

"Not if nobody knows about it," Cypress said.

"Nobody *does* know about it," she said, her moon-kissed eyes widening. "The police like to act like she doesn't even exist."

"No humans involved," I grated and clenched my jaw.

"That's about the size of it," Hex agreed.

"I'm sorry, but I don't follow," Alina murmured, and the strain in her voice made me turn and look as I hit the switch to get the coffee to brewin'.

"It's what they say when folks like us disappear or die," Cypress explained.

"Your friend's extracurricular activities put her in the 'no humans involved' category. Known problems like drug addiction and hooking, be it high-class hooking or not... when it comes to folks like us that don't tow the company line or fall all over ourselves to choke on authoritarian cock? Well, we ain't considered human to the people in charge," Hex explained.

"But Maya's his *daughter*," she tried to argue.

Cypress snorted, and I sighed, trying to be as gentle as possibe when it came to explaining people like what we was dealing with.

"Not according to the political machine," I said. "When it comes to people like Councilman Bashaw, all his little girl is, is a liability."

Hex grunted in agreement and Alina's eyes flickered from me to Cypress, to Hex and back to me.

"Okay, I understand the point," she said. "But can we please not talk about her that way?" she asked and she looked hurt.

"No, cher. We ain't judging her," I promised her. "An' we'll keep the disrespect out of our mouths when it comes to her from now on," I said as gently as I could.

"We don' think on people like that," Hex agreed. "We just tryin' to make it clear that the people we dealin' with, *do*."

She looked from Hex's face to mine and her keen mind picked up on exactly what I wanted to hide.

"You don't think she's alive, do you?" she asked. She sounded deflated, glum.

"Probably not," Cypress said, and I coulda cursed him.

Alina's face crumbled, and she demanded, "Why not?"

"Men like Bashaw, they don' let anything get in their way or 'cause 'em problems on their climb to the top," Hex explained.

Alina covered her face with her hands and shook her head. She took several deep breaths and absolutely *refused* to fall apart, which I was proud of her for that.

"You're trying to tell me you think my best friend's father, her *own father,* had her murdered? And for..." She gestured with her hands emphatically as though trying to dredge the words she was looking for out of the very swamp beneath us. "For what? Political aspirations? That's nuts! That stuff doesn't happen in real life!" she protested. "How did you even reach such a wild conclusion?" she finished, her tone demanding as she wrestled with denial and tried valiantly to reject the notion that I think in her heart she knew... Her friend was a goner and she wasn't coming back.

Hex sighed and I could tell he hated to be the one to break it to her. "We called in a favor, a connection to somebody inside Nawlin's finest," he said. My first thought was Hope, Cutter's girl from out there in Florida.

"Now, our contact reached out within the department and asked a couple questions about the status of your missing person's report... an' they did a little pokin' around in the system. They say they ain't find one."

She sank into the tired recliner in my living room, her hands folding into her lap and asked, "Didn't find one?" Her voice sounded like she was far away. Her thoughts must be goin' a mile a minute, and I pushed off the counter and headed in her direction.

"But I made one," she said, and she sounded like she was in disbelief. "Went down to the police station *several times* and *everything.*"

Hex nodded, and I put my hand on her shoulder to lend her some strength. She sounded hurt, like a child finding out for the first time that the Easter bunny wasn't real when they still wholeheartedly believed in it.

"I think that's enough for now," I said. "Any leads on who she was meetin' that night?"

Hex and Cy shook their heads almost in unison.

"Boys are still chasin' down the minutiae," Hex said. "This is just the big picture that makes the most sense, given what we know."

She looked bleak and nodded weakly. Her heart hurt, and I vowed right then and there, I would avenge that hurt a thousand times over. Her friend was dead. I was damn certain of that. Keeping her alive when politics and politicians were involved? Nah, too risky. No way they'd leave her alive to talk.

"You supposed to work tonight?" I asked my little Alina softly. She looked up at me, her hair draping over where I had my hand on the back of her neck.

"Yeah, I get split days off," she said. "Next night off is in two days."

I nodded. "I'll take you home then so you can get ready."

"Okay, what happens now though? You aren't giving up on her already, are you?"

"No, cher. We don't give up. That's not how we work," Hex said kindly and Cypress nodded.

"Okay," she said and the coffee maker gurgled in the subsequent weighted silence.

I gave the back of her neck a gentle squeeze and she looked up at me.

"A bargain is a bargain. I ain't quit until you have the answers you need. They might not be omething' you wanna hear, but I'm gon' find 'em," I promised her. She nodded, her eyes a little wide, and I thought to myself, no matter what the answer, someone was gonna burn for puttin' her through it like they was.

∽

I took Alina home after coffee and some breakfast; the boys giving her an education on some of the club life, like how it wasn't alright to ask a man how he got his name. Shit like that when she'd asked 'em. Hex and Cypress were good sports about it, but we gave her warnin' that it wasn't okay to ask just anyone. That usually, you wait long enough, the story would come out on its own.

She'd blushed furious when Cypress flexed his neck when she asked about his.

"That's so *mean*," she'd said, outraged on his behalf, and Hex and Cy had laughed.

"That's what happens when you hang around a pack of assholes," Cy'd said.

I could see the curiosity in her eyes when she looked at me, and I knew that some time, someday, when we were alone again, that she'd want to know about mine.

She'd hit the nail on the head back in her bar, though. Ruth done give me my name; said I reminded him of the seltzer she'd referenced. That it sounded French Cajun enough to make my big ass fit in, but that I was just like the beverage; you expect somethin' refreshing, but all you got was flat, boring, and somethin' that tasted like despair.

I couldn't argue with that last part. I mean, for most of the motherfuckers I came up on? I was woe and despair personified.

Leaving her at her place was hard, and it did something to me when she'd let her hand linger in mine, towed herself up to me, and stood on her toes to kiss me goodbye. Her fingers twined in the cord through her great-grandmama's ring and she plucked at it, before finally letting it go.

"You'll get it back," I'd promised her. "When the time's right."

"When will that be?" she'd asked softly.

"When I decide and not a minute before," I said, and I'd kissed her again, one final time, and I'd left her there.

Now, I was back at the club and lookin' forward to getting' in it with the boys and figurin' this shit out.

Hex looked up when I came through the door and threw me some chin as he talked on the phone.

"Ah-huh, alright now. Thanks, cher, we got it from here, I think."

He hung up, and I cocked my head.

"Cutter's woman," he said. "Said her boy inside the NOPD got pulled in by the brass for even lookin' up Maya's name an' huntin' for that report. Had to do him some fast talkin' to get hisself outta trouble."

"Phew, you smell that?" I asked.

"Ah-huh. That's the distinct odor of bullshit," Hex agreed. I nodded.

"Probably coverin' up a body," I said, and he nodded.

"I think so, too."

"Any luck chasin' down who she hooked up with that night?"

"That was the other thing they all let me know," he said, sliding a notebook down the bar at me, the pages ruffling some before settling back down. I picked it up and looked.

"Name and address, alright," I said, nodding.

"Not so fast. That might not be who met up with her. That might just be who booked the room." He spun around on his bar stool and took up his glass, chasing back whatever he had in it. "You want I should send some of the boys to handle it?" he asked.

I shook my head. "Naw, I gotta confess, I'm feelin' violent."

"Chatty too," he said with a wink. "I think your girl's got you loosened up some. This is the most I heard you talk in a while."

I scowled at him and tore the page out of his book, sliding the notebook back down his way.

His laughter followed me back out into the daylight, which only had a few hours left to it.

I took Saint and Cy with me. We took the van, slapping a magnet up on the side for some fake-ass handyman business, inconspicuous in the neighborhood. Just some handy guys here for an evening emergency repair – nothin' to see here.

Nothin' at all to see…

CHAPTER TWENTY-THREE

*A*lina...

My phone started to blow up inside my jacket pocket the moment we'd returned to an area with cell service. I worried about it, wondering what it could be about, but didn't have the nerve to look until I was home and after La Croix had gone.

It was Dorian and Marcus both freaking out, and I immediately called them on Dorian's phone.

"Alina! Where have you been?" Dorian barked on the other end of the line.

"I am *so* sorry," I rushed out. "I was out, and I didn't expect it but I found myself out overnight where there wasn't any cell service. I'm at home right now."

"She's home?" I heard Marcus ask anxiously in the background.

"Yeah," Dorian answered him.

"Tell her we're on our way," Marcus said and Dorian came back on the line.

"Stay put," he said. "We're coming over."

"Okay," I said, and I sighed as the line went dead. They sounded so mad.

"Oooo, I fucked up," I muttered into my empty apartment and I sucked in a breath between my teeth.

It took ten to fifteen minutes to make it from their place to mine and Maya's, but they made it in a little less than eight, my door buzzing incessantly and repeatedly until I crossed the apartment and hit the button.

They made it up to my door breathless and sweating. Dorian immediately wrapped me in a tight hug. I'd never seen Marcus look so anxious in all my life.

"I'm so sorry!" I repeated. "I didn't think."

"Where *were you*?" Marcus demanded. He looked downright distraught. I waved them inside and shut the door.

"Out in a swamp," I told them. "But I really need to start from the beginning."

"Yes, please, by all means!" Dorian said, throwing up his hands and bringing them back down with a crack against the tops of his denim-clad thighs. I don't think I'd ever heard him so mad and so exasperated with me at the same time. It made my heart ache to know he was only likely to get angrier by the time I got done telling them the whole story, which I did.

"Was the sex at least good?" Marcus asked, sitting there wide-eyed and clearly at a loss. The first thing that came to his mind during situations that were stressful was to cope with dry humor and I seized on the opportunity to somehow make this all sound less awful than it kind of was.

"Oh my God, out of this world," I said with a grateful smile at his attempt to lighten things up. I was even more pleased to say, "And that's the God's honest truth. No bullshit."

Dorian was standing off to one side of where Marcus and I sat on the couch, his arms crossed over his chest, one hand pinching his nose bridge like he had the *worst* headache ever. He didn't laugh or join in with mine and his boyfriend's banter at all. The moment of levity was gone, just like that, snatched out of the air and all the way to the Mississippi River.

"I can't believe you," he said through gritted teeth. "The fucking

Voodoo Bastards? Are you fucking kidding me?" His voice rose an octave on each question. I could tell he was beyond mad and was careening right into a level of upset that may be permanently damaging to our friendship.

"Did you honestly have a better idea?" I demanded, knowing I was being defensive but unable to stop myself.

He shook his head and looked at the ceiling. I knew when the tears gathered at the corners of his eyes that he wasn't *mad* mad, he was *scared* mad. Scared for me... like out of his mind terrified for me, but he didn't need to be... I didn't know how to explain it in such a way that he might understand right now.

I think Marcus picked up on that before his boyfriend had – the whole not needing to be afraid for me. I think he was working it out some more, the way he was looking at me with empathy in his eyes. He just didn't know how to explain that to his irate boyfriend without putting himself in the line of fire of that ire.

"And you," Dorian said rounding on Marcus, anyway. "You're seriously going to sit there and crack jokes and encourage this madness? Those guys are no joke! They're bad news! They *kill* people!"

Marcus got up, went to Dorian, and hugged him tight.

"The police weren't listening. No one else was looking, and La Croix said he could do it," I argued, getting teary myself with fear and frustration. "He's already done way more than the cops."

"Yeah, like what?" Dorian demanded and I could tell he fully expected I would be grasping at straws here, just to keep him from being mad.

Instead of arguing or fighting, or letting the high emotions get the best of me, I just tried to remain calm and told them what I knew – the theories that Hex had put forward that morning, and how the club was out there running those theories down as we spoke.

Thankfully, my friend *listened,* and the more he listened, the more he thought about it, the more he started to calm down.

"You work tonight," Dorian said after almost a full minute of silence. It wasn't a question but I was confused anyway.

"You don't?" I asked. This was supposed to be our night on together.

He shook his head. "I took the night off, worried about finding *you*," he said. "Called in about an hour before you called me, fixin' to start up a fuckin' search party if I had to."

"Oh, shit," I muttered. "I am *so* sorry!"

"Don't be," he said, waving me off, and I could tell in that moment, he was hurt.

"I am," I swore. "I didn't think," I said and then I *did* start to cry. "Please don't be mad at me," I begged. "I don't want to lose my only other friends."

"Oh, baby." Marcus pulled his chair around the kitchen table over next to mine and sat down, pulling me into a hug and reassuring me, "That would never happen."

Dorian came around and rubbed my back. "He's right," Dor said. "You may have pissed me off all to hell, pulling a stunt like this, but I get it. You'd do anything to get her back. I would too. I just don't think the Voodoo Bastards are it."

I sniffed and said, voice warbling a bit, "What's it say that La Croix treats me better than any man I've ever been with before?"

"Right now," Dorian said. "I just worry about later." He sighed then, and I looked up at him.

"I'm not mad, I promise," he said. "I'm just really scared, Alina. I don't want to lose you, too."

I sniffed and nodded.

"You won't," I promised. "I mean it. He's good to me, and I... I know it's weird. This is all so, so, fucking *weird*, but I trust him."

"I have a show tonight," Marcus said, changing the subject, "And while it'll be nice to have Dorian there, you need anything, and I mean *anything*, girl, you *call us*."

I smiled. Marcus was one of the better drag performers in New Orleans which is what he meant by saying he had a show.

Dorian looked at me and his face was crumpled into lines of worry, compassion filling his eyes as he put on a brave front and scoffed. "Even if you *don't* need anything, I want you to check in more," he demanded. His bravado softened and he asked, "Do you think you could be happy with this man?"

It was my turn to soften.

"I don't know," I said after a long silence in which I thought about it. "I don't know him at all really. I'm hoping that with time, I could *learn* to be happy, but all of this is just so *rushed* and backward and *weird*... like some plotline to some movie or a book, not like real life."

I sighed.

"He ever hurts you, you *run*," Marcus said, and I nodded. "You run and we will do *everything* in our power to get you away and safe."

"I honestly… I honestly don't think he ever will," I said, and it was with a definite certainty I knew I shouldn't possess this early on in the game, you know?

"I don't know," I went on. "I just have a gut feeling about him or I don't think I would have ever agreed in the first place. There's just something about him…"

"Alina, you always have this way of giving people the benefit of the doubt and of seeing the absolute best in people. If you didn't, I don't think you would be such close friends with Maya because, *girl*…" Marcus gave me a look, and I laughed a little. I understood what he meant. Maya was a tough cookie and her resting bitch face was something to behold sometimes, but the girl could be *drama,* too.

"Don't let your trusting nature get the better of you is all we're saying," Dorian said, and I gave him a look like he was nuts.

"Trusting?" I echoed incredulously. "Me?" The disbelief continued. *"Ha!"* I barked with the absurdity of it.

He gave me a look like he was unimpressed.

I sighed and told him what he wanted to hear, but I also meant it. "I won't. I'll be careful. I promise."

We talked a little bit more, ironing out the ruffled feelings between us. When they left, I sagged against the inside of the front door.

At this point, I was both mentally and emotionally exhausted and with work ahead? I was likely going to be physically exhausted before the night was through. Still, at the end of it all, if all of this drama brought Maya back to us? Well, it would all be worth it, then, wouldn't it?

I looked at her open bedroom door and sighed.

I know that La Croix and his men were certain she was dead, but I just couldn't give up hope. Not yet.

I took myself in for a shower. I had just enough time for it and to get dressed before work.

CHAPTER TWENTY-FOUR

*L*a Croix...

"Saint, you an' Cy look less out of pocket than I do, brother. You go on an' git 'im," I said. I hated that I had to wait in the van.

"We got this, boss. No worries," Cy said easily, checking his gun.

"Don't get cute," Saint shot back at him curtly and I gave 'im a nod, backing up his assertion.

"Make sure it's 'im," I said. The boys nodded and bailed out of the van, heading on up the steps to the moderately fancy house.

"Shit," I muttered. We was in the area around Harrison and Argonne. Upscale. Nice. Way richer 'n the likes of us should be hangin' around. All it took was one patrol comin' by and running the plates on our van and we were sunk; because, of course, the plates were stolen.

We didn't care so much about gettin' popped for that, aside from the embarrassment. If we was gonna get locked up, it'd better be for somethin' worth it and not somethin' so petty.

I waited for what felt like entirely too long, suckin' in a breath and letting it out harsh, drumming my fingertips and thumbs against the steerin' wheel as I shifted in my seat. I hated waitin' on the outside. Hated giving up control.

It wasn't long before Saint and Cypress came out of the place with a rolled-up carpet over their shoulders. Saint turned and hollered somethin' jovially while Cy gave a polite nod in the direction of the house and shut the front door.

"Heh." I huffed a laugh. I knew a bullshit charade outta my boys when I saw it. There weren't no one in that house they was talkin' to. Nah, you looked close enough at the rug they was haulin' out, you would see the irregular lumps in it.

I got out and opened the doors of the van and they tossed the rug in. The rug grunted, and I smiled.

"Slicker 'n owl shit!" Cy said with a grin from the passenger seat as Saint took up behind the wheel.

"Get us out of here nice an' easy, brother. We ain't outta the woods just yet," I told him as he turned the wheel and pulled us out and away from the curb.

The carpet made muffled noises, and I punched it.

"Shut the fuck up," I snarled low and quiet. "I'm fixin' to deal with you in a minute."

Fuck. I hated it when they whined.

We rode outta the city right quick and got out onto the two-lane highway to get us into the swamp. Somewhere where our quarry couldn't be heard screaming.

"Smokehouse?" Saint asked, and I nodded.

"You know it."

The smokehouse was almost always the place we took 'em to ask questions and make 'em sweat and this was no exception.

Once we got there, we made quick work of unloadin' the dude and gettin' him inside. It was still light out, but that light was failing. Plenty of time yet before Alina was off work for me to meet her.

The fool pissed himself when Saint pulled the bag off his head after gettin' him hung up. I admit to participatin' in a little theater. When the dude's eyes adjusted, it was to me standin' there naked.

Not that I was interested in boning the motherfucker – nah, it wasn't nothin' like that. No, it was a DNA thing. The blood was easier to wash off skin and there wasn't no risk of takin' anything incriminating in the fabric of my clothes. That and it tended to send the fear of God into 'em – a dude especially.

"Let him talk," I said and looked to Saint who stepped up and tore the duct tape off from over dude's mouth. He worked the bandanna out of his mouth with his tongue and immediately started babbling.

"What do you want? What're you gonna do to me?"

"Well that depends on you," I said easy. "You cooperate, you tell me what I wanna know, and things go easy."

"What do you want to know?" he demanded, complying quickly.

I grunted and gave a nod. Dude was a pussy, that was clear – a skinny gopher boy, fetch and carry, fawning all over big daddy politician's boots.

I hated the type. We may share a penis in common but he weren't no man.

"A little while back, you booked a hotel room," I said. "At the Ritz Carlton there downtown, yeah?"

"What?" he demanded.

I sighed and hung my head.

"A hotel room!" I barked. "You booked a fuckin' hotel room at the fuckin' Ritz a while back!"

"Yes! Yes! The Ritz!"

"You didn't stay there, though, now, did you?" I asked.

"No! No! It wasn't for me! I just booked it."

"For who?" I demanded.

"F-f-f-for a donor! A donor to Mr. Bashaw's campaign!"

"What's his name?" I asked.

"I don't know!" he cried, his voice high and shrill.

"Wrong answer." I punched him in the eye.

He screamed and cried, hollering like a little girl.

I looked up at Saint and Cypress behind him. Saint shrugged his shoulders over the wailing and weeping of the scrawny, pathetic, little man. Only thing runnin' for the hills faster than his constitution was his fuckin' hairline. Fuck, I hated these little weasley types.

"Now let's try this again," I said coldly.

"Please don't hurt me!" he begged, like I hadn't heard that before.

Cy rolled his eyes, a notepad and pen in his big hands, ready to take notes.

"Tell me what I wanna know, then," I said without mercy.

It was fixin' to be a long night at this rate.

In the end, we wrung everything we was gonna outta that boy and we didn't get no closer.

He was a lackey for the gubernatorial campaign for Maya's daddy. He'd booked the hotel at the behest of Mr. Bashaw's lawyer, a one Bryan Cornelius; and that was it. He was told to book it for that specific night at that specific time, for a Mr. Daryl Winters. That Mr. Winters was comin' into town for a night from Shreveport an' was supposedly a donor for Mr. Bashaw's campaign.

One traded look with Saint over the man's head told me I wasn't the only one smellin' bullshit; but that bullshit wasn't comin' off this guy. He'd just bought it hook, line, and sinker.

One of the things about bein' in the business we were in, was knowin' all the players when it came to the underworld dealin's in and around the city we called our turf. Be it drugs, money, or pussy, we knew who all was involved and we damn sure got our cut to leave 'em the fuck alone or to deal us in.

Was just a fact 'o life livin' in the Big Easy.

You lived here, you dealt with us one way or another… an' we had never heard of this Winters guy. Cornelius did ring a bell, though.

I took no joy in killin' the son of a bitch we held captive; but there weren't no way we could leave his ass here an' alive. Not when he could ID us. Just weren't no way. He was just another name on a long list of missing that included Maya Bashaw's name at the moment.

Still, as soon as Cypress and I was done choppin' him up and scatterin' the parts out there in the Bayou for the gators to finish, we looked at each other.

"What now, boss?" Cy asked me.

"Seems I'm stayin' in the city tonight," I answered.

"An' tomorrow?" he asked.

"Let's just deal with tomorrow when it gets here," I said. "For now, let's just get back to the club."

I wanted to run some of the thoughts and ideas I was havin' through Hex. Then, I wanted to swing by my girl's bar, see about pickin' her up.

CHAPTER TWENTY-FIVE

*A*lina…

I was just *drained* by the time the tips had been counted out and closing was finished. Leaving the bar was a relief, and I couldn't tell you why it was, but finding La Croix outside the bar when I got out was an even bigger one.

I felt my shoulders drop, and he cocked his head. He asked in that deep voice of his, "What's wrong?"

I shook my head and was just so overwhelmed with all the things that despite my best efforts, tears sprang to my eyes and my lip trembled with the effort to keep it together.

He strode forward and put his hands on my shoulders.

"What's wrong?" he repeated as I hung my head.

"Nothing," I said. "Everything. I don't know!"

He rubbed his hands up and down my arms and sighed.

"Somebody say or do somethin' to you?" he demanded.

"No, nothing like that," I told him. "I'm just so… *tired*."

He swore softly and nodded, steering me gently but firmly by one shoulder in the direction of home.

"Parked the bike up near your place," he said. "Should'a thought better."

"No, it's fine," I murmured, and we struck out along the cracked sidewalk.

"Did you find anything out today?" I asked, and he pursed his lips.

"Yes and no," he said. "Took a lead in a direction. It didn't do much for us but put us on another one. We're trying."

I nodded and said, "I know, and I appreciate it." He put an arm over my shoulders and tucked me into my side. I leaned into him. It felt good, and I was *so* tired, just absolutely dragging ass. No term was better apt to describe me right now than *wrecked*. I was just *wrecked*. The stress of it all catching up to me and overwhelming me completely.

I mean, I really meant it. I didn't know *why* I was crying exactly, other than just being on emotional overload and just being so grateful to be *done* for the night, and to find him waiting? It really had done my heart good. It was such a *relief*, which I knew that *had* to make me some kind of crazy... didn't it?

It felt strange being his, whatever that meant. I mean, we clearly had differing ideas on the subject which was confusing in and of itself.

You would *think* it meant I was some kind of a slave, or that I would feel like some sort of trophy or object to him – but I didn't. I mean, you didn't go to the lengths he had to genuinely *care* for something you considered a thing – property in the traditional sense of the word.

In fact, I would even hazard to say that he had gone far *out of his way* to care for me versus *expecting* me to care for him, which honestly made me want to I just didn't know how. At least, not yet. I understood through some of my own, personal healing journey from my childhood, and through deep discussions with my best friend, that *caring* and *love* looked different and felt different to different people.

It was why we had this whole love language thing, and everybody's love language was different. Both giving and receiving... I didn't know what his reception of love or caring looked like, but I did know that I was curious about it. Everything he'd done and shown me in the last day or two made me want to reciprocate something fierce. I just didn't know what that looked like yet. Not with all the chaos going on around me.

"Here, give me that," he muttered and took the keys from my hands, sliding it into the lock at the front of my building to let us in.

"Sorry," I said, a little flustered at not getting my brain to cooperate and my body to function quite right. La Croix just shook his head.

"You're tired," he reminded me. We took the stairs in the old building up to the third floor where he keyed us into the apartment.

Everything was untouched and just as I'd left it, which *boy*, was that both equal parts a relief and soul-crushingly disappointing.

"What was that?" he asked me, shutting the door behind us, and tossing my keys into the bowl by the door.

I set my purse by it and took my tips out of my shallow hip pocket, tossing them into the bowl as well.

I had *a lot* of money stacking up and I needed to do something with it like take it to my damn bank.

"You need to do something with that," he said, reading my mind. "But first thing's first. What was that big sigh about?"

"Mm, I was just thinking how every time I come home, it's a mix of relief finding everything the way I left it followed by the biggest feeling of soul-crushing *disappointment,* that she's not here."

La Croix nodded his head and fixed me with those wall-to-wall dark eyes of his.

"I'd ask what you do when you get home but I already know the answer," he said, stepping up to me.

"Mm?" I looked up at him and he raised a hand to my jaw, cradling it gently, bringing his lips carefully to mine.

He kissed me sweetly, which was so out of step with his fearsome appearance that it mollified me, sending my thoughts and feelings tumbling end over end, like Alice did into Wonderland.

I didn't understand, and so when he finished, I said as much.

"You are so confusing," I breathed.

His lips twitched, something like a smile trying to break through before he suppressed it.

"Yeah?" he asked.

"Yeah," I said. "Your appearance, and how you are with anyone else screams you don't like people and you don't want anything to do with them... and yet..."

"And yet?" he prompted when I fell silent.

"You're so nice to me," I said, looking away and shrugging.

Something darker than even the ink surrounding his irises slid behind his eyes as he said, "And God help anyone that *isn't* nice to you, cher."

I swallowed hard, robbed of speech, and simply nodded.

"Go take your shower," he ordered gently, and I smiled.

He *did* know what my after-work ritual was. I turned in the direction of the bathroom and halfway there, I stopped. I turned and asked, "Join me?"

His smile broke free and got away from him that time, and he nodded.

I started the water before meeting him in my bedroom where he was undressing. Before I could much get past taking off my shoes, he was there, his hands so careful and so sweet as he finished undressing me, his lips twitching once again when I giggled through a few slightly awkward parts.

In the shower, his demeanor didn't change. I sort of figured it would, you know? I mean, I thought for sure he was here for sex. That was the deal, right? But no, once in the shower, he backed me under the spray and threading his big hands through my hair, tilted my head all the way back to soak it.

He was so gentle, and it felt like... it felt like it brought him *joy* to care for me like this. Some measure of peace.

I mean, was he hard? Yes. But he didn't seem at all interested in doing anything with his erection. No, he was wholly focused on me and what I needed. It was like he knew what I needed even before I did myself.

He washed my hair, and me, and wouldn't even hear of me doing the same for him; instead, wrapping me in his arms and simply standing in the steam and the spray, holding me while I soaked in his strength while my own reserves were just so depleted.

"Thank you," I whimpered, and he kissed the top of my head.

"I told you, I take care of what's mine."

I nodded, but I couldn't help but still tense, to bristle at the notion inwardly. I know I agreed, and I know how I felt, but the wording still gave me that knee-jerk reaction of *ugh*.

He held me just a little bit tighter, and I felt a wave of regret for said reaction.

"Come on," he murmured, and he had me shut off the water. He got out and dried off first and then held out his hand to me to step out. I did, and he took up a fresh towel and dried me, wrapping me from armpit to past my knees with the big, big bath sheet.

"Sit," he urged and pulled out the bench from beneath the makeup table Maya and I had in here.

I sat, and he took up my brush. Holding my tail of hair in a tight fist, he began working out the tangles at the end.

"It's like you've done this before," I said and he looked over my head, peering at me in the mirror.

"No," he said.

"Then how did you know to hold the hair to keep it from pulling?" I asked.

"Watching you," he said with a shrug.

I had to ask, "How did you see all that from downstairs?"

"Dunno, but you would stand right in front of the window, lookin' at the sky, doing things all the time. If it wasn't the one you would read at, it was the one next to it."

I blushed, not realizing how much I took for granted that no one was watching or that nobody out there cared about me.

He stood silent sentinel behind me, running my brush through my hair and soaking up extra water with his towel. I handed him my leave-in conditioner spray, and he used it a bit sparingly, checking with his eyes in the mirror until I smiled and murmured, "Thank you," to signal that it was enough.

He lifted his chin, handed it back, and resumed combing and brushing my hair until it was dry.

It was a pleasure I almost couldn't describe. A tingling wash all along my scalp and down my back that after enough time left me totally relaxed, bordering on sleepy. I don't know how long I sat and let him brush, but it was a good long while. My hair was barely even damp by the time that he set the brush aside.

"C'mon, cher," he murmured and held out a hand for me to take. I got up and followed him to my bedroom, where he went to the drawer that held my nicer things and pulled out the nightgown he'd said he liked best. I smiled and put it on. I mean, it was such a little thing to indulge him in after he had spent the better part of the last two evenings positively spoiling me.

He tucked me in and got into bed with me, switching out the bedside lamp I always left burning while I was out, in anticipation of coming home in the dark.

I laid my head on his shoulder, his arm around me encouraging me to get close and I did, because honestly? It felt nice. It felt nice to be cared for the way that he cared for me, and it made being his seem so much less daunting than when I'd first agreed to it.

I felt like maybe, just maybe, I'd misjudged this man and his MC as a whole. I mean, after dealing with the police the way that I had and after some of the stories Maya had told me about her father… I had to question who was really the bad guy here? Certainly not the one that held me in his arms. I mean, right?

CHAPTER TWENTY-SIX

*L*a Croix...

She fell asleep on me almost immediately, and even though it took me a while, eventually, I fell asleep right alongside her. I think it was sometime around noon when I woke up, and *shit* did I feel like I'd overslept, as in I'd slept way too much.

"Hi, good morning," she murmured, and I finished stretching, looking to her doorway.

"What time is it?" I asked, my voice rough and gruff with sleep.

"Eleven-thirty," she said, and handed me a steaming mug of coffee once I'd sat up.

"What you doin' up before me?" I wondered out loud and held up my free hand, dropping it by my hip and patting the mattress. She came around the bed, her own cup of coffee in her hand, and set it down on her bedside table. She got up next to me, lifting the satin fall of the floor-length skirt of her nightgown as she did. A distinctly old-fashioned gesture that was the type of feminine that – shit, I don't know, it just *did things* for me.

"I don't know," she murmured with a smile. "I guess I just am." She lifted a slender freckled shoulder in a shrug.

"C'mere," I said, and she leaned in to put her mouth against mine.

I palmed her waist over the slick material she wore and my cock twitched beneath the sheet. I groaned into her mouth and she made this soft sound into mine that riled me up even more.

It surprised me when she took my coffee from me and set it aside. Lifting the long skirt of her nightgown, she threw a leg over both of mine to straddle my hips.

"Cher?" I asked softly, and she responded by crushing her mouth over mine all over again.

I felt her body through the satin covering it, and whew, was that a thrill. She kissed me like a woman starved and I definitely felt that. I wanted her like nobody's business, but I respected her choices about her body and I didn't have a fuckin' condom with me.

"Cher, mm, baby..." It was hard as fuck to talk with her biting my bottom lip like that. Harder still with her pullin' the sheet off my lap and gathering the satin of her long nightgown up out of her way. I stroked my thumbs over that slick material covering her hips and finally managed to find the strength of will to jerk my head back and say, "I ain't got a condom."

"Mm, don't judge me," she said breathlessly, throwing herself off to one side and yanking open her bedside drawer. She extricated a foil-wrapped package, and I already knew it was gonna be too small – but at the same time, I didn't care. I'd take it. Any port in a goddamn storm, you know?

I took it from her, ripping it open with my teeth as she leaned back, holding the satin material back out of my way so I could roll it on.

It was a bit of a fight, and a little uncomfortably tight at the base, but that was soon forgotten as she repositioned herself, and took me... and the *way of it*, holy shit.

The bright room, the copper spill of her hair around her face, the feel of me sinking into her tight, wet, hungry little pussy, and the way she looked at me with those heavy-lidded silver eyes of hers? *Fuck.* I grunted, and she dug nails into my chest to keep me down when I tried to sit up.

She wanted to drive? Okay, okay. I lay back and let her ride.

I looked up at her, relaxed, and let her take her pleasure. She rose and fell in a gentle easy cadence and I liked that. I liked that a lot. Smooth and silky, her body surrounded mine, snug and so perfect.

At some point, she added this roll to her hips that'd like to make my eyes roll back in my head and I found my breath matching her rhythm.

"Fuck, yes, like that, baby. Just like that," I praised her and the tremulous smile that touched her lips at the small praise meant the world to me.

"Bring that mouth down here to mine," I ordered and with a smile that grew as sweet as the sunrise over the horizon, she kissed me.

I held her tight against me, kissing her back and loving the way she felt. When she slowed even more, starting to feel like she was on the verge of tiring, I rolled her over lightning quick. She cried out in surprise into my mouth and rolled with it. I pushed myself *deep* inside her, fucking her proper good.

"*Oh!*" she cried, arching beneath me, and I sat up to give myself better leverage.

She writhed under me, her pussy gripping my cock and I licked the pad of my thumb and pressed it against her clit, giving it some easy swipes to watch her come alive. She raised her knees all on her own to take me as deep as I could go an' I loved that.

She was my angel in the streets and was provin' to be a siren in the sheets. I couldn't tell you how much that fuckin' turned my ass on.

"There you go, cher. That's it," I grated when I could see just by the look on her face, could hear by the sounds she made, that she was wicked close and I needed it. I needed her to come around my cock, because I wasn't liable to hold my own back much longer.

"Yes!" she moaned when I hit the right place. "Oh, yes!"

God *damn* watching her come apart beneath me was a thing. A thing more powerful than when I held a man's life in my hands.

My God, she was perfect. Perfect and *mine*, all mine.

She panted beneath me, shuddering as I pulled outta her body, because now that'd I'd filled the condom. the damn thing just *hurt* around the base. I stood up and stripped the damn thing off and groaned, putting my hands on my knees, and catching my breath.

"I gotta get some of *my* brand for that drawer of yours, cher," I said breathlessly, and she giggled, putting a hand over her mouth.

"I'm sorry," she said. "It's not funny, but it's funny, you know?"

I cracked a rare smile and nodded, discarding the used rubber in the trash, and said, "Yeah, sure. I get 'cha."

"Mm, thank you for that," she said as I got back up on the bed with her, bringing my mouth to hers.

"*Mais non,*" I told her. "That was all you, baby. So, thank *you.*"

"Mm." She kissed me, her arms going around me. "What does it say that you treat me better than anyone has before?" she asked quietly.

"Tells me you was datin' boys, not men," I replied.

She smiled, and it held a touch of sadness. "Is that what we're doing?" she asked softly. "Dating?"

I could catch her meaning and I nodded. "If that's what you need it to be, then yeah, we can call it that. We can call it whatever you need."

She searched my face, arching so I could delve my arms beneath her as I settled between her thighs, resting my chin on her chest above the sweetheart neckline of her gown.

"There's nothing normal about catching feelings for your stalker," she said. "But I am and that seriously makes me wonder about my mental health."

I heard what she was saying and she wasn't wrong about the stalker part but I was stuck on the part where she said she was catchin' feelings.

"Depends," I said carefully. "Those feelin's good ones?"

She gave me a puzzled look and said, "Would I have just done what I did if they weren't?" she asked, and I simply stared at her, at a loss for words. Her face changed, losing its playfulness and she touched the side of my face gently and said, "Yes, they're good. I mean, I think they're good. You, um… you…"

"I what?" I prompted when she blushed a bright crimson and her bravery faltered.

"You want me to fall in love with you, don't you?" she rushed out.

I blinked in surprise.

"I mean, I didn't expect it," I told her honestly. "And I don't get into the habit of hopin' much anymore."

Her look crushed down into something like sympathy which I hated. I reared up and smacked a kiss on her lips, not much likin' how I was feelin' in that moment.

"I need to get a shower and get movin'," I said. "More work to be done findin' your friend."

She sat up, her expression suddenly closed off and unreadable. I vaguely worried that I may have hurt her, but there weren't nothin' for it right now.

"What's on the agenda today?" she asked and the lightness to her tone sounded forced.

"Gon' talk to Hex and then we maybe gon' see about gettin' us a lawyer."

"A lawyer?" she asked, her head jerking back with the unexpected comment.

"Can never have a good 'nough lawyer hangin' around," I said. I went out to use her shower, leavin' her lookin' mollified on the bed.

~

HEX WAS WAITIN' on me when I got to the club. leaned up against his bike, his own cup of coffee from inside the clubhouse in his hand.

"How's your lady?" he asked when I shut off my bike.

I nodded. "She's good," I told him. "Catchin' feelings already – her words, not mine."

"Heh." He hitched up a little with his laugh. "Well, I'll be damned. An' you thought you'd need my ass to coach you."

I lifted one shoulder in a shrug. Knowing him like I did, I sniffed and confessed, "I thought she was on the verge of havin' a mental breakdown last night." His easy teasing smile fled his face.

"Oh yeah?" he asked. "Makes you think that?"

I shook my head and heaved a sigh. "She was losing it, started crying and couldn't even tell me why. The stress was gettin' to her, for sure," I said.

He nodded and sighed. Without any real wisdom to offer on the subject, he just changed it.

"Been thinkin' about this lawyer," he said. "Can't be droppin' more bodies surroundin' this fucker's campaign without settin' off any alarm bells. An' to be honest? A lawyer's always a good thing to have around. 'Sides that, I thought the name sounded familiar, and I went back 'n looked. Cornelius is the guy that got ol' Snowball off on that assault with a deadly and attempted murder charge scot-free about five or six years back. Baby Ruth done had him in his hip pocket somehow."

I hated bein' anything but clean, and clean meant leaving no one behind to rat on you or to fuck you over down the line. Still, Hex wasn't wrong. Couldn't go stacking up bodies like that without ringin' some bells and getting law enforcement sniffin' our asses. I rubbed the stubble along my chin and had to scowl.

"Be right back," I said, getting up off the bike. "I'ma go shave. By the time I get my ass back out here, you think of a way to get this motherfucker in *our* hip pocket, because like it or not – you're right. Dropping more bodies surrounding Bashaw's campaign is apt to get the wrong kind of attention and we don't want to do that."

"I might have Benny workin' on some of the rest of this mess right now, to put that off or make it unnecessary," he said.

I said, "Tell me about it when I get back out here."

I went on in and back into the back to the bathroom we had in the clubhouse with a shower and shit. I opened one of the four lockers we had back in it along one wall. It had my lock on it and I kept a bunch of shit in there. Some towels, some clothes, and ah – there it was. I took out my shaving kit, hanging up my cut and pullin' the faded black muscle tee I had on off over my big head.

I shaved my head and my face and took my time about it, thinking to myself all the while about the problem in front of us of finding my girl's girl.

I knew in my gut Maya's daddy had somethin' to do with this, and I was determined to get my girl closure on this deal, no matter what it took.

When I came back on out, Bennie was with Hex at the bar.

"Beignet, what you got for us, boy?" I asked.

Ol' Bennie gave me a dirty look, and I fought not to break it off in his ass about him bein' a sensitive-ass pussy. He was a small guy, short, but built. Keepin' himself in fine shape – but the man had one of those little-man complexes. A what do you call it? That short shit from France. Napoleon! He had a Napoleon complex, and that shit got goddamn annoying, *fast*.

"I was just down at the Ritz, greasin' some palms and got a hold of their security footage the night your girlfriend's friend was there."

"Shit, you got it? Bennie, my man!" Hex slapped him on the back of the cut.

"That's good work, brother," I said.

Bennie asked, "Got a laptop around here somewhere?" He held up a flash drive.

"Shit yeah," Hex said, sliding down off his seat and heading on back to our office. He came back with the slim profile black laptop and handed it over to Bennie who set it up on the bar and unfolding it, switched it on.

He worked at the keys, punching in the password to open the desktop. When it was awake and ready to roll, he plugged that flash drive in.

It had several clips on it – the first in the lobby, the second in the bar, and finally in one of the upper floor hallways.

"Now, let's just see if that's that rich feller your boy from last night says he booked the room under," Hex said, pausing the screen on a good shot of the dude's face.

He pulled up the web browser and looked up Mr. Daryl Winters out of Shreveport, finding a picture of him and putting it up there next to the window with Maya's John's face.

"I'd say it'd take a fuck ton of surgery to make that into this," Bennie said, clicking back and forth between the two screens, full-sized one over the other, back and forth between the man with Maya and Daryl Winters.

"Take a fuck of a lot more 'n that to turn a fucker from sixty to thirty," Hex said.

"Well, we know Cornelius is in it," I said. "Room was booked on his order."

"Print that out for me, would yah?" Hex asked Bennie of the closeup screen cap of the dude whose arm Maya was on.

"No problem," he said and did what was asked, running the laptop back to the office and grabbing the photo for us. He handed it over to Hex who let his eyes rove over it.

"Don't much like the size of that suitcase with him," he remarked. I shook my head.

"Me either," I said. It was a big, checked bag. Probably empty. Perfect size to transport a body in, out of the hotel – no one the wiser.

"To the blood-sucking lawyer's?" I asked.

"I figure," Hex said, nodding. With his down-home country-fried accent it came out sounding more like "figger."

So that's what we did; Hex, Bennie, an' me all headin' on down to the lawyer's office. We parked where we could find it, meaning a fuckin' spot in the general chaos and crush of Central Business District traffic. I told Bennie to stay with the bikes and holler if he saw somethin' we should be concerned about – cops and the like. Never could tell with these crafty bastards if they had some kind of silent alarm or somethin'.

We'd had ol' Bennie call ahead and fake bein' somebody interested in an appointment. It was just our luck; Mr. Bryan Cornelius had an opening today, and here we were. Still, I know his ass ain't expectin' *us*.

He sat up straighter when we walked into his office, Hex shutting the door behind us as the lawyer swore. "Well, hell, I thought my business was done with you boys when ol' Ruth died."

"No such luck," Hex said without missing a beat. "With any luck, your dealin' with us today is gon' be easy as pie."

"Oh, yeah?"

Bryan Cornelius was a weasel by definition and by looks – a tall, skinny motherfucker with a big nose and close-shaved silvery graying hair. He wasn't that old lookin', though. Maybe mid-forties? Which made me wonder just how he was wrapped up with Bashaw.

"A week or so back, you gave the order to one of Bashaw's campaign lackeys to book a hotel room," Hex said.

"Did I now?" Cornelius looked smug, leanin' back in his big office chair with a shitty smile, pushin' his expensive rimless Oakley glasses up on his big fuckin' nose.

"You did. Told 'im to put it under some rich feller's name from all the way up there in Shreveport."

"Ah-huh," Bryan said nonplussed. "You gotta question comin' in all this? Because, gentlemen, I am expecting an appointment any minute now an—"

"I suggest you shut the fuck up and listen," I said and Hex gave me a nod when Cornelius did just that – shut his fuckin' mouth and opened those stupid ears stickin' off the sides of his head.

I fuckin' *hated* lawyers.

Good for nothin' most the damn time.

"Now, I don't know about you," Hex said, pulling out the printout from the security camera. "But that there don't look nothin' like Mr. Daryl Winters from up there in Shreveport. You understand what I'm sayin'?"

Cornelius looked over the image and I swear, he turned a little green around the gills, pullin' his collar away from his neck. He tried to recover but one sideways glance from Hex told me he'd seen it too.

"Well, what do you want me to say, boys? That certainly isn't Mr. Winters, now, is it?"

"So, who is he?" I asked. "And don't fuckin' lie to us."

"Well, fellas… I wish I could help you, but that may or may not be breeching attorney-client privilege. I simply cannot do that – you understand."

"I don't think you quite understand the position you're in here, Mr. Cornelius," Hex said. "You either tell us what we want to know, or you're just sittin' there puttin' a target on your back. You feel me, son?"

Bryan stilled in his chair, his watery blue eyes losing their sparkle.

"I don't think *you* understand, boys," he told us. "I tell you, and I'm dead either way."

I shook my head. "Motherfucker in that photo already signed his death warrant the moment he touched her."

"Well now, ain't that interesting," Bryan declared. "Who knew the girl in the photo had friends in such low places?"

"Oh, she don't. A friend o' hers does and paid us pretty fuckin' handsome to find out what happened to that girl in the photo," Hex said. "An' that's just what we aim to do."

"Tell me this," Cornelius said, steepling his fingers in front of him. "You mean to deliver that man's head on a proverbial plate, to, ah, your client?" he asked, and the wheels were turning in his head.

"Metaphorically speaking," Hex said with a wink. "We just lookin' to put a name to a face is all. We ain't vigilantes now, that would be illegal."

Cornelius laughed outright at that.

"All we need is a name, and at least one of your problems disappears," I said evenly. I knew I was treading a dangerous path.

"You boys are bein' awfully candid," he said, eyeing me.

Both Hex and I just stared at him, lettin' the bottomless pits we had inside show out our eyes.

"I give you a name, you keep me out of it an' we free an' clear?" he asked.

"Until we need your services for somethin'." Cornelius raised his eyebrows an' Hex held up his hand to stave off whatever the lawyer was gonna say. "An then we'll pay you fair an' proper for your services. You help us, an' we'll help you. No favors now, but you'll be at the top o' our list for lawyers to call an' you know the kind o' trouble our boys are apt to get into."

"Five-thousand-dollar retainer, right here, right now," the lawyer said after a moment of judicious silence.

I pulled my billfold outta my cut and started counting. I only kept around half that on me at any given time. I happened to have around twenty-seven hundred on me right now. I slapped down twenty-five hundred of it and said, "Twenty-five hundred now, the rest *after* you give us what we came for."

He leaned forward and picked up the stack of hundreds, counting them out. Hex gave an almost imperceptible nod when Cornelius wasn't lookin' – as in he had the rest and he'd spot me.

"Alright, then," Cornelius said. "The man who asked me to ask the lackey to book the room was none other 'n Kenny Wells, Bashaw's right-hand man an' campaign manager. As for the man in the photo?" He gave a gallic shrug. "He goes by a lot of names, has a pretty high body count, too, from what I understand. He's a professional, ex-military type. I guarantee, if he's in the picture, the girl ain't."

Fuck.

"You know any of his aliases?" Hex demanded.

"Jacob Landry is one of 'em, but I'm tellin' you – I don't know his real name. I mean it about you boys lookin' out for my ass in trade for this information. I ain't fixin' to die young."

"This conversation never happened as far as we concerned," Hex declared, pulling out his billfold and greasin' the lawyer's palm.

"Well now, consider me retained," he said. "Y'all stay outta trouble now. An' if you can't do that? At least don't get caught."

I glanced at Hex who glanced back my way and nodded.

"Pleasure doin' business with you, sir." Hex tipped an imaginary hat.

"As always," the lawyer said, giving us a half-assed little salute.

We got the fuck out of there with our connections and treasure trove of information.

Now we just had to figure out how to get a hold of a professional assassin. I mean, we'd never needed one. We'd always done our own dirty work.

"One last thing," Hex said just before we went out the door an' I swear he was reading my mind. "You know how to get ahold of this Jacob Landry?"

"Now why would I know a thing like that?" the lawyer asked.

"The company you fuckin' keep," I rumbled.

He had a good laugh over that one, too.

"Oh, that's a good one," he said, wiping a tear from his eye. "Whew! I wish I could help you boys. More out of self-preservation than anything, but I couldn't tell you. I would if I could, truly, I would."

I nodded, and Hex nodded, too.

"Have a nice day, now," Hex declared and we left.

"You believe him?" I asked when we hit the sidewalk.

"Fuck no, not completely," he said. "I'll keep Bennie on 'im and send Axeman out this way. Make sure he don't go runnin' to the wrong people."

"I don't think he will," I said, shaking my head.

"How's that?" he asked.

"I could smell his fear, brother. He's way more scared of us than he is of some paramilitary boogeyman."

"You got a nose like a bloodhound for fear, so I'm gonna believe you on that one," he said and I nodded.

We were gettin' closer, but *goddamn*. By the same token, it was feelin' like we was paintin' ourselves into some corners.

CHAPTER TWENTY-SEVEN

Alina...

I was more alive when I got off work than I'd been last night. When I stepped out the front door with Dorian, La Croix was waiting. I smiled. I couldn't help myself, and I touched Dorian's arm to let him know we had company.

I'd been able to let him know all about how things had been with La Croix, but he still didn't like it. He was wary, and I couldn't blame him, really. I mean, with each passing day, my hope for Maya's safe return was dwindling. I just didn't want to admit it out loud. I felt like my waning hope was failing her somehow.

"Hey," Dorian said when he caught sight of La Croix.

La Croix, to his credit, gave Dorian a nod before reaching his hand out to me.

"Hey, cher," he said to me and towed me in for a hug.

I was beginning to relish his hugs. They were so warm and tight, and I felt so safe and protected in his arms.

"La Croix, meet Dorian. Dorian, this is La Croix," I said.

"Been tellin' stories about me, girl?" La Croix asked, and he didn't sound entirely happy about it.

"Be glad she did," Dorian said with a worried smile. "She didn't, I would be more worried about her than I already am."

La Croix smiled, but it wasn't a nice thing. I maybe was a bit *too* familiar with him when I pinched him. He looked down at me sharply and raised an eyebrow. I gave him a meaningful look right back that I hope conveyed – *don't antagonize my friend.*

La Croix's face split into an affectionate smile then, like I had done something cute. Like the same kind of smile you would turn onto a kitten that was trying to be fierce, or like… like a Pomeranian. I scowled and his smile only grew bigger.

"Wow," Dorian said. "Okay, then."

"What?" I asked.

"You two have known each other, what? Two days? Three?" he asked.

"So?" I asked carefully, thinking that *technically,* I had only known La Croix a couple three days, but La Croix? La Croix had been watching me for what had to be a very long time. I think he knew far more about me than I could even begin to imagine.

"So, y'all giving some serious long-term couple's vibes already," Dorian said. "And I wouldn't believe it if I hadn't seen it with my own eyes just now, but it's… it's kind of cute."

"Confusing, isn't it?" I asked softly, and he nodded, giving me a look of understanding and empathy rolled into one.

"Hopefully it's good, though. Hopefully, it *stays* good," he said.

La Croix simply gave Dorian a nod and something passed between them. I wasn't sure what, though. Gay or not, Dorian was still a guy, and it was like I had just witnessed something under a strict guy code.

"You walkin' with us, brother?" La Croix asked and Dorian nodded.

"How was your night?" La Croix asked me as we struck out, his arm around my shoulders, Dorian walking on the other side of me.

"Oh, my God! We had a bridezilla and I swear her bachelorettes were like mini velociraptors," I said.

Dorian regaled La Croix with tales of drunken fuckery out of the bride and her party and the absolute meltdown that ensued when it came out that the maid of honor had been fucking the groom-to-be for like the last six months. Predictably, the bride had lost her shit. A catfight had ensued and before the bouncers could wade in, the mother-of-the-bride had broken a martini glass and had stabbed the maid of honor in her boob. Somehow, in doing so, she'd managed to go deep enough to pop the poor girl's saline breast implant. So, *she* ended up packed off in an ambulance. The bride was carried off by the rest of her girls, and Momzilla had been taken away by NOPD, screaming about suing the bar; for what, we had no idea but good luck with that, I guess.

La Croix had just shaken his head and had glanced down to me and asked, "You were safe enough, right?"

"Of course! I was behind the bar the whole time and the bar is like Fort Knox. You have to know how the switches work to get back there."

"Unless someone jumps over it, but you'd have to practically be a gymnast to do that," Dorian added.

"Exactly," I said.

We reached my apartment building and La Croix said, "I plan on takin' Alina with me out to my place. Y'all got a way to talk via the internet? Ain't no cell service out that way."

"I can hit you up on social media to check on you," Dorian said, and I smiled at him.

"I'll be sure to connect to the internet this time and stay in touch," I promised. I gave Dorian a hug. "Give my love to Marcus."

"I will," he said, giving me a squeeze.

"Later," he said to La Croix and La Croix nodded at him.

We went inside, and as soon as the lobby door was shut, I said softly, "Thank you."

"For what?" he asked, following me up the stairs.

"For being nice," I answered, and I swear I heard him chuckle.

"Not my usual deal, I promise you," he said.

"I know, which is why I said 'thank you,'" I replied as I unlocked the apartment's front door.

His chuckle was unmistakable that time.

"You feel up to a ride tonight?" I asked.

"Tonight? Sure, I guess," I said.

"Gear on up, and pack an overnight bag, yeah?"

"Sure."

"Havin' a good ol' fashioned Cajun cookout at my dad's place tomorrow," he said. "All the boys from the club, a bunch o' hunters and such. Families from out that way and in the bayous."

"Okay," I said carefully, nodding.

He touched the side of my face and stared into my eyes and I felt moved. I don't know why.

"I have to warn you, cher, my daddy, he let's his mouth get away from him sometimes."

"I understand," I said.

"Well, you been warned," he said. "Understandin' is sort of up in the air until you see it for yourself."

I stood on my toes and kicked the door shut behind us, twining my arms around his neck. He bowed his head and met me halfway. I kissed him, and thought to myself, *nobody had better say anything mean about you. Not in front of me.*

His arms went around me and he pulled me tight against his hard body, tearing his mouth from mine and whispering, "We'll ride tomorrow. I want you tonight."

"Mm," I moaned softly, the raw need in his voice thrilling me down to my toes. "Okay," I murmured and his mouth crashed down onto mine, much needier this time and I relished it.

At some point, I gave a little jump, trusting he would have me, and he did; hauling me up his body so I could twine my legs around his hips, gasping as he tore his mouth from mine once again only to attack the sweet spot on the side of my neck.

I held the back of his head, pressing his mouth closer as he somewhat blindly carried me to my bedroom. He hip-checked the corner of the back of the couch and grunted, but barely broke stride.

"Are you okay?" I asked, and he just grunted in assent that yes, he was fine, and kept right on going. He laid me down on the bed and immediately pressed his cock against me through our jeans. I moaned against his invading tongue.

He shrugged out of his leather vest and tossed it aside on the bed, following it up with a crushed box of condoms out of his back pocket.

"Oh, thank God," I uttered against his mouth and he let out a rumbling chuckle.

"Wasn't about to do *that* again," he said, straightening and pulling his shirt off from over his head.

"Mmm." I smiled and wriggled my shirt over my head, tossing it aside. I hesitated only slightly when he pulled the gun out of the back of his waistband and leaned over to set it on the bedside table.

This is the man he is… never forget it, Lina, I reminded myself, but it was oh, so easy to forget when he kissed me like that, when he held me close and let his lips roam over my skin. The way his hands were so gentle, and the way he was so careful when he put his cock inside of me.

He didn't fuck me. There was passion there, for sure, but he didn't get rough with me – no. If anything, when we had sex, it felt as though he was making love to me.

I couldn't help but believe wholeheartedly that despite his fearsome appearance, somewhere deep inside that tough and frightening exterior, was a sweet and gentle man.

He'd proven it to me with every touch, every look of concern, and his gentle loving care of me.

He treated me better than any man I had ever known before him, and it was so at odds with everything else about him.

He was such an enigma, a mystery to me, but I didn't back down. The deal was to be his, and so I figured that went for as long as he wanted. And the things I had learned about him so far? They told me that I had plenty of time to figure everything out. That once he settled on something, it was a long time or even a forever kind of a thing…

There was a certain sense of security in that. One that'd I'd craved, probably, since the day I'd been born. There was a part of my heart that'd been broken since childhood, a part of me that had longed so hard, had positively yearned to be wanted and to be loved – the unconditional and fairytale forever kind of love.

Maya had been the first to show me what unconditional love was. She loved me like a friend, and a sister. No matter how big or small the disagreement, if I would freak out? She'd bring me right back down to earth, always quick to remind me that yeah, she was pissed, but that didn't mean shit. That didn't mean she was giving up and abandoning ship.

Dorian and Marcus loved me like family, too… but deep down, I'd always craved what La Croix was giving me.

That romantic partnership. Not just a lover, confidant, and friend… but the promise of safety. And not just physical safety either… but emotional safety. Even if he did bring it to me in the strangest of ways.

We stripped each other naked and kissed. It felt so good to have his skin on mine, our nude bodies writhing in concert, but not penetrating; not yet. He was determined to kiss, lick, and suck on every inch of me and I enthusiastically encouraged him with the feral noises pouring from my throat.

When he went down on me, I swear I saw stars. I wasn't even close to orgasm yet – he was just getting started.

Feeling bolder, and braver than I did our first time together, I put a hand on top of his inked scalp and pressed his mouth to my pussy as he delved his tongue between my lips and inside me.

Fuck, that was good, but I craved a deeper touch.

I panted and gasped, gripping the covers with one fist, the other pressing his mouth to me as he rolled those alien eyes up to gaze all the way up the long length of my body.

God, the view between the valley of my breasts at those eyes looking up at me, penetrating me all the way down to my soul, was *so fucking hot*. When he shoved two fingers inside me, I almost lost myself in it completely, my eyes closing, my head tipping all the way back, as he wrung a cry from my throat that painted the town red with my lust.

He held one of my thighs, and with that hand, did something no one had ever done before – he reached around over the top of my leg and pressed the heel of his hand on my lower stomach, just above my pubic bone and *holy shit! Oh, shit!* It was like he brought that place inside me down in contact with his fingers inside of me, the sensations going from zero to absolute goddamn *magic* in the blink of an eye.

It was so quick, so unexpected, I very nearly died a real death. I can't tell you how I was ready to go with a smile on my face.

He tortured me so sweetly, so completely, and I found myself spiraling high and higher; just like one of those fireworks, that once lit, shot spinning into the sky with its shower of sparks and *bang!* I was coming, knees snapped together, body curling, his fingers still inside me, wringing every last drop of pleasure out of me until it clearly became far too much for me and he stopped.

I felt suddenly empty, my legs shuddering uncontrollably, my body shivering like a junky too long denied a fix and the drug was definitely La Croix at this point.

He sat up, and picked up the box beside us, tearing it open and then tearing open the gold foil packet with his teeth. He rolled the condom onto his jutting cock, and rather than come to me, he did the hottest thing ever and wrapped those strong arms around my still trembling thighs and dragged me bodily to him.

With a grunt, and a deep fast stroke, he was all the way inside me, and *oh,* it was good. He hooked his arms behind my knees, folding me back until my legs touched my chest and he slid himself even deeper inside me. There was only one word to describe it – *exquisite.*

"Yes, harder," I moaned, and he drew back and drove deep. I cried out and writhed, the intensity unreal but oh, so, delicious that I found myself begging him for more.

He didn't disappoint. I don't think he honestly ever could – not in the bedroom. He was careful about it, but at the same time, he let some of the dark savagery I knew he was capable of out on me. He drove into me deep and swift, and every time he did, he bottomed out against my cervix in such a way that it was a darkly sweet pain that'd like to drive me crazy.

"Touch your pussy," he demanded, and I liked that. It was so deliciously dark, the kind of dirty a girl reveled in, and I reached between us, pressing my fingertips to my clit, and *oh, God yes...*

I moaned out from behind pursed lips and concentrated on my breathing.

The darkness swirled out of his eyes and danced with my soul in a decadent nightmare's waltz among the stars. The stars that were gathering at the edges of my vision, the stars that dispersed through my very veins in an effervescent building rush. As though I was a vessel and filling slowly from my very womb, the weight there an erotic thing made even more erotic by the persistent rolling thrusting of his hips, the way his cock parted my folds and delved deep, hitting all the right places.

"That's it, baby. That's it, cher. You come for me," he ordered gently and I just didn't have it in me to disobey when he asked me so nice like that.

I arched, his cock slipping and riding so perfectly over that one spot, and it was all over. I slipped from his grasp and fell from the heavens. The rush and the thrill of falling from so high was so damn beautiful, tears gathered at the corners of my eyes with just how hard I came.

The only thing more perfect about coming so sweetly were the sounds he made as he came with me.

CHAPTER TWENTY-EIGHT

*L*a Croix...

She whimpered in her sleep several times, waking me out of my light doze. I would hold her a little tighter, pull her a little closer, and she would settle but her sleep was uneasy today. I got my rest, but it was broken. When she finally did wake, I'd already been eyes open for a few minutes.

She gasped, and jerked against me and looked up, startling slightly when she met my eyes.

"You okay, cher?" I asked her and she nodded mutely. But by the white showing around those luminous eyes of hers, I knew she didn't speak lest a tremble in her voice betray her.

I cocked my head and told her, "You ain't need to hide nothin' from me, you know that, right?"

"No, I know," she said quickly. Maybe a little too quickly, y' ask me.

I reached up and smoothed a thumb over her porcelain cheek dotted with the star scatter of her freckles and she lent me a brave but tremulous smile.

"What you dreamin' about?" I asked and she looked away fast.

"Nothing," she lied to me.

"Alina..." I know my voice held some warning, but I didn't like this feeling, the feeling that something ain't right between us.

She pushed away from me and sat up. I let her go, dropping my hand back down to the bed and considering her.

"I... I had the worst dream," she murmured. "About you... I mean, about *us*," she said, and she looked at her lap. I reached out and took her hand and gave it a little squeeze. Her eyes flickered back up to mine.

"Sure it was a dream?" I asked, and she looked a little sad then.

"If I ask you a question, you promise to tell the truth?" she asked.

"Silence is better 'n bullshit," I told her, but I knew she knew that about me. She was smart though. I knew she'd catch my drift. The grim set of her lips in a thin line told me that she knew I knew what she might be askin' about any second now.

"Did you... did you hurt someone the night you brought me home? The night Maya disappeared."

I remained silent rather than feed her a line of bullshit.

She let out a shuddering breath and muttered, "I thought so."

I raised my chin just a little, and she said, "The only time I ever faint is at the sight of blood and my dreams..." She sniffed and looked at the sun coming in around her window blinds as though it would burn the memories away that'd haunted her sleep.

"Felt like memories," I finished for her and she looked back at me.

"Yeah," she said.

"What 'cha feelin', cher?" I asked softly.

She swallowed hard. "Grateful," she said finally after a long pause. "Grateful that you were there," she finished.

I nodded slowly and reached out, reassured when she didn't flinch from my touch as I gripped her shoulder, swiping a thumb over her so-soft skin.

"He touched what was mine, baby," I said. "I can't have that. Nobody touches you with ill intent *ever*, you get me?"

She swallowed hard and said, "You protected me."

"It's my responsibility to protect what's mine," I said.

"I don't think I fully understand," she murmured, and I nodded slowly.

"I think you're startin' to, yeah?" I asked.

She nodded, and I couldn't help but smile.

"Few things in this life are *mine*," I said, emphasizing the word. "My bike, my club, and now you."

"You don't count your house?" she asked curiously.

"A house is just a thing," I said. "It burns down, or sinks, I just build another one. *You*, on the other hand... *you* are my everything. Worth dying for, worth fighting for, worth killing for. You understand?"

Her eyes were so very wide and glassy, and those twin tears dropped down her cheeks, glittering in the light coming stronger around her blinds and draperies.

"I... I don't know what to say," she said.

"You ain't gotta say a thing, baby girl. Just know that's what you signed up for. Not just the sex, not just to find your friend. There's a lot of bad parts to this life, sure... but there's some good parts too, and—"

I didn't get to finish. She threw herself at me and kissed me something fierce.

"I don't know how to feel, knowing, I mean, *remembering*... having seen it with my own eyes. I just don't."

"Take all the time you need, huh?" I smoothed a thumb through the wet track left behind and said, "Just don't dwell on it too hard, and know that I've got you."

She nestled her way into my arms and pulling her long red hair behind her ears, laid one of her cute little ears against my chest.

I stared at the back of her copper hair and worried a bit. I'd been pretty raw just then and my fate was in her hands. If she went to the cops, she could maybe have my ass locked up.

"I don't understand, am I crazy?" she asked.

"Crazy for what?" I asked softly, petting her hair, stroking my fingers through it as much to comfort her as to relish in the sensation of it through them.

"For feeling so safe with you like this, after... after knowing... after seeing?"

"I like to think your heart knows and your head just ain't caught up yet," I said.

She turned her head and shifted her body so she could look at me.

"I think that's as good an explanation as any," she said and I nodded slowly.

She sniffed and said, "He was going to really hurt me. I was so afraid, and then you were there..."

I nodded and she said, "Maybe my head always knew and it was really my heart that needed to catch up."

I smiled at her then and put my hand back to my side.

"Maybe just."

"Thank you," she whispered, and I chuckled then.

I don't think I'd ever been *thanked* for killin' someone afore.

"C'mon, baby, let's get cleaned up," I whispered after a minute and she nodded against my chest.

We showered together and got ourselves dressed. I rushed her a little, as I had at least one stop I wanted to make on the way out of the city. It was still early yet before the all-day festivities got going out there on my daddy's land.

She packed a bag enough for two or three days even though she was only stayin' for tonight and it made me smile on the inside. My girl liked to be prepared, and while somehow, I knew that about her, it was still nice to see.

Slinging her canvas backpack that looked some kind of vintage over her slim shoulders, we locked up and headed down to the bike. She put her helmet on while I got it started and then making sure the straps of her bag were secure, she climbed on after me.

I rode us on over to the bookstore first. I knew my girl had a love of reading and that she was feeling down after a rough night sleeping and her memories coming back. Her friend was still missing, and the weight on her shoulders when it came to worry and heartache was growing with every hour of every day that passed that Maya couldn't be found. She needed an escape, and I aimed to provide one or some for her.

I knew today would be hard, lost in a sea of people that she didn't know, but Hex had suggested this little community get-together with a purpose in mind. It was a damn good idea as we climbed up the ladder of fuckin' lackeys in this little melodrama full of backstabbing and intrigue.

"What are we doing here?" Alina asked when I killed the bike's engine in a shady parking spot out front of the bookstore. She got off the bike and I did too, fishing my wallet out of my back pocket on its chain. I opened it up and further fished out a hundred and handed it to her.

"Go on in and get what you want, cher," I told her. She looked from the money in her hand and back up to me, confused.

"You need a break," I stated. "I told you, I take care of what's mine. Now go on, now."

She stood up on her toes and kissed me, shrugging out of her backpack as I said, "I'll be right on out here when you're through. Take your time. I'm gonna make a call."

"Okay," she said softly and handed me her bag for safe keeping. She took herself inside with no more questions asked.

I rang through to Hex.

"Where you at, brother?" he asked.

"Made a quick stop," I said. "Headed your way next. Everybody there?"

"Oh, just about," he said. "Folks are playin' and the crawfish'll be boilin' here soon."

"Good," I said.

"Just a warnin' to you," he said, his voice lowering. "Yo' daddy's in his liquor already."

"Fuck," I muttered. "He'd better watch his mouth where Alina's concerned," I said and Hex made a noise like he'd sucked his teeth.

"Agree wit you there," he said. "She seems like a nice girl from what I've seen."

"She is. She certainly deserves better than th' likes of me," I said, looking through the front of the bookstore's windows to see if I could spot her, but no luck. Displays were in the way.

"Alright now, we'll see you when we see you," Hex declared. "I already got the boys workin' the party, lettin' your kin an' the locals know to keep an eye out for what we're lookin' for."

"Appreciate it," I said, and I meant it.

"Shit, these here are good people. Some are already thinkin' about takin' the boats out on a search," he said.

"Doesn't surprise me," I declared.

"Ride safe, brother. Keep the shiny side up for me."

"Will do, man."

My girl came out a little while later with around three or four books and tried to hand me the change. I just said, "Keep it," before mounting my bike. She took her bag from me, stuffed her books in the top, and re-shouldered it, getting on up behind me again.

The ride on out to my daddy's place on the edge of the Bayou out there was nice. It was still early enough in the day the real heat ain't set in yet. I'd told Alina when she'd been packing to pack something cool to change into, that we'd be outdoors most of the day. She'd made a bit of a face but complied.

With her fair skin, I can't say as I blamed her for the look. Bein' a night's dweller like she was, it was probably out of a sense of self-preservation. The sun had a habit of gettin' brutal out here, but my dad's land had enough shady spots and I'd make sure she'd get the pick of the litter.

When we arrived, I took her into the house and down to the bathroom to change before I made any introductions – because when those started rollin', they'd be rollin' on for a good long while and I wanted her comfortable for it.

"Yo, La Croix!" someone called when I came out the back door. They lifted a mason jar full of hooch in salute in my direction, and I threw the brother some chin and stood sentinel, shaking the hand of any man that come up to me.

When Alina slipped out the back door, she looked much cooler, wearing an earthy green tank top over a white one, a nice, layered look that'd keep her good and cool along with a short pair of denim shorts. She had some light leather sandals on her feet and one of her new books clutched in her hands, a tassel of a new bookmark dangling from the top in a green I didn't think she realized matched the outer tank top she was wearin'.

"You good?" I asked. "Anybody bother you?"

"No, not at all! Why?" she asked, handing over her pack that'd been stuffed fuller with her riding gear, and her leather jacket. Her helmet was back with my bike.

"Just makin' sure," I told her, taking the gear from her. "Come with me," I said. "I'll stow this shit down in the boat."

"You want sweet tea or lemonade, cher?" one of the women called out to her as we neared the folding tables at the edge of the shade of the porch where the drinks were being kept.

"Oh, sweet tea if you please," Alina said with a smile.

"Lizzy this is Alina, Alina this is Lizzy Baudelaire. She's with one o' the Baudelaire boys on over there," I said, pointing at the trio of brothers at the edge of the canal running the length of the back of my family's property.

"Nice to meet you, 'Lina," the woman greeted and Alina wrinkled her nose with a big smile.

"Likewise!" Alina chirped back, accepting a mason jar packed with ice and loaded with tea. Lizzy knew what I liked and handed me a half and half – an Arnold Palmer or whatever you liked to call it.

"Thank you, sweetheart."

"No problem, Lenny!" Lizzy chirped and Alina looked at me, curiously.

"The Baudelaire boys an' I 'ave known each other for a lifetime, now. Neighbors since we was kids. Lenny is my government name," I told her.

"It feels like I should ask 'how could I not know that?' but I already know the answer. I guess it just feels like we've known each other longer somehow."

I nodded. "Fair 'nuff," I said.

Before I let her step out into the yard, I set her book and her drink aside with mine and sprayed her down hard with a can of sunscreen. She smiled and laughed as I made sure to get ever inch of her fair skin and shook my head as she tried to return the favor.

We made our way through the gauntlet of locals and my boys alike as I ushered us in the direction that I wanted to take her – to the edge of the yard with the hammock set up between the only two trees we had back here. It was the one I tended to crash in when I was too damn drunk to navigate the waterways to get to my house.

I settled her in, bringin' over a couple of old crates to stack up and give her a place to set her drink and her book if she'd like.

"You relax here, cher. I'll fix us some plates," I said.

She shaded her eyes and smiled up at me and purred, "You treat me like a queen."

"Now you're gettin' it," I heard Hex call out, and turned to catch him wink at my girl.

"Have a minute?" he asked me.

"Course, you can help me carry some food over," I said, and Hex laughed and gave a nod. We went over to where plenty was startin' to come out the pots to feast on.

"Word's out," he said, careful of the kids runnin' around playin' and I nodded.

"Good thing," I said.

"Made sure to play careful, warnin' everyone to keep mum in front of 'Lina. Don't need her upset, now."

"Thank you, brother." He looked past me in her direction.

"She's a beauty," Hex said, and I stiffened slightly. "All the boys are sayin' it."

I nodded carefully, and he chuffed a laugh. "Ain't none of 'em stupid enough to make a move."

I nodded again, and he smiled at me.

"Seems you got it in the bag, brother." He clapped me on the back and I looked back to Alina who was lying back, her book propped open in her lap as she read. The hammock was swinging gently and the cool breeze sweeping through was a relief to the heat and humidity that pooled in the air today.

"Was there anything else you wanted to tell me?" I asked. "Any word on our killer or the lackey that hired 'im?"

"Not yet. Got Louie tailin' him. Chainsaw's wit 'im."

"The political cocksucker or the man on the video?" I asked and Hex laughed.

"The cocksucker," he said, and I nodded.

"Think we're gonna have to pay him a visit to find the triggerman," I said and Hex nodded. We dished up three plates as we talked, going on down the line and fillin' 'em with good things – shrimp n' grits, fried alligator, gar cakes, and some mud bugs, corn and hushpuppies, and a few taters on the side.

"Think her daddy's behind it?" I asked suddenly, a few moments later as we took up our plates to go on and deliver.

"Hard to tell, man. All we can do is keep climbin' the ladder."

I nodded, and we worked our way out to Alina, Hex runnin' interference with chatty folk stoppin' us to talk an' catch up on things.

"Catch up with you," Hex said, stopping at a cooler. "Grab us a couple 'o beers."

I threw some chin and went on over, handing my girl a plate. She set down her book an' took it, turning and sittin' up, patting the hammock for me to sit beside her.

"Room enough for three if that line holding it up is strong enough," she said, and I chuckled.

"That's over a thousand-pound test line," I told her. "It's plenty strong enough."

"Good to know," she said, wrinkling her cute little nose and smiling bright.

CHAPTER TWENTY-NINE

*A*lina...

There had to be at least fifty or sixty people in La Croix's childhood home's backyard.

I didn't know how I was going to *possibly* remember everyone's name. I recognized Hex, Cypress, and Saint but there were several other men wandering throughout the throng in their leather cuts. That was what they called their motorcycle club vests, I guess –the ones with the brightly colored skeleton leering under its purple top hat through its monocle, bursting out of the gold fleur-de-lis that was the symbol of the entire region.

They looked like a fun bunch with their purple, gold, and green bandannas, and their big smiles as they chugged their beers. Unlike the people of the city who would cross the street to avoid any of them, the people out here in the swamp embraced them with open arms and even bigger smiles.

I found that curious to a degree, but the people out here? They were just built different – sturdier, more adaptable. Despite how much the rest of the folks in the city loved to treat them like they were dumb or stupid hicks? I knew better. They could make just about anything you could think of work in their favor with what they called just a little Cajun ingenuity.

So, no; stupid they were not.

Wary? Now wary they absolutely were. You could see it with the way they looked at me with curiosity but also with how they wouldn't dream of approaching me to talk with me. I was alright with that. I was peopled out. With how much the kids looked over at me and pointed in my direction only to have their parent say something and turn them around from me? Well, I had to think La Croix had something to do with telling them not to bother me.

On any ordinary day with Maya in my life, I would have been hurt. With Maya missing, and possibly dead? I was a little grateful for my solitude. I just felt emotionally and mentally tapped out right now. It took everything in me to pretend things were normal enough to go into work and work took *so much* out of me.

We ate and made small talk. Cypress, Saint, and a smaller brother they called Bennie; although his name patch on his vest read *Beignet*, came over and joined us after a little while.

"Headin' out here in a bit," I tuned in to Cypress saying. "Saint and I just wanted to get somethin' to eat before riding out and relievin' Louie an' Chainsaw."

"Where they at?" La Croix asked.

Saint looked in my direction then back to La Croix and tipped his head as though to ask if he should really say anything, which mildly annoyed me. But then I harkened back to some of the previous discussions La Croix and I had… about certain things being safer if I just didn't know.

"You can say where they are, man. Just keep what they doin' outta your mouth," Hex said.

Cypress thought about it and nodded. Saint was the one to answer. "They out at some fancy golf course not too far away, actually," he said and Hex raised an eyebrow.

"Good enough," La Croix rumbled, giving my knee a squeeze.

I'd met a lot more of the club today than I had previous.

There was Bennie, who like I said, was a small man, not much taller than my five foot three, maybe by only like an inch or two. What he lacked for in height, he made up for in looks. He was all sleek, hard muscle with rich brown hair and a neatly trimmed brown beard. The real showstopper, for him, was his thickly lashed soulful brown eyes.

Axeman was similarly colored in that he too was a brunette, only a little ashier than Bennie. Likewise, he too was bearded, but it was much longer, hitting just above the middle of his chest. His hair was likewise longer, swooping down in front of his eyes and reaching nearly to his chin.

His eyes, where they peered out from behind all those bangs or whatever, were what was striking the most, however – icy blue, and as wintery as I had ever seen. Cold and apathy radiated from them in such a way that if I were a woman walking alone and he passed me and took a second look? I would most definitely quicken my pace or cross the street altogether.

I didn't need to ask about his road name, either. Axeman was likely a homage to New Orleans' most famous serial killer. He was active just past the turn of the last century, from like 1918 to 1919. He invaded people's homes and killed them with an axe, usually their own from their shed or out by their woodpiles. No one was spared, really. Not man, woman, or child; and he just absolutely reigned terror never to be caught. He had a fondness for jazz and writing letters to the papers which is what made the Axeman of New Orleans such a sensational case. He wrote a letter to the papers, stating he would avoid any house that played jazz on a certain set of nights, and as a result, the city's streets had been filled with music.

While I hoped that the Axeman of today simply had a fondness for jazz – I didn't think that's how he got his name. Not with that look in those eyes, which were somehow more terrifying than La Croix's had ever been, at least to me.

Finally, there was a quiet man – average height like La Croix, except not nearly as imposing or big. He had been introduced to me as Collier but everyone just seemed to call him Col. He had a Tennessee accent and was downright wiry, his hair long, and a dishwater blonde.

He had a goatee and a sort of somberness that hung around him. A stillness he wore like a mantle.

After a while, Cypress and Saint left and sometime later, when our plates of food were finished and disposed of and our drinks refreshed or traded for something stronger, two more men of the club rode up and dismounted their bikes.

I guessed they were the Louie and Chainsaw the rest of the men had been speaking of earlier.

"Be right back, cher," La Croix murmured against my temple and I sat up with my book in my hands, to let him get up out of the hammock. We'd switched to lounging in the shade, me with my book in my hands reading, while he'd simply rested with his eyes closed while I'd lain on him.

I looked back over my shoulder at the small huddle of four. Hex had joined La Croix and the two new men, and eventually, La Croix made his way back to me, the other two splitting off in the direction of the food.

An older man shouted from over by the house and La Croix threw up an arm, waving him off as he came back my way, head bowed as he listened to Hex. La Croix nodded, and Hex split off from him, and that seemed to be that; for now – the older man grumbling and turning to a knot of other older men to seemingly bitch. I noticed a few looks from those men cast our way – some amused, and others sympathetic. I could only imagine the angry old man to be La Croix's father. Don't ask me why, but if you know you just know – you know what I mean?

I pulled my bookmark from the back of my book and stuck it between the pages, closing the cover.

"Everything alright?" I asked, as La Croix returned to me.

"Aw, yeah," he said, shaking his head. "He's just up from his nap. Been tyin' one on since sunrise. It's his fuckin' way."

"Ah," I said and nodded my head knowingly.

"Chainsaw an' Louie be here any minute to meet you," he said, and I smiled warmly.

"Everyone's been lovely," I confessed.

"They know you goin' through it," he said and dropped into a vacant camp chair near me, palming the inside of my thigh.

I squeezed my legs together, trapping his fingers and chuckled a little and he smiled at me faintly.

"You needin' some cock already?" he asked, and I laughed and nodded.

"I can wait, I promise," I said.

He wiggled his hand and squeezed the top of my thigh and said, "You can ride me as long as you need to tonight, cher."

"I like the sound of that," I confessed softly, as plates loaded, Chainsaw and Louie made their way this way, beers in their other hands.

"Boys," La Croix intoned. "Meet my little Alina. Alina, these are the last of my boys. The big bastard here is Chainsaw, and this one's Louie."

I shaded my eyes. "Louie has to be only the second normal sounding name I've encountered so far," I said.

"Ah, yes ma'am, but it's short. It's short for Loup Garou," he said.

"Goodness!" I said. "I'd ask, but I know it's improper."

Louie grinned at me and said, "It's 'cause I seen one."

Chainsaw sat down on the ground and rolled his eyes.

"Sure, you did," he said and shoveled a gar cake in his mouth.

"You ain't got to believe me," Louie said. "I know what I saw, though."

I smiled a little bigger and held out my book. "I was just reading about swamp lore and just got to the part about the roux-ga-roux," I said.

Chainsaw was big, like La Croix, only taller and with a layer of fat over his muscle that made him appear softer somehow. I didn't believe he was for a minute. Not with a name like Chainsaw. Although he seemed a lot more jovial than the rest of the men of the Voodoo Bastards, sort of along the lines of Hex and Saint.

La Croix's daddy shouted something our way again and La Croix ignored him.

"Worthless bastard," came out of his mouth and I stiffened, sitting up.

"Did he just—?"

"Just ignore him, cher. He's drunk as fuck." La Croix shifted in his seat and gave my leg a squeeze.

"I don't care!" I said. "You're his son. He shouldn't talk about you like that."

I scowled and stared past the men sitting with me in the direction of the bitter old man.

"Eh, yeah, they got history, sweetheart. Don't you worry about it," Chainsaw said.

"Nobody fucks you like family," Louie declared quietly.

I looked from one to the other and settled on Louie who looked mighty uncomfortable.

La Croix's dad started shouting again and La Croix made to stand up. Chainsaw stood up swiftly and put a hand to La Croix's shoulder.

"Whoa, brother. No sense in doin' somethin' rash now. You already went to prison for beatin' some sense into that cocksucker once – it ain't work. No sense in doin' it again. Besides, you got your lady here."

"Why don't you go sleep it off? Ain't nobody here care or wanna listen to your bullshit! Nice to meet you too, you drunk fuck!" I shouted, and the party fell silent. People stared openly at me. La Croix's dad jerked back and blinked like he'd never thought a woman'd speak to him in such a way, and I didn't care.

It was one of the other women who laughed first, and then a ripple of laughter spread out throughout the partygoers and the tension eased. One of the old-timers put a hand on La Croix's daddy's shoulder and spoke low and insistent to the man.

I settled back in my seat and looked to the three Voodoo Bastards around me who all stared like I'd sprouted a second head or something.

"What?" I demanded.

"Did you—?" La Croix looked from me back to his daddy.

"If I'm yours, you're mine and nobody talks to one of my friends that way, let alone my man, without me saying something." I sniffed. "It's something I learned from Maya," I said.

"Well alright, den," Chainsaw said with a nod of respect. Something like pride shined in La Croix's eyes.

"You don't wife her up, I will!" Hex yelled across the yard, a girl in his lap who was laughing at him.

La Croix made a deep, bass growl in his throat at that, and I hid my smile with my book.

CHAPTER THIRTY

*L*a Croix…

The party went on into the night, and Alina was exhausted and a little pink despite the sunscreen I had on her and sittin' mostly in the shade all day. She'd finished the one book she'd bought and her demeanor was much more relaxed after a day around so many people.

After she'd told off my dad, more people came around to meet her and talk with her. I'd like to think my girl'd made a few new friends.

Word had spread about why I'd called everyone together before we'd even got there, but I'd had some questions come my way. I'd done my best to answer them away from my little Alina. After all, I was trying to instill some peace and calm; not damage whatever she had left beyond anything.

I had a feeling that'd come sooner rather than later.

With every day that passed, the outlook on my girl's girl bein' alive was gettin' dimmer and dimmer. The image of that fuckin' suitcase the dude was wheeling alongside them as they went down the hall in the security footage haunted me.

I got Alina back to my place and drew her a hot bath, lighting the candles in the bathroom for her and calling up to my room where she'd taken her stuff, to go on an' bring down another book to relax.

She came down with the book in her hands and I took it from her. I leaned her up against the edge of the tub as it filled, taking first one then the other sandal from her feet, working my way up her body, taking a piece of clothing at a time.

She watched me, mute and eyes alight with curiosity. My girl couldn't keep a thing off her face, and I could see the gears turning in her head.

"What?" I asked.

"You're so curious," she said. "As in Alice in Wonderland curious. Curiouser and curiouser." She smiled, and it was adorable.

"Yeah, what makes you say that?" I asked, genuinely curious about why she would go there, myself.

"You killed that man without a second thought," she said softly. "By your own admission, beat your own father to within an inch of his life," she added. "And yet, you're so careful with me."

I looked up at her and stood, grasping her tank tops at the hem, and lifting them over her head. She raised her arms obediently, and I stared down into her face, drawing her closer to me by a gentle grasp on her hips with either hand.

"The blood of the covenant is thicker 'n the water of the womb," I said. "At least on that last one."

"Then why do you launch from his house and keep going around him?" she asked. "If he treats you like that..."

"My daddy is a broken man, cher," I said, cupping her face and stroking a thumb along her cheek. "He has been for a long, long, time."

"And yet?" she asked softly.

"I guess a man can only take so much afore he snaps... and I snapped," I answered her.

She shuddered slightly, and I cocked my head. "I can't promise you I won't never yell, or say somethin' cruel even. But what I can and I will promise right now, is if we ever don't see eye to eye or you piss me off that much? I'll walk the fuck away before I'd ever lay a hand on you."

Her eyes were wide as I stared into them, my own eyes fixed on hers, my mouth set in a grim fuckin' line. I was never more serious than I was right in that moment.

Her mouth closed where it hung open in surprise and she swallowed hard.

She put her arms around me and leaned into me some and plucked the ring off of my chest that she said belonged to her grandma or something. She turned it in her fingers and said, "You know, my great-grandma was the only person who was ever happy to see me until Maya," she said and I focused on her face that was intent on the ring and her memories.

"My mamma didn't want me, and my grandma had to raise me," she said. "But my grandma didn't want me neither. Told me all the time how much of a burden I was and how she was wasting what was supposed to be her life and her time on me." She sighed and let go of the ring.

"My great-grandma, though? She was great. She was so wonderful to me. Listened to me, was happy to see me, and taught me how to escape a lot of the bullshit through books." She tore her eyes from the ring around my neck and looked up at me, meeting my gaze which was intent on her face. "I guess I'm just trying to say I'm no stranger to the ones who're supposed to love you saying mean things and breaking you down, you know? I get it, though. What you were saying about the whole blood is thicker than water thing. Maya is my sister of the heart. She's the one who taught me what unconditional love and loyalty are supposed to look like. I guess… I guess the same way your club does for you?"

I nodded, and she smiled a little. I leaned down and kissed her forehead.

"Best test that water and stop up that tub," I told her. "I'll get you a drink, and come in here and sit with you, if you like."

She smiled a little bigger and nodded. "Absolutely I'd like," she said.

I went into the kitchen and got the bottle of my good bourbon out of my freezer and poured a couple of stiff drinks. When I got back into the bathroom, she was huddled in the tub, her hair twisted in a knot on the top of her head.

"Gon' grab a shower," I murmured, handing her down her glass and sipping on my own. She sniffed and closed her eyes, an appreciative smile curving her lips.

"I love a good bourbon," she said, and I smiled on the inside. Well, hell, if it was gon' be like that, she really *was* the perfect woman. One I should and would have every intention of wifing up if it came to it.

"You sure you don't want to join me down here?" she asked after a long sip.

"Nah," I said. "I'm just not feelin' a bath tonight."

She nodded. "Okay."

I started up the shower and got in with my glass, taking a sip and setting it on the little shelf on the far side, well away from the spray.

The water beating on me felt real good. The bourbon went down smooth, and the sound of her dulcet voice as we talked over the rush of the showerhead just made all the things that much better.

It was a nice way to cap off the night, but the best I hoped was yet to come.

I got out of the shower and dried off while my little Alina lounged back and relaxed and that was nice, too. I stood at the sink and shaved my head and my face as she chatted with me some more. Just quietly talking, we learned some about each other.

Finally, I went over to fish her out and dry her smooth skin.

"You got some lotion or somethin'?" I asked, and she nodded.

"Got to get your skin hydrated, boy – or this burn liable to really sting tomorrow."

She smiled and asked teasingly, "You want to put the lotion on my skin?"

"Damn straight," I told her, and she giggled like somethin'd just gone over my head.

I wrapped her up, and she helped me blow out the candles I had going down here. We went on upstairs to the bedroom.

I rubbed her down from head to toe with that lotion of hers, which led to me making love to her, slow and sweet. I left her trembling and quaking in our bed with all the passion and devotion I could show her, and that was mighty fine.

If it was one thing that I *did* learn from my daddy it was this – nothing else in heaven or on earth beat the love of a good woman. Only I aimed to do right by mine and if it came to it, any children she might bear me.

There weren't no way I would ever be him. Not that way.

I slept hard and deep with her in my arms that night, and it was all good.

I ain't have no one calm my soul like she did.

∽

I DROPPED Alina off and rode up the way before pulling over to make my calls. I got a hold of Hex and asked, "Where are they?"

He knew what I meant, knew right away what I was talkin' about, and told me where our boys were at.

"Thanks," I said, and put up my phone, pulling back out into traffic and the throngs of tourists that were a fixture in this part of the city.

I rode out to where Saint and Axeman were sitting on our quarry.

"Boys," I said when I pulled up next to 'em and cut my engine.

"Hey, boss." Axe gave me a nod.

"What's the rundown?" I asked and they gave it to me. He'd been home all day, but from what they knew, listening as they had with the surveillance equipment we had, he was planning on going out to dinner at a fancy place off Chartres.

"Thinkin' about grabbing him?" Saint asked, handing over the parabolic mic he had pointed at the house and the earpiece to go with it.

I nodded.

"Axe, go back to the club an' get the van. Gonna need it to haul this hog to the Smokehouse," I said.

"You sure, boss? This ain't no little hog," he said.

I nodded, my eyes fixed on the fancy house he was in.

We lucked out. We were in one of the neighborhoods where folks with six figures worth o' income were housed right next door to a workin'-class family on government assistance or a dude on a fixed income and Medicare. There were parts of the city that were a real crazy mix like that, and this was one of them. It was enough to keep us sittin' here off the radar. Weren't no reason for us to be here, but there weren't no reason for us *not* to be, either.

"You got it," Axe muttered, and he kick-started his classic ride.

Wasn't long before our prey was pullin' out his driveway and went right on past us without a second look. We looked like we were just talkin' and smokin' a joint, but he paid us no never mind which was a test in and of itself to see if Cornelius had been talkin'.

Didn't look like it.

We rode out, keeping a healthy distance as we headed on down to Chartres. We found a place to park, and Axe rolled up. We got in the van and circled the block a while, casing the joint, possible points of exit and, the best spot to potentially ambush our boy.

It was dicey kidnappin' a man off the street like this; but we'd done it in broad daylight afore and right now we had the benefit of the cover of darkness.

We had our chance, and things went smooth as butter.

We threw open the side door, hauled his ass in, and tazered the motherfucker until he was out. A hood, some flex cuffs behind his back, and we were good to go.

"Anybody spot us?" Saint asked Axe as our chests heaved with the struggle to subdue the little shit.

"Don't look like it," Axe declared.

"Drop us up the block," I said. "And git on to the Smokehouse. We gotta get this little piggy ready for the market."

Axe pulled up in a loading zone ahead and Saint and I bailed out to walk back to our bikes.

We rode out to the Smokehouse, and I contemplated how I was gonna play this.

I kept thinking about my little Alina, and how she'd spoken about her friend. She had a thing with Maya that was as close as a citizen could get to what I had with my brothers that rode with me.

Despite my girl's lonely upbringing in the face of massive dysfunction, she had a deeper understanding about what *family* meant than any other person I'd known – and for her, her only family was Maya. If indeed this motherfucker had taken Maya away from my woman? Well... there would be hell to pay, and I had no trouble bringin' hell with me wherever I went.

The humidity was so thick you could cut it with a knife, and still it'd be a bitch to get it off the blade when you were through. So, it stood to reason, it was going to be one hell of an uncomfortable night at the Smokehouse. Not nearly as uncomfortable as it was going to be for Kenny boy, though.

"He's still out," Axeman said calmly when we pulled up. He lit the spliff in his mouth and sucked in a lungful of green.

"You get him settled into his new accommodations?" Saint asked him.

"I got him trussed up like a Thanksgiving turkey," he shot back and I nodded.

"You good, boss?" Axe asked me, looking my way.

"I'm good," I declared darkly.

They exchanged a look as I passed them to walk down the trail. A dubious look, if I ever saw one myself, and I didn't give a fuck. They weren't who I was mad at. The guy in the shed? He had whatever I was bringing coming. I had no doubt that Cornelius was tellin' the truth. Granted a man like that would lie his fuckin' ass off to save his own – but if you didn't think we'd been checkin' up on him, then you were a fool.

He was still going about his business in the city like nothin' happened. Hadn't packed up or tried to make a run for it and truthful men didn't run.

If he said this guy had given the order, then he'd given the order, and there wasn't no way to get to this assassin without his knowledge. There also wasn't no way to find out how far up the political food chain that this order had come from without him, and so here we were, the moment of fuckin' truth on that.

He was just waking up, just starting to struggle when I got up into the shed.

I took off my cut and hung it on the peg on the far wall where it'd be out of sight and worked on getting myself naked. That shit always freaked a motherfucker out when the hood came off; and it was the easiest and most efficient way to get cleaned up and carry no evidence away. Axe and Saint came in a minute later and took themselves off to the far corner before lookin' to me curiously. I ripped the hood off the motherfucker in front of me and his eyes widened.

"What are you doing?" he demanded, struggling against the shackles we had him in.

"Fixin' to get answers," I grated and went over to the table of implements and tools we had against the wall by the front door. "Scream all you like," I told him when he started hollerin' for help. "Ain't nobody out here to hear you."

"What the fuck?" he demanded. "What do you want?"

"A name to start with," I said.

"Whose name?" he demanded.

"Let's start with the assassin you hired to take out poor Maya Bashaw, yeah?"

He went very still and said, "I don't know what you're talking about!"

I cocked my head, the sharp blade in my hand, and finally shook my head. "You can't bullshit a bullshitter, Mr. Wells," I said. He glared at me defiantly.

"Wait, what are you doing!?" he demanded as I approached him with the blade.

"Getting answers," I said darkly, and I started to cut off his expensive clothes. He thrashed and screamed and hollered about it, but I didn't care much about that. We was just warming up.

The real fun had yet to begin…

Question was, was this little hog gonna squeal before the blade kissed his flesh or, was he gonna hold out until the pain started?

Answer was, he held out way past the pain starting. Had to respect a man who wouldn't break, but *goddamn*… this was one tough son of a bitch. Surprising really, but not in a good way.

BOURBON & BLOOD

I looked to Saint and Axe. Saint's eyebrows raised in something like a measure of boredom, Axeman's icy-blue eyes gleaming with a mix of contempt and excitement. I knew the excitement was for gettin' tagged in on this – Axe was a master at his craft and breakin' people was his specialty. He dug it when they fought as hard as this dude did.

I threw him some chin, and he stripped out of his cut. Only thing Axe didn't like was getting naked for this shit; and so, he didn't. Instead, he preferred the disposable Tyvek suit that was hangin' alongside the empty pegs for cuts and clothing for the guys, who like me, didn't mind airin' our skins.

It was too fuckin' hot in here to put anything else on over clothes and skin cleaned up so much easier.

"Get the buckets," Axe told Saint and Saint sighed and hung his head.

"Fetch and fuckin' carry," he grumbled, but took up the pair of metal pails and went on down to the dock to bring us up some swamp water.

I went over and got the weight bench and set it up behind ol' Kenny to get this party started.

The waterboarding did the trick. Nothin' like the fear of drowning after a round of painful torture to get a man singin' like a fuckin' canary.

"Alright! Alright!" he screamed. We doused him some more just to make sure he'd stay loose and talking.

He sang like a little bird, giving up the killer, spillin' the tea that Daddy was sick of his little girl out there doin' what she was doin', worried about the fuckin' fallout when he ran for governor and what his darling little girl would come out an' say. Worst of all, he came out with the real reason why Maya hated her daddy beyond anything. It was going to be worth killing a few men for that alone; even though they were sins committed well before little boy Kenny's time. Finally, he said how the solution to all of Bashaw's problems had been all little Kenny Wells' idea, somethin' he'd said when his tongue was loose with some good liquor – but also how he'd never expected Bashaw to agree with it, let alone run with the idea, expecting Kenny to make it happen.

How they'd never dreamed that Maya had friends or even chosen family that would care about her and would press the fuckin' issue like my little Alina did.

That last part caught my attention, sending up red flags. I shook him and demanded if they had plans for Maya's friend – the one who kept going to the police.

"Not if she keeps her mouth shut!" he cried. "We already paid someone, some low-level street scum, but he's dead!"

I raised my eyebrow at that and glanced at Saint who nodded and took off to head right on back to the city. He knew what I expected – head to the Quarter and sit on my little Alina's pad an' watch for trouble.

I got every bit of information there was to get out of the son of a bitch on Maya's killer. Axe nodded from behind his mask and goggles that he was gettin' it all. That man had a brain like an iron trap – I could bet he had it alright.

"Run it down when we get out of here," I said, and he nodded.

"You need to go. I'll finish this off."

I took my knee up off the weeping broken man.

"Hamstring him, leave him out there for the gators or the heat to finish him off. He don't deserve to go quick," I told Axe.

"You got it, boss."

I went out into the daylight and the heat, taking myself down to the dock with my bar of Ivory soap. I washed up, rage flowin' through my veins, albeit sluggish at the moment.

I took my time cleanin' myself up and went on back in to get myself dressed. Axe was talkin' to the stripped and bloody, half-drowned man sweatin' in the heat of the Smokehouse. Yeah, this hog was properly smoked and ready for market, but I didn't much care how long Axe took with it. I let the man have his fun. Kenny sure fuckin' deserved it, followin' through like he did after knowing the why of Maya's ways.

The knowledge of it stuck in my craw something fierce as I left

Axe to it and went out to my bike. I rode a ways away from the Smokehouse before pulling over and takin' up my phone, turning it on.

It immediately started blowing up with messages and shit, the first from Saint sayin' he was headin' home – that Hex had shown up to my little Alina's in his truck, had her in hand, scooping her up and taking off with her somewhere. The way Saint described it? They lit outta there like their ass was on fire.

I didn't look at anything else. I was just about to call Hex directly when my phone lit up and started buzzing in my mitt with his name on the screen.

"What?" I grunted by way of greeting, my brain going faster than my mouth and just condensing my "what the fuck is going down" into the single word. I could hear road noise in the background as he filled me in.

"Yeah, where you at bro?" he asked me.

"Smokehouse," I said, keepin' it short.

"I got Lina with me. We on our way out to St. Mary's medical examiners – they want her to ID a body," he told me.

I was closer than they were to Saint Mary's Parish by a fair bit, bein' out the way I was. I lowered my phone and searched the medical examiner's office address in the navigation pane.

"I'm on my way." I ended the call and started my bike back up, pointing myself up north toward St. Mary's Parish. I was closer bein' out at the edge of the Atchafalaya Swamp like I was, but there was no tellin' how far Hex was into the drive from the city.

I had a sinking feeling in my gut that bein' along the basin, that Maya's body had been found. Not by our people, but by somebody.

Fuck.

My only thought and concern was about either beating my woman and my VP to the morgue or at the very least, narrowly making it there just in time.

Damnit to hell, I thought to myself. I didn't realize I'd started to share so hard in my woman's eternal optimism and I'd found myself hoping against better sense that Maya was somehow alive.

I knew how much this kind of shit didn't have a happy ending. I lived it every day. Yet still my woman made me want to believe in happy endings enough that I nearly had myself fooled.

Now she was about to get one of the roughest lessons life ever had to serve up... I mean, I hoped not, but *damn*. I just had this sinking feeling in my gut that told me she was just in for it... and no, it wasn't fair. It wasn't fair by half.

It was all so much fucking bullshit. Another ballad on how the rich fucked with the lives of the ordinary and the poor – of how they thought they were above the law, and they were if I was being honest. They absolutely were.

What no one was above? Not even a rich and powerful fucker like Bashaw and his cronies?

Good ol' fashioned street justice. If I was late, if my little Alina wound up hurt in any way by that rich bastard's machinations? Well, I aimed to deliver some of that justice sure and swift.

CHAPTER THIRTY-ONE

*A*lina...

First thing in the morning, I connected to the houseboat's Wi-Fi and checked in with Dorian and Marcus. They were relieved to hear from me, and both expressed surprise when I regaled them with the tale of our stop at the bookstore the day before and the big Cajun cookout at his father's place.

I didn't share anything about La Croix's dad and his treatment of his son; that sounded too personal and just not like something that should be shared.

La Croix did some things around his place, got some laundry going in his single washer/dryer combo – which I had never seen one before. I especially had never seen one in the kitchen like his was – but it worked, I guess. I mean, spared some extra plumbing drama I guess when it came to the location of his pipes and stuff.

It thunderstormed outside, and we spent part of the day on the couch. He streamed something on television, while I laid back on the couch with my legs over his lap and read another of my books. It was nice, low key, and I loved how he smoothed his hand up and down my leg absently as he was engrossed in whatever he was watching.

It was nice.

Very domestic...

...and it did my heart good.

I almost wished I could have two days off in a row to indulge in it more fully. I admit a sort of wistful regret when it came time for him to run me home.

It was cutting it close once we reached all the way back to the city and he pulled up in front of my apartment building. I got off the bike and turned, but he didn't kill the engine or make to follow me. I gave him a questioning look, and he said, "Come give your ol' man a kiss, baby. I got business to attend to."

I pouted but kissed him goodbye.

"Be careful," I warned, and he nodded. I got myself up to my apartment just in time to change and really hoof it in to work.

∼

I WALKED HOME, and it was the first night in a while I had done it myself – no La Croix outside waiting for me. When I got up to my apartment, I checked my phone for texts and had one from him.

La Croix: Sorry cher, tomorrow night, I promise. Stay safe, lock your doors.

I smiled faintly, texted him back the kissy face emoji, and fixed myself some dinner before settling on the couch to watch a movie.

I woke up to my phone buzzing across the coffee table and light streaming in through the windows.

I winced and shaded my eyes with one hand while groping for the phone with my other one.

"Hello?" I answered, before it could go to voicemail even though it was an unknown number.

"Hello, Miss Bouchard? Miss Alina Bouchard?"

"Yes, speaking," I said politely to the authoritative voice over the line.

"This is Margaret Torrance out of the St. Mary Parish's medical examiner's office," she said. "I'm so sorry to have to ask you this, but

I'm going to need you to come in for an identification if at all possible."

My heart seized in my breast.

"Identification?" I echoed.

"Yes, ma'am."

"I-I live in the city," I said, my brain screaming big red warning sirens, a sound like static rushing through my ears.

"I could arrange a ride if you need—" she said.

"Um, yeah, let me see what I can do," I said. "You need me now?" I asked.

"Yes ma'am, if at all possible—"

"Okay, let me see if I can get a ride. I'll call you *right* back, okay?" I said out loud. In my head I said, *oh, shit.*

As soon as I got off the phone, I immediately tried to call La Croix. It went straight to voicemail. I swallowed hard, and hands shaking, scrolled through my numbers – he'd added a bunch yesterday while we'd sat on the couch.

I landed on Hex, who I'd been instructed to try next and he answered on the first ring. "Hey, darlin', what 'cha got going on?" he asked by way of greeting and he sounded like I'd woken him up.

"St. Mary's Parish medical examiner's office just called me," I said. "They're sending someone over to come get me if I can't get a ride myself – they want me to identify a body." My voice cracked despite me trying so hard not to let it.

"I'll be right over," he said. "Call 'em back, tell 'em you got a ride."

"Okay," I said, my voice shaking. "Thank you."

He ended the call before I could and trying to remember to breathe around the boulder sitting on my chest, I called the unknown number that'd called me. They said they understood, gave me the address, and said they looked forward to seeing me which I tried not to laugh hysterically at that. Seriously? You're a freaking *morgue*, and you look forward to seeing *anybody*?

It echoed of when you went to the doctor's office when you were sick and the nurse brightly asked how you were doing today – like, I'm sicker 'n dogshit and here so you can fix it. How do you think I'm doing?

I got up and whipped through a quick shower and changed my clothes into something much more presentable than my dirty bar uniform.

By the time I was pulling on my boots, there was a knock at my door.

I blinked and went to it, looking out the peephole and letting out a breath when I saw Hex through it.

"Hey," I said when I unlocked the door and he lifted his chin. "Sorry, cher. I piggybacked in on somebody who was leavin'."

"Oh, no, it's fine," I said, snatching up my purse and my keys.

"Gotta hurry, though. I'm double parked down there," he said and I was already pulling the door shut.

"Let's go," I said firmly, but I couldn't stop my full-body shaking.

When we got downstairs, there was a big black pickup on the other side of some cars parked at the curb and an irate dude standing between the cars and the truck on his phone.

He pulled the phone away from his face and demanded to know, "This your truck, asshole?"

Hex's expression darkened and he went to the passenger side door and opened it for me, ushering me in. I skirted the dude who was saying something along the lines of "Great, just fucking great. You know you're not the only dude on the planet, *right?*"

Hex straightened, shut the truck's door, and turned on the guy.

"I would shut the fuck up if I were you," I heard him say through the glass.

"Or what?" the dude snarled.

"Or I'll burn your fuckin' house down with you in it," Hex said, walking around the back of the truck. "Today is not the day and I am not the one, bro. I'm leavin' and I suggest you do too," Hex said over the top of the truck as he got in.

I blinked, and he settled into the driver's seat.

"Seatbelt, Lina, or La Croix will have my ass," he said as he stepped on the brake and pressed the button on the dash to start the truck.

We pulled away from the curb smoothly and got on the road. I felt sick – like sick to my stomach.

"Where's La Croix?" I asked a few seconds later.

"Handlin' some business, baby, but I got you," Hex said.

I nodded and accepted it for what it was.

Partway there, Hex tried getting through to La Croix and he seemed to have better luck than I did.

"What?" La Croix's voice blared through the truck's speakers.

"Yeah, where you at, bro?"

"Smokehouse," La Croix grunted, and I gave Hex a quizzical look. He waved me down and said, "I got Lina with me. We on our way out to St. Mary's medical examiners – they want her to ID a body."

"I'm on my way," La Croix said, and the line went dead. He didn't sound happy from the word go when he'd answered the phone.

I wondered why.

"I think you best call in to work now," Hex said, and I blinked.

"Why? I mean, what if it's not her?" I stared at him and his hand tightened on the wheel, making a creaking sound where his hand rubbed against the material of it.

"I think it's best you call in anyway, Cher. Her or not, this ain't gon' be an easy thing."

I swallowed hard and did what he said, or tried to. Clyde, my manager, was giving me an absolute ration of shit over it. Finally, he relented, but not before cursing me out. I lowered my phone to my lap, red-faced and sniffed.

"He always talk to you like that?" Hex asked.

I simply pursed my lips and shook my head.

Hex grunted, an annoyed but at the same time skeptical sound, and I hunkered down in my seat, turning to stare out my window.

Please don't be her, please don't be her, please don't be her, I chanted in my mind the whole way there. I swear the rest of that drive went by in a blur.

I walked down the hallway with Hex at my side but I wanted La

Croix. I wanted my frightening, stolid, sentinel of a lover at my side to hold my sweating hand and to lean on.

I was in a fog, terrified, and everything on my insides rebelling and trying to spill on the outside of me as I went back with the doctor. There would be a window between me and the body. As I stopped in front of the window, Hex at my back, I tried very hard not to look like I was going to hyperventilate.

"Are you ready?" the doctor beside me asked, and she sounded like she was down a long hall with an echo. I didn't trust myself to speak, and simply nodded instead.

I steeled myself, took a deep breath, held it, and made eye contact with the person on the other side of the glass. They nodded at me in their surgical gown and their scrubs, the mask over their face. All I could think was that their eyes were kind, empathetic and so sad for what I would go through, which just served to ratchet up my level of dread even further.

Hex gripped my shoulder to steady me as the person behind the glass pulled back the sheet…

CHAPTER THIRTY-TWO

*A*lina...

The sheet peeled back and anything I'd held in my heart resembling hope shattered into parts so fine it might as well have returned to the sand that the glass of it had been made of.

I crumpled, and screamed, at the bloated mess on the cold and sterile table. Her face so distorted, the only way I'd truly recognized the thing in front of me as my best friend was by the filigree black-and-gray tattoo along her collarbone and shoulder on the one side.

Hex caught me before I hit the floor and the curtains on the other side of the glass whisked closed at the touch of a button by the medical examiner out here with us. She'd been quick on the draw, the curtains whisking along their track before the morgue attendant could even pull the sheet back up to cover my friend.

I didn't hold anything back, screaming my pain at the linoleum floor as Hex tried to hold me up and then, out of nowhere, he let me go and the arms I really wanted were around me. La Croix was suddenly there, as though appearing by magic. I looked up into his darkly inked eyes and his face was as stone – impassive, even as security and another doctor in a white coat loomed behind him.

I didn't care. I was grateful. I wrapped my arms around him and practically crawled into his lap right there on the hallway floor.

I felt like I'd just been rent from the hollow of my throat to the top of my pubic bone, my heart, my guts, all my hopes and prayers to the goddess I believed in, spilling out onto the shiny linoleum floor. All the best parts of me, all the worst parts of me, seeping out across it to touch their shoes. All while my friend's bloated rotting shell sat on that unforgiving table on the other side of the glass, covered only in a sheet, hidden only by a curtain.

Empty, like I was emptying out right here; except she didn't have anybody to put it all back in. She didn't have the ability to smile or laugh or tickle me or throw popcorn at me, or cry with me during the sappiest part of the romance movie, or positively drool over the male lead, or hug me, or slap some goddamn sense into me when I started one of my pity parties, or… anything! Anything anymore! Because she was gone… gone forever, and I felt like I was the only person out here looking for her, and I didn't understand that!

I didn't, because out of the two of us? Maya was better. Maya was stronger, and braver, and the baddest bitch I had ever met in my life, and I didn't *want* to miss her like this. I didn't *want* there to be a world without Maya Bashaw in it.

"I got you, cher." La Croix's deep soothing voice broke through my frantic thoughts, broke through the shock and the pain, and I took it from him. I took from him the offered strength, the offered stillness, the numbness chasing the panic and the heartache away, if even just momentarily. I wept, and I knew there would be some more weeping to come, but for now, the initial storm was passing and it was thanks to La Croix's steady presence, his arms wrapped around me and rocking me gently.

I sniffed, and the pressure he had on the back of my head, pressing it to his chest beneath his chin eased up. I drew back and looked up at him. He looked down at me and smoothed a thumb through the moisture slicking my blotchy face from my deeply ugly cry.

"There you go," he murmured encouragingly. "That's it."

I dove into the shelter of his big arms and he held me tight for as long as I needed to finish getting it together.

There was paperwork, because of course there was, and then the devastating news that when they were done with my best friend's body, that I wouldn't be able to take her home or have anything to do with anything, really... that was up to her father. Her father who wasn't interested in her at all so long as she did anything that was perceived as untoward.

Her daddy didn't give a fuck about her. Not like I did. Not one little bit, unless she was doing something that was making him look good.

It was bitter. Extremely bitter.

La Croix took me back outside to Hex's truck, Hex staying behind for some reason.

"I want to ride with you," I protested as La Croix thumbed the fob and the locks disengaged on the truck. He turned me to face him and caressed my face, standing so very near and sheltering me from any prying or curious eyes from the building, with the truck's door.

"I don't have an extra helmet with me, cher, or I would," he said.

I sniffed and nodded and he sighed.

"Just tell me what you want me to do, baby, and I'll do it," he said, and I looked up into those eyes and realized – La Croix was a villain by his own design and that was something that I needed right now.

What was it they said?

A hero was a person who would sacrifice you to save the world, while the villain? The villain would burn the world, lay waste to it, to save *you*... I didn't need to be saved, though. What I needed was *revenge*, and a villain was good for that, too.

I took a deep breath, and then took another, and then I thought to myself, *what would Maya ask for in this moment?* And I knew. I knew with my whole heart what she would say. What she would want, and right or wrong, I was here for it.

"Find them," I begged. "Find them and kill them. Every last one of them that had *anything* to do with this," I said and La Croix raised his chin, his nostrils flaring as he took a deep breath in of his own.

He kissed me fiercely, and I kissed him back as hard as I could. When he broke that kiss, we were *both* breathless.

"I planned on it, sugar. I planned on it," he said.

To Hex who came walking up, he turned and said, "Take her home, pack up her things, an' talk to ol' Saint. Get as many of the boys as you can in to help."

"You make it sound as though you mean we should pack up the whole apartment," I said startled.

He nodded. "That's exactly what I mean," he said.

"What?" I asked, startled. "Why?"

"Just trust the man on this one, cher," Hex declared, and I met La Croix's eyes and nodded.

"Alright, but where will I go?"

"We'll get you taken care of. I'll be right on by before you know it," he said. "Just need to stop on in the club first, an' make some calls."

"Okay," I agreed, and he put his hands on my hips and lifted me easily into the truck. I swung my legs in and he gave me a nod, a pat on my knee, and shut the door.

He spoke with Hex a little way away, their voices low enough that I couldn't hear them. Hex looked up from the ground and over to me and back to La Croix, his hands settling on his hips. He didn't look any happier than La Croix did, his expression darkening.

I swallowed hard. Hex gave a nod and then jogged around to the driver's side of the truck as La Croix strode to his bike.

"What was that about?" I asked.

"Club business, cher. Now just you sit tight now while I get you home."

I nodded and huddled in on myself, pulling my seatbelt across me. Hex took it and fastened it. I couldn't even give him a watered-down smile. I just looked at him, and he gave me a nod, an understanding one.

"We've got you, baby," he said. "You go on and feel whatever you need to feel. We'll take care of everything from here."

"Thank you," I said, and he made a sound like he'd sucked his teeth. My eyes were fixed on the brightly colored patch on La Croix's back as he roared away from me, swooping gracefully around a bend in the parking lot. I twisted as Hex backed us up, to keep him within view, and he raised his hand to wave at me as he took another turn to point himself and his bike out the driveway. He hesitated for only a second before turning out onto the road. Twisting down on the throttle, he shot forward and disappeared.

"Someone gon' feel the pain for this, baby girl. I promise you that," Hex declared and I let my unfocused gaze remain out the passenger side window.

"I certainly hope so," I said. He turned his head this way and that, checking for traffic, before turning out onto the same street La Croix had just gone up.

"You best believe it," he said, and I took some measure of comfort in that. An immense measure of comfort, actually.

CHAPTER THIRTY-THREE

*L*a Croix...

First thing I went to do was head back to the club. I trusted Hex had my little Alina in hand, but after hearin' what ol' Kenny Wells had to say about her bein' on Bashaw's people's radar for raisin' a stink over her best friend? Yeah, nah. I expected Bashaw's people already knew about the body. Bet even more they was just seein' if Alina was gon' show up and make the ID. Now, she was goin' back to the apartment that, by her own admission, belonged to Maya's *family*.

I didn't know if it was her daddy's family, or her momma's, but I weren't about to take no risk.

So, with all that weighin' heavy on my mind, I pulled up at the club.

No one was here, which didn't much surprise my ass. It was in the week, and fellas had day jobs. I got off my bike and unlocked the gate, running it back and open so I could pull into the club's courtyard.

I further unlocked the club's door and disengaged the alarm before I headed on back to the office.

I made some calls an' got a hold of the boys I could. Some were out there in the swamp. Not just Axe, but boys like Cypress who made their livin' out that way.

It took a while, repeatin' the story to get some of the boys mobilized. There was some bitchin, but despite it, they all left their jobs and headed on over to my girl's. I didn't think much of it had to do with a fear of me. Or, at least, I'd like to think it had more to do with them liking my girl now they'd had the chance to meet her.

The calls completed and messages left for the boys who couldn't pick up, I got into the safe and pulled out two fat stacks of cash and stuffed them in my back pocket.

Time to grease some fuckin' palms.

Back outside, I set and locked everything back up and strode out across the street and up to Alina's old building. I buzzed the office, and the door buzzed and unlatched. I walked on in, past the stairs down on to the end of the hallway and up to the old door with its frosted and pebbled glass with *Office* painted on it.

I opened the door and an older big black woman stood up, alarmed, from behind the desk.

"Now what you want?" she demanded, and her tone was defensive. She must have buzzed me in without lookin' at the camera first.

"The apartment up there on the third floor." I pointed up. "3A. You rent it back out yet?" I demanded.

"No, got someone comin' to look at it right now," she said and crossed her arms. She was gonna be tough, I liked that.

"The girl who used to live there, you liked her as a tenant, right?" I demanded.

She eyed me suspiciously, and I repeated myself, "Alina Bouchard, you liked her as a tenant, no?"

"I liked Alina just fine," she said, nodding.

I pulled out the two stacks of cash and said, "First, last, deposit – whatever the hell you want, and at least two years rent. You let it to her again?" I demanded and her eyes went wide.

"Alina?" she said. She nodded. "Mighty fine girl, was so glad she decided not to move out," she said, sweeping the stacks off the desk.

I nodded. "The apartment fit?" I asked.

"Right as rain. My boys just got finished with it yesterday," she said. "'Lina was fixin' to leave it in mighty fine shape. I'm sho glad she changed her mind."

I nodded to her and said, "Pleasure doin' business with you."

"Rent's due at the first of the month," she said with an arched eyebrow and I raised mine.

"Don't get cute," I said.

"You good for a year," she said with a smile, and I raised my chin.

"You good for eighteen months," she said, and she squared up.

"Eighteen months," I finally agreed. "Rent's due the first of the month…" I paused and did the math and rattled off the year and month payments would resume if we were still using the place.

"No refunds," she added, just to cover her bases.

I held out my hand and her eyes dropped to it.

She took it and gave me one hell of a hearty handshake.

"We have an accord," I said.

She nodded and turned around to a little metal cabinet mounted to the wall. She pulled down a little ring with two keys on it, leaving a second behind in the box and handed them to me.

"Have her stuff squared away tonight," I said, and she nodded.

"Won't be here, after hours an' all," she said.

"Yes, ma'am," I said with respect.

By the time I got back on over to Alina and Maya's place, I found Hex's truck parked at the curb and spotted Saint, Bennie, and Louie's bikes backed against it a little further up. I found a spot for my bike and strode down the sidewalk.

I buzzed Alina's apartment, and somebody buzzed me in.

I took two of the stairs at a time and walked through her open door to sheer chaos – boxes and packing shit strewn all over the fucking place.

She looked up from some of her books that she was carefully packing away, face still red and blotchy, sniffling and tears staining her cheeks.

"Hey, cher," I murmured, and she broke down crying all over again, reaching her arms up for me.

"Oh, hey now," I said, and I went to her, pulled her into my arms, and dropped my big ass down onto the floor beside her. She cried it all out again and steady after the tempest of her tears, she looked up at me and said brokenly, "I don't know where I'm supposed to go."

"I got you, cher," I told her. "I always got you," I said, hugging her tight.

She sniffed and nodded and I sighed.

Wasn't this just a big ol' mess?

∼

FIRST THING FIRST. We boxed up a bunch of Alina's shit. That done, we took it on down to Hex's truck once there was enough to fill it and let him and Louie take off and take it on over to her new/old place.

Hex made sure I gave him the keys. I was more focused on my girl than the details like that.

Dorian and what had to be his boyfriend Marcus showed up after a while and they'd gone to my little Alina. All three cried in a huddle while the rest of us kept on hauling shit out.

"What can we do?" Dorian had asked me, and I'd swept an arm out.

"Help us get her the fuck up outta here," I'd said and the two gay boys pitched right on in.

More of the Voodoo boys showed up, an' finally Axe with the van. Between the van an' Hex's truck, we started takin' down some of the big shit – her bed and dresser, her bookcases which she tried to stop us on that. I'd just stared at her a minute and she'd sat back on her heels and nodded.

"Those are Maya's" dying on her lips almost as soon as she'd spoke it. My silent, *Maya don't need 'em no more,* going unspoken.

"You take what you need of hers, baby," Hex said. "We'll make sure ain't no one come after you on it."

She took all the photos, and certain other things, but left Maya's room intact for the most part and didn't touch her friend's jewelry or nothin'.

I thought about her great-grandmamma's ring around my neck and vowed to get it fixed soon. I went and found a necklace out of her friend's box and stowed it away in my cut for later – a day when I knew she might regret not having more of her friend. Why? I knew my little Alina was honest, and a good girl, and despite those facts, I knew she had just enough of the dark in her that she would regret not snagging *something* of her friend's.

I knew, because I'd seen it in her eyes when she'd begged me to kill every motherfucker that had a hand in her friend's death.

The darkness, the anguish, the pain in her heart, and the desire to inflict that pain back on someone tenfold. I knew what that felt like and it chapped my fucking ass like nothing else that she was feeling it now.

She wanted some motherfuckers to suffer and die? Well, in that regard, I was but my dark queen's instrument.

I would make that shit so. I just needed to see her safe, first.

Hex'd told me how her manager'd spoke to my girl on the phone and that was another thing I had on my list of shit to do. That transgression was likely to cost ol' Clyde some teeth.

It was after midnight afore we finished moving all her shit out and up to her old apartment. I'd ridden behind a load and left my bike at the club and drove back with the truck. When it was the last run and Alina was ready to go, I put her in the passenger seat and watched out the corner of my eye as she waved at Dorian and Marcus stayin' behind on the sidewalk before they walked themselves home.

I'd let 'em know where she was going, and I also let 'em know not to even speak it. That there was far too much at stake and I'd give 'em the all-clear as soon as we had it.

"Where are we going?" Alina asked, and she sounded so tired.

"Back where you belong, cher. Don't you worry. I got it all in hand."

She turned to me, her eyes wide, when we took the familiar streets around her old apartment.

She sank back in her seat with relief when I pulled the truck up outside and the boys started pullin' shit out of it to take it upstairs.

It wasn't perfect, boxes and furniture all over and in no sort of order, but it was all up here. We'd help her get it done, but for tonight, I'd be taking her home to the swamp where it was quiet and calm.

I borrowed Hex's truck to do it. I couldn't trust her to ride.

"Shower?" I asked as we stepped off the boat onto the barge, and she shook her head, looking half-dead on her feet.

"I just want sleep," she said, and I nodded.

I took her upstairs, undressed her, and tucked her in.

"Where are you going?" she asked, holding onto my hand.

"Babe, I been sweatin' my ass off," I chided gently. "I *do* need a shower, okay?"

She nodded and let me go.

I took a long one, and with the lack of any decent rain beyond the one thunderstorm that'd we'd had lately, I worried marginally about the tanks, but not too hard.

When I got back to the bed, she was sprawled out and fast asleep. I honestly couldn't wait to join her. I would be sore tomorrow.

CHAPTER THIRTY-FOUR

Alina...
I woke up to sounds of sizzling and the most delicious smells permeating the small house. Then I took another sniff of the air and *oh... coffee.* I shifted, the bed creaking, and I had to wince. The combination of so many emotions, the frantic boxing and moving my shit, and La Croix's awful, awful, bed did my body in. I was so sore.

He appeared at the top of the stairs and handed me a cup of coffee and crouched by the bed, tracing a middle finger along my hairline and pushing my hair behind my ear, out of my face.

"Hey." His voice was rough but gently sweet.

"Hey," I murmured and sipped the coffee between my hands. It was good, just the way I liked it. He was a quick study where I was concerned. Observant.

"Don't get up," he said. "I'll bring you breakfast up here."

"You're too good to me," I said, and I felt my lip tremble. He leaned in and kissed me sweet. Without another word, he got back up and went down the stairs again.

I drank my coffee and tried to wake up, and soon he returned with two plates.

I set my mug aside and accepted one, famished while at the same time not hungry at all. I took a bite of bacon and looked over at him as he settled on the bed beside me. I said, "It's good, thank you."

He nodded and chewed quietly, and we simply ate together in silence, which was nice.

"You just tell me what you need and it's yours," he said.

I nodded and finished my food, believing him.

As I finished, a ringing came from downstairs.

"Aw, shit," he muttered and got up, double-timing it down and back into the kitchen beneath me.

"Yeah?" I heard him answer, and it was rough. "Ah-huh. Yeah. Good to know. No, we'll be in. Yeah."

There was a clatter as the phone was put down, and I had to imagine it was his satellite phone. He came back up and said, "That was Hex. I gotta go back, but if you want to stay out here you can, otherwise, I'll take you back to your apartment or the clubhouse with some of the guys."

"The apartment is good," I said. "I need to unpack. It'll keep me busy so I don't go crazy."

He nodded and said, "I'll see if some of the guys can help you, set it up how you'd like it."

"Thanks," I murmured.

We went back to the lower ninth ward, to the club, and my old apartment with all my things in it, looking like some kind of whirlwind moving bomb went off in it. As I sank down sitting cross-legged in the middle of what was the living room floor, I had to admit – *a bomb had gone off*, a hurricane *had* swept through, and my heart was the thing that was truly obliterated from it.

La Croix had gone down to make a call that he didn't want me to hear, so I just sat up here, alone for a minute, and tried to decide just where to begin… because all of this was *a lot*. I mean, a *lot,* a lot.

"Hey." I jumped and turned around to my open doorway, Collier leaning into it. "Shit, sorry, I didn't mean to scare you. I'm here to help. What can I do?"

I smiled and gave a broken little laugh. "Honestly, I don't even know," I said. "I feel like my brain just isn't working. Like I have a one-track mind and that track ain't here, you know?"

He slipped inside the door and nodded, surveying the carnage of mishmashed random furniture, boxes, and shit just *all over the place* in here.

"Okay," he said. "First thing's first… boxes in the rooms they're labeled for. If it ain't got a label, let's open it up and figure out where the fuck it goes."

I nodded. "Okay. Okay, yeah. That's a good start," I agreed. "Thank you."

"No sweat," he said, and I tried to smile. He went for a box, looked at it, and with a nod, carried it off to the kitchen.

I pulled a box to me, checked the scrawled writing, and ultimately decided it read *bathroom* on it.

We'd only shifted a few things around to where they belonged in their respective rooms, when La Croix returned.

"Hey, what're we doing?" he asked.

"Uh, just moving things around, shifting them into the rooms they belong in," I said meekly. He nodded.

"Okay, you keep on keepin' on with that, cher. I'm gon' steal Col here and we're gon' put your bed together. Call you when we got it to find out where you want it."

"Okay," I said. "Before you do, can you put these two bookcases against that wall?" I asked, pointing.

"You got it," he said and waved at Collier to come help him.

The bookcases out of the middle of the living room and up against the wall by the door eased some of the tightness in my chest for some reason. I started shifting boxes of books over in front of them, so that I could unload them in a bit, while La Croix and Collier disappeared into the bedroom.

Once I'd been set to a task, I found my groove, the one small task leading to the next and the next.

I worked methodically, a room at a time, starting in the living room until the boys came out of the bedroom and needed me to point where I wanted the big furniture to go.

They'd already laid out my bedroom area rug, which I appreciated, and then immediately felt a little bad for having them completely shift it and the bed to a different position within the room.

I sat down on the unmade bed and sighed. It was a box-topian nightmare in here, too. A lot of these boxes only like half-full, and labeled everything from kitchen to bathroom. We got everything not marked bedroom out of there and then it was just me and La Croix for a little while, pulling things from boxes and folding them silently.

He would hand me piles, and I would secret them away into the dresser where I wanted them.

"How you doing, bro?" Saint asked, sticking his head and upper body through the bedroom doorway after a while. I glanced up just in time for La Croix to give Saint a meaningful look and then to glance in my direction as though to say *you should really be asking her that.*

Saint looked over at me on the floor hidden by innumerable boxes, my very own cardboard fortress springing up around me. He slipped more fully into the room and said, "Hey, 'Lina... I didn't see you down there."

I smiled. "It's okay," I murmured.

He didn't ask me how I was doing, instead pulling a knife from where it was clipped to his pocket and taking up one of the piled empty cartons.

"Let's get you out of there, huh?" he asked with an easy smile and I forced a smile back as he sliced through tape and folded the first box flat.

By the time he was on the last one or two boxes, everything clothing had either been folded and put away, or had been hung up in the closet.

"This is your sewing machine?" La Croix asked, and I looked up.

"Oh, oh, no... that was Maya's," I said. "I make my own paper and bind books. Sometimes I paint watercolors. Maya was the one who sewed."

"Oh, shit. Well, oh, well. Uh, where did you want me to put it?" he asked and lifted the machine in its carrying case out of the box.

"Front closet floor?" I asked.

He nodded. "You got it."

He went out into the chaos outside the bedroom and I sighed.

We'd set up all the furniture in here – the nightstands, their lamps, the dresser, my desk, my easel and watercolors which had been a housewarming gift at the new apartment from Maya and was a *very* fancy and portable setup... but somehow, we just couldn't find my bedroom sheets for the bed. They were lost in a box somewhere or something, maybe even back at the old apartment. It was frustrating.

"Hey, 'Lina. Heard you were looking for these."

I looked up and Louie stood in the doorway with my sheets.

"Where were they?" I asked and I smiled.

"In a box labeled 'Kitchen' with some pots and pans," he said. "We just started opening everything until we found them." I laughed, and he held down a hand to help me up to my feet. I took it and sighed, dusting myself off a little. He pried the sheets apart and handed me the fitted one, dumping the rest on the dresser then coming over to help me make the bed.

"Thanks," I murmured. "Just trying to make this room livable for tonight so I can just shut out the rest of everything – you know?"

He nodded and after the fitted sheet was on, he turned back with the top sheet and said, "You know, I know it's not the same but I... I- uh, I lost my momma real recently and so I just wanted you to know that I sorta know what it feels like... except, you know, my momma didn't care about me like your friend did."

I felt my shoulders drop and said, "That's awful, Louie. I'm really, really, sorry."

He nodded and said, "Yeah, me too." He sighed.

I bit my lips together and caught his hand as he flung the top sheet over the bed and I gave it a squeeze in solidarity, letting the compassion flow for a minute. He met my eyes and his were a startling light green. He gave me a brief, weak smile, and I saw how much it hurt him. Maybe not the fact that she was gone, but definitely the fact she didn't care and boy, could I relate to that too, with my own upbringing.

"Nobody really cared all that much about me when I was a kid, either," I murmured. "I don't think that's a hurt that ever really goes away."

"I don't see how," he said.

"Don't see how what?" I asked.

"How anybody couldn't care about you," he said and his ears turned red.

I smiled. "Well, thanks for that – but my mamma was a teen who didn't want me, and my grandmamma made her have me because of her," and I made air bunnies with my fingers in the air at this next part, "'deeply held religious beliefs.' So as soon as I was out, my mamma abandoned ship and my grandmamma ended up raising me, and…" I gave a low whistle. "She never let an opportunity pass where she didn't let me forget it, I'll tell you what."

"That's shitty," he said, and I smiled.

"That's where my great-grandmamma came in. She's the one that taught me what real love was supposed to look like. Then Maya finished my education and threw in a bunch of lessons on strength and tellin' the people in my life who didn't add to it in positive ways to kick rocks."

Louie considered me a minute and said, "All I've got left is the club, now."

I smiled. "And me," I said with a bit of false brightness.

He grinned and looked shy, his ears turning that bright red again as he said, "Yeah, well, I like my skin attached Ms. 'Lina, so I wouldn't say that too loud."

"Say what too loud?" La Croix asked, winking at me from behind Louie who straightened up and blanched a little.

"Nothin', boss!" he said quickly, and I stifled my giggles behind my hand. La Croix put a hand on the back of Louie's head and rough-housed with him a little bit. Louie was finally like, "Gah! Quit it!" but he was smiling again.

"Less talk, more work, boy!" La Croix said and tossed me one of my pillows. I took up one of the pillowcases from the dresser, while Louie went back to putting on and smoothing the top sheet.

The blankets and bedspread were still missing in action, but I think that's because they were wrapped around a couple of fragile things that were taking up their own box somewhere.

About twenty minutes later, my bedroom was as put together as I could make it for the moment, and I was sighing in a bit of contentment. One room down, only the rest of the apartment to go.

I stepped out and found things much neater out here – the dishwasher running, the bathroom nearly complete, and the boys standing in a huddle in the living room, which was mostly arranged, the area rug down and the couch situated.

"What's going on?" I asked and La Croix, Saint, Louie, and Hex sprang apart, looking a little conspiratorial.

"Nothin', cher," Hex declared.

"Why don't you go finish your bathroom so you can have a shower tonight?" La Croix suggested gently and I could tell they'd been discussing something serious and that it wasn't something I needed to be present for.

I nodded, and went into the bathroom, finding a box of cleaning products and sorting which I wanted in here under the sink versus what I wanted under the kitchen sink. I fished folded towels out of another box and put them on the built-in shelves in here, all with the door shut in the cramped space while the boys talked outside.

Did I like it? No. It felt like they didn't trust me, and I think that was, more than anything, what bothered me so much about it. But I understood it, which had to be good enough for me. At least right now.

La Croix stuck his head in a minute later and said, "Boys and I gotta go across the street and have church."

"Church?" I echoed.

"It's what we call it when we have a club meetin'," he answered.

"Ah."

"You gon' be okay on your own up here for a while?" he asked, and I nodded.

"I think so," I said. "It's not like I don't have plenty to do."

He smiled at me and slipped into the room far enough to kiss me.

"You need me, you call me," he whispered against my lips.

I nodded.

"Okay," I murmured. "I'm going to need a ride into work," I said, and he shook his head.

"You got the rest of the week off," he said.

"Oh, do I now?" I asked, and he smiled.

"You do," he said. "Ol' Clyde and I are about to have a talk about respectin' my lady."

I smiled and asked, "Okay, but on that one can you at least *try* to keep it to just talking?" He eyed me a little suspiciously, his face stone and I laughed a little. "He's really not always like that. He's all bark and no bite, really…"

"Well, I'm all bite, and probably not enough bark," he said, and I kissed him a quick one.

"Well, maybe this is a perfect time to work on that bork of yours," I said and I tweaked his nose. He jerked back and tried to scowl, but his smile ruined it.

"You make me happy," he said a second later, and he scraped his bottom lip between his teeth, giving me a meaningful but still cryptic look.

"Right back at 'cha," I said softly, and he punched the doorframe to the bathroom lightly, giving it a couple of taps before disappearing.

I sighed and surveyed the rest of the bathroom. If I put my mind to it, I'd have this room done in no time and could maybe take a rest and go through and shelve my books, which is honestly what I really wanted to do.

CHAPTER THIRTY-FIVE

*L*a Croix...
Everyone gathered around the big metal industrial table and took their seats.

"To order, I guess." I smacked the gavel on its disc. Never much liked the thing. Too citizen justice for my taste.

"So, this is to catch us up on the situation with your lady, right?" Chainsaw asked from down the table.

"Well, first off, I want t' thank you all for everything you've done so far for me an' my little Alina," I said. "But yeah, the shit's got real and Hex an' me figured now would be a good time to get everyone on the same page."

"That an' we wanted to ask the hivemind if y'all had any good ideas for next steps, because this sure all is one gigantic shitstorm," Hex said.

"How bad we talkin'?" Saint asked.

"Hex," I said.

He looked over and gave a nod, since I gave him the floor. He picked up his glass and sipped whatever he had in it and swallowed, stretching his lips in that rictus grin of a smooth burn going down on first take. He cleared his throat and said, "Yesterday, I had to run La

Croix's ol' lady all the way out to St. Mary's Parish to ID her friend's body," he said. "Now, I got to talkin' to the examiner on the preliminary findings and whew." He huffed a breath. "Boy. Mm-mm-mm." He shook his head.

"Has to be pretty bad for you to go on that way about it," Cypress observed.

"That little girl didn't deserve t' die like that," Hex said. "The doc said she was strangled to death, or so the killer thought. He found out different when he broke her leg to fit her ass in the damn suitcase. She said Maya fought like a wildcat, that there was skin under her nails, and that she'd definitely been raped during the first attempt to choke the life out of her. Dude's jizz was up inside her and she had 'signs of vaginal trauma.'"

"Shit." Louie looked a little green around the gills and I can't say as I blamed him.

"He broke her neck the second time around, her hyoid bone was snapped, probably from the first time he choked her out. Anyway, she didn't go quiet and the dude that killed her? Brutal is an understatement." He waved all the technical shit away. "He put her through all kinds of hell and bein' a pro? I have to think he did that shit on purpose for his own gratification, you know what I mean? Anyway, he broke her legs to get her body folded up in the suitcase, used it to get her out of the hotel, like we figured," he said, eyeing me. "But the dumb fuck *left* her body in the suitcase when he dumped it - which is how a couple o' gator hunters found her. They hooked it with their treble hook, thinkin' they got themself a moderately good-sized gator and pulled the damn thing up on their boat. An' well... the rest there is history."

"Fucking dumbass," Axeman muttered. I agreed on the principal of it. You want the gators to disappear a body for you? You had to make it accessible. It was a big mistake on his part, but a fortuitous one on ours that the gators couldn't get into the Tupperware container of a hard-shelled suitcase he had her in.

"Hope to hell she put the hurt on 'im," Bennie said, staring off into space and then said, "Maybe she did. Enough that it was too much of a hassle for him to unpack her out there in the swamp."

"Good possibility," I said, having not thought of that. "I hope you're right."

"What else?" Col asked from down the table. "Anything? Or is that where we're at?"

I heaved a sigh and looked at Axe who looked back at me.

"Ol' Bashaw's campaign manager had some interesting things to say about ol' daddy dearest," Axe said and I nodded.

"Oh yeah? What's that corrupt fuck into?" Chainsaw asked.

"Sellin' his baby girl to climb the political ladder," I said with a sigh.

"Do what now?" Chainsaw's eyes went as big as saucers.

"Seems ol' Maya was no stranger to bein' a whore," Axe said tiredly. "Daddy had her turnin' tricks with some high rollers since she was somewhere around six years old."

"What the fuck? *Six?*" Cy's jaw dropped.

"Anything for political gain," I grumbled.

"Jesus fuck, these assholes." Saint huffed an incredulous, angry, scoffing laugh. A single barked note that was an iron spike, pinning Maya's secret pain to the center of our table for us to pore over and make some decisions on what we was gonna do to serve some justice for her. If my boys chose to, that is. But judging by the looks on their faces? Oh yeah, justice was absolutely fixin' to be served.

"*The whore that daddy made her...* that's what she called it here."

Every one of us startled and turned to the narrow doorway where Alina's broken voice filtered over the table.

"Aw, shit..." Hex mumbled but I don't think she'd heard us. At least not really. Because she clutched some kind of a book in her hands and a sheaf of papers on top of it.

"cher, you ain't supposed t' be here," I said gently, and she sniffed.

"No, I know, but I found this," she said and broke into a smattering of sobs, holding out the book and the papers.

I got up from my seat as Bennie took them from her. Setting the book down, he started going through the papers.

"Oh, shit," he said. "This is a lot."

"A lot how?" Hex asked, looking over Bennie's shoulder.

I went over to Alina carefully, while the boys started spreading the papers out over the tabletop.

"Shit, this is big," Hex said.

I pulled Alina into me while they were distracted.

"Baby, you can't just come in here like that," I whispered and she clung to me.

Her voice muffled by where she pressed her face into my chest, she said, "No, I know. I'm sorry but I tried to call and I just didn't know what else I should do! It's just so awful!"

I held her tight and several of the guys' attention was got and on us.

"We all gon' let it slide," Hex said. "Aren't we boys?"

"Yeah."

"Too right," echoed around the table and I nodded, grateful.

"This is real damn big, boss," Bennie said to me and I nodded.

"Alina," I said gently, and she nodded.

"No, I'll go," she said. "Um, Dorian and Marcus are on their way. I called them."

"Good, that's good," I said, nodding.

"Hey, boss, I'm still so new, I'll go sit with her 'til they get here so she's not alone. I think y'all know where I stand on kiddie diddlin'," Louie said, and I nodded.

His momma had sold his ass when he was a boy for a fix here 'n there until he got strong enough, she couldn't do it no mo'. We all knew about it. We also swore we'd never speak on it again after the night he'd come apart after a hazing stunt gone wrong. There were certain things you didn't fuck with, no matter how big of an asshole you were.

I passed Alina off into Louie's care and watched him, arm around her shoulders, lead her on out through the club.

"Sorry about that, boys," I said, turning. Hex was lookin' at me just a little excited.

"Nah, bro. She brought us a fuckin' treasure trove of information the likes to shake up the political system from here to kingdom come," he said and I scowled.

"Just what kind of names you got in there?" I demanded.

The papers were a sort of salt the earth, raze and ruin that Maya left behind just in case somethin' were to happen to her. She left it right where she knew Alina would find it. Handwritten in her own hand that she knew Alina would recognize and be able to have authenticated. We had somethin' radioactive on our table.

This shit was something that was gonna have some far-reaching consequences and needed to be handled with some kid gloves.

We came up with a couple ways of dealing with things and put them to a vote. Surprisingly enough, the boys voted to error on the side of caution this time around and decided not to leverage what was in those pages for our own gain. I had mixed feelings on that. On the one hand, I was a little relieved – I mean, this wasn't good trouble. This was as down and dirty and in the fuckin' slop as you got. Add to that, if it ever reached my little Alina's ears that we'd done leveraged her friend's pain and the reason she'd been murdered to our own benefit?

I would lose her. I was sure of it. There wasn't no way I would let that happen. She meant too much to me.

Instead, we decided to play it smooth – anonymously report it to the *Times Picayune* and a couple of the leading television news outlets and see who bit first.

As for the hired gun? We called in the big dogs to sniff that trail and cashed in our chips on a big favor with The Kraken who had more computer know-how than us, who in turn cashed in some chits of their own with the crew they was friends with up north – an outfit far bigger than the Voodoo Bastards and The Kraken combined. The Sacred Hearts.

They was working on it, and we'd have our assassin by the time they was done, come hell or high water.

That just left dear ol' daddy dearest for right now, and boy howdy would we handle his ass.

That left just one thing for me to do for right now, and that was go to my lady and hold her tight.

I walked across the street and looked up, catching a glimpse of her in her window as she whirled to go for her door. She was just on the other side of the glass as she took the last couple steps to open the lobby door for me to fly into my arms.

I held her tight, her shelter from the shitstorm a brewing out here.

"Come on upstairs and we'll talk," I told her. She nodded quickly and gripped my hand in some desperation as she led the way back up to her apartment.

"What's happening?" Dorian asked, standing up from the window seat my girl so loved.

"Will you let the man get in the door, baby? Jesus…" Marcus rolled his eyes and turned the page of a photo book in his lap as he sat cross-legged in a skirt on the floor.

"Thanks," I grunted at the fabulous queer and he smiled happily and wiggled back and forth in a little dance before turning another page.

I dropped onto the couch and pulled Alina down onto my lap, sighing hard.

"I can't tell you when, or how, but shit's gonna get really real in the news and real soon. We're just waiting on some callbacks."

"The media?" Alina asked astonished.

I nodded. "Things are in the works," I said. "We don't want just Daddy and the hired gun to pay. We want 'em *all* to pay, and the best way of goin' about it is gettin' the truth out there as far and as wide as we possibly can and givin' 'em no place left to hide."

Alina looked thoughtful, and Dorian looked shocked. Marcus looked pleased.

"Maya would be *so* proud," Marcus declared. "She could be a petty bitch. The pettiest of petty bitches, and this is gonna make *all* her petty bitch dreams come true. I can't tell you how much I am *so here for it!*" He snapped out a rainbow-colored fan and fanned himself and I smirked.

"There was a Louisiana *senator* on that list," Alina said. "Like, a currently sitting Louisiana senator," she said.

"Shit, you don't think dear ol' dad's gubernatorial seat was bought and paid for?" I asked. "This weren't no election," I said. "This was his just rewards."

Dorian looked sick.

"I can't believe she didn't tell any of us," he said.

I shook my head. "And put y'all in danger? No. I don't think that was your girl's style."

Alina shook her head too. "It wasn't," she said in agreement.

The boys stayed a little while, but then had to get going to get to their respective evening jobs. It was Dorian's night off, but he was going in anyway to cover Alina's shift to quote, "Head Clyde's bitching off at the pass."

I liked him for that, but don't think for a minute ol' Clyde was off my radar, either. I'd see if I could keep it to just barkin' for now, but I still had my bite I'd keep in reserve to make that bark have some meanin'.

Finally, after the boys took their leave, it was just me an' my girl – we were alone. It felt both strange and exciting to be up here in what was her space for so long, and now it was again. She laid draped over the top of me on me on the couch, and I massaged the back of her neck where it met her skull while she did.

"You gon' put this place back to the way it was, or you gon' do something different?" I asked.

"I mean, it pretty much *is* the same except for the better heavier bookshelves along that wall instead of the cheap ones from the big box stores that were there," she said, lifting a finger and pointing vaguely.

She sighed. "My bedroom is the same," she said. "I can go back to taking the bus to work and catching a ride home like I did before."

"I can get you," I murmured.

"This is all so crazy and exhausting," she murmured.

"Yeah," I agreed. "How you doing?" I asked. "Really?"

She cuddled closer. "I don't think I would be doing half so well if it weren't for you and the rest of the guys," she said. "Missing Maya is going to hurt forever, though."

"It hurts less with time," I said, raising a shoulder and dropping it. "Or at least you get used to the pain in such a way you just don't notice it anymore."

She sniffed and nodded against my chest and said, "I think that second one is more accurate."

"I'm so sorry you're going through it, cher." I kissed the top of her head and she hugged around me tighter.

"Me too," she said.

"You eat anything yet today?" I asked.

"Breakfast," she said.

"Look, I know it's gettin' late and all, but we need to get you somethin' to eat an' I'm starvin'. Let me take you out. We'll get some food, maybe get some shit to go for tomorrow so you ain't gotta cook." I jiggled her a little in my arms and she sighed and nodded.

"I need to call and get the utilities back in my name, the internet hooked up and all that sort of thing," she said.

"That's all tomorrow," I said. "I'm talkin' about tonight. We ain't even on one day at a time right now, cher. We on every minute at a time, an' that's okay."

She looked up at me and said, "Okay. Take me to eat, then bring me back here," she said. "But then, can you do me a favor?" she asked.

"Anything," I said.

"Make me forget for a little while?" she asked.

I smiled at her and nodded. "I can try to do that," I told her.

"Thank you," she whispered.

CHAPTER THIRTY-SIX

*A*lina...

We took a ride, my man and I, and I knew he took the long way; cruising around the city with its vivid nightlife, looking around for what looked good food-wise. We ended up at a bar and grill, *shit*; somewhere that was still serving – I didn't know. The menu looked pretty okay, and we sat at a little two-person table and just sort of stared at each other while the music blared from the jukebox.

We ate in companionable if tired silence, just sort of trapped in our own little bubble, which I was *absolutely* okay with. I didn't want to deal with anything, anyone, or anymore. I just wanted a nice meal with La Croix, to go home, and to feel his hands on my skin. I wanted to *rest with him.*

After all of this? I just wanted a little while to settle into this life, and for us to find our normal.

Alas, it was not to be.

A jock-looking guy was arguing with his girlfriend nearby, and he grabbed her by the arm, hard, jerking her up hard against his body as he yelled in the woman's face. I scanned the bar, dabbing my lips with my napkin, and ah, yeah... bouncers were at the back separated by the man up here and his girlfriend by the crush of the crowd. I sighed. Just sick of all of it, I got up.

I smiled down at La Croix, who frowned and looked up at me in confusion. I walked up behind the guy, wound back, and kicked up right between his legs with everything that I had, dropping him, who in turn dropped the hold he had on the girl's arm, and silencing the crowd in like a twelve-foot radius – or at least everyone that'd seen what'd just went down.

I turned back to La Croix, gave him a bit of an apologetic look and lifting my shoulder in a shrug, made to step back over to our table when he stood up and squared up at something behind me.

I glanced over my shoulder and *ah...* bouncers.

"Hey, now, we don't want any trouble," the bouncer said, putting his hands up and stepping back from where, apparently, he'd been about to grab me by the arm.

"We don't either," I said in a tone that sounded bored, but I was far from it. I was just absolutely sick of everyone's shit right now and I think it clicked with me in that moment how Maya had felt.

Why she'd had no fucks left about taking that serving tray to Larry with the hands who'd been trying to back poor Mikayla, the fifteen-year-old server, into a corner.

I think Maya was just as sick to death as I was about good people being treated poorly by bad people who just never seemed to face any consequences for their fucked-up actions. Like the man just now, that had stood in the middle of a packed fucking bar, treating his girlfriend like that in front of God and everybody, *knowing* that no one was going to stop him.

Well not to-fucking-day, bro.

I felt a gentle hand on my elbow and I turned, La Croix looking down at me confused.

"You wanna tell me just what the hell *that* was all about?" he demanded.

I looked back at the tableau in front of us. The girl was now rapidly explaining to the bouncer that the man still on the ground, clutching his family jewels, had indeed just been *assaulting her,* and that I was just trying to help. The bouncers, thankfully, seemed to be listening, but La Croix? He deserved an explanation.

"I don't know," I said. "I just... I just *reacted*."

He sat me down and kneeled in front of me, looking up at me.

"Why didn't you get my attention?" he asked, and I eyed the big, tall guy on the floor, the bouncers trying to help him up and get him out of the bar. I shook my head.

"I didn't want you to get hurt?" I asked, and I quailed a bit, knowing just how stupid that sounded.

His eyebrows shot up and he searched my face, his mouth flattening into a grim line. Finally, his expression turned completely mystified, and he said, "I need to get you home. You aren't thinkin' straight. In fact, I'd even hazard t' say you're absolutely out of your goddamn mind."

I sputtered a laugh, like it caught me so off guard that'd if I'd had a mouthful of liquid, I would have spit it all over him.

He threw down more than enough to cover our meals and a healthy tip onto the table and took my hand.

"C'mon, cher, before the bacon gets here."

I followed him out, one of the bouncers calling after us, but we were gone, striding up the sidewalk in the direction of the bike.

We pulled into the gate outside the club a short ride later and I hopped off the bike. La Croix backed it in with the line of other bikes and cut the engine, his dark eyes fixed on me like a predator looks at its prey and I felt my heart sink just a little, worried he was mad at me.

He got off the imposing machine and stalked toward me in a way that scared me enough that my body started backpedaling before my mind caught up to me enough to say, *that's crazy! He promised to never hurt you!*

I fetched up hard against the fence and he came right up against me, pinning me to it, the chain link rattling, his knee coming up between my thighs and holding me as much as the rest of my body, my toes barely touching the ground.

He grabbed me by the chin, his grip firm, but gentle, and his mouth covered mine.

The relief swept through me so complete when he kissed me, I sagged against the fence and him, kissing him back with the same fierce energy he kissed me with.

"That was hot," he growled against my mouth. "But don't you ever do it again."

"I'm sorry," I whispered breathlessly.

"Just what were you thinking?" he demanded, his big hand palming my waist, his forehead pressed to mine.

I closed my eyes and confessed.

"I was thinking I am so *fucking sick* of men doing whatever they want. Of bad people doing *whatever the hell they choose,* out in front of Goddess and everyone; knowing there won't be any consequences for their being shitty!"

"All you had to do was get my attention!" he snarled, but I realized he wasn't mad. Not at all. I'd scared him. I'd scared the hell out of him. "You're *mine*, Alina. You point and I fucking pull the trigger! Do you understand me?" he asked, and he was the most intense I'd ever seen him.

"Yes," I whispered, and he shook me a little. "Yes!" I cried a little louder, and he pulled me to him, wrapping his arms tightly around me.

"I swear to God, you're losin' it, babe," he said, and I nodded against his shoulder.

"I feel like I'm losing it," I told him and he sighed.

Clearly, it was not my finest hour.

"What do you want me to do?" he asked, and I looked up at him.

"I don't know," I said. "I don't have an answer for you. I don't know *what* to do. I just know I'm... I'm... I'm so *angry.* I'm just so fucking *sad* and *pissed* then pissed some more and then sad some more and I just feel like I'm fucking *drowning* and I don't know what to do. I don't know what to ask for to make any of it better. I don't even know if I *want* anything to be *better* per se. I just want a fucking break from it all!"

He listened to me spill my feelings onto the pavement in a rush of word salad that I didn't even care if it made sense.

"You need to yell, you yell. You need to hit me, you hit me. I can take it, cher. Whatever you need," he said. "Just tell me what you need."

The last sounded beseeching, like he was begging for any guidance, and honestly, only one thing came to mind.

"I want you to take me upstairs and fuck me," I said and I like to think I knew what I was asking... but with La Croix, there honestly was no telling what you would get.

He crushed his mouth over mine and his tongue forced its way past my lips and teeth which just weren't relenting fast enough. The sheer *power* in that kiss, by all that was everything, it was like plugging directly into a thermonuclear reactor.

I was suffused with energy, as though he lifted me up out of this... this *muck* and *mire* of despair momentarily and I *craved it*. I craved it so hard. I needed some light, some love, just *something* with which to thrive for just a moment rather than just survive.

He pressed me back against the fence, his hand trailing from my waist to my thigh; lifting my leg over his hip and *Goddess,* I could feel him – the hard hot length of him pressing against my sex through the layers of denim and the thin cotton panties I wore next to my skin. The cotton grew uncomfortably damp with every touch, every caress, every bit of pressure of his body against mine.

I don't remember making the trek across the road or keying our way into the lobby. I don't remember taking the flights of stairs to the third floor or keying my way into the apartment's door.

The next thing I remember was being pressed up against the unyielding wood on the *inside*. La Croix's hand up my shirt, squeezing my breast, as I shoved his cut off his shoulders and reached for the hem of his white wifebeater to pull it up over his abs, my hands following the contours of his muscular body as though learning him by braille.

"Like this?" he growled, biting into the side of my neck, but not hard; no, just extremely arousing.

"Harder!" I begged, and he sank his teeth a little harder, laving my pulse point with his tongue.

"Oh, yeah!" I pulled him tighter against me, and writhed against him, and he growled against my neck.

"Fuck," he gasped, and he looked at me as though I was the sexiest thing that he had ever laid eyes on and *that?* That made me feel so very powerful.

"Yes," I said, my voice like iron and stone. "Fuck me."

He grabbed me by my throat, not choking, but definitely controlling, and pulled me away from the door and my mouth to his.

I kissed him, hands to my sides, trusting him not to take it too far, and he didn't. Instead, he curved the hand around my throat around to the back of my neck and he marched my ass in the direction of the bedroom.

CHAPTER THIRTY-SEVEN

*L*a Croix...

She was fire, she was smoke, and I could feel it thrumming through her – her divine feminine *rage*. I kissed her, coming in hot, and she kissed me back just as fierce, but her actions in the bar, *they just weren't her* and they'd caught me off guard.

I felt like she'd become fire and I needed to be ice, to somehow cool her down before she flamed out into oblivion on me.

Once back upstairs and in her apartment, I captured her by the back of her neck and brought her around to kiss me again, shoving her up against the inside of her door as I had against the inside fence of the club's courtyard downstairs. *Fuck, did she turn me on!* She did, making this low and feral groan into my mouth that had my inner predator stalking through the trees, coming up to the surface like a gator about to strike.

I hauled her up against my body by her hips and her hands went to my chest, but she *melted* into me and didn't try to push me away.

It was in the blink of an eye that I had her nude and bent over her bed, her wrists pinned behind her back with one hand, the other against her hip, pulling her back onto my cock.

I looked down, pulling out of her, the sight of the condom snug around the base of my dick a fucking a turn on in and of itself. Just as much as her glistening pussy juices coating me with her arousal took things up even higher on the heat scale. The feral noises poured from her lovely throat with every thrust I made, and I swear to fucking God, it sent my ass into a fucking frenzy.

I looked up at our reflection in the window, her face heavy-lidded and filled with ecstasy as I filled her, globes of her fucking perfect tits swaying as I drove into her, the sweat pouring off of me. We were far enough back from the window, we weren't giving anyone a show – but god*damn* it was a powerful thing, watching myself fuck her like this.

"You like that?" I demanded, and I drove forward as far as I could get inside her. She cried out, and her face twisted into something akin to pain, but the bliss that flooded her expression when that initial look faded away was the best thing I'd ever seen.

"Yeah, like that?" I asked her again, and she arched down, laying her body low, pressing her hips back to accept my forward thrust into her deeper, harder, maybe even faster.

Oh, yeah. Just like that, I thought, and I gave her just what she wanted, just what she asked for.

I fucked the shit out of her, made her come twice, pushed for a third time before I even thought about taking my own.

She was on her back now, her legs up along my chest, her ankles crossed over one of my shoulders. I hugged her thighs and rolled my hips, driving into her at a slightly more sedate pace, feeling every feeling, snatching at that spark that was just there, just out of reach. I stared into her soulful gray eyes, like mist in the morning, the darkness receding in her gaze as she looked up at me.

The softness returned to her smile as she moaned and her head turned, as though she were listening to the finest music, and I realized that for her; she was. She was listening to *me*, to the sounds I made as I drove into her sweet wet heat and I felt as though some of the darkness left my soul – fleeing in front of her returning light, scrambling back and away as though afraid of being burned by the awful goodness she represented.

I smiled down at her, and her smile grew for me. I closed my eyes and let everything go for just a little while, gasping, crying out softly, as I spilled inside her snug little pussy, filling the condom I wore, and cursing that I wasn't in a position to be skin on skin with her.

Not yet...

...but *oh*, someday I would.

∼

I JOLTED awake a little while later, the night still dark outside the glass of her bedroom window. I looked down, unsure what'd dragged me from my sleep, and found my little Alina awake. Her head was on my shoulder, her great-grandmother's ring plucked from where it'd rested on my chest. She was turning it in her fingers, her silvery eyes unfocused and vacant as she played with the ring absently, her thoughts a million miles away from here, from me, from now...

"You alright, cher?" I asked her and she startled.

"Mm?" She dragged her head off my shoulder and pushed herself up so she could look at me, searching my face, in the vague light from the streetlights down below her window.

"Asked if you were alright," I repeated gently when it was clear she didn't know what I'd asked.

"Mm, I'm fine," she lied, and I reached up to trace some of her fiery copper hair back behind one of her cute little ears.

"No lies, baby girl," I told her and she smiled, and the smile held sadness.

"I just wish I could be there," she murmured.

"Be where?" I asked, and I had a feeling.

"Be there when you kill them," she said.

"Oh, no, cher..." I shook my head a little and smoothed a hand over her hair, stroking a thumb along her pale cheek. "I know you wish that now, but you don't need to see what I'm gonna do to the likes of these assholes. That's not for you to see. That kind of ugly is for me an' me only, baby."

She nodded and she said, "I just want them to hurt. I want them to be afraid and to see the end coming and—" her voice broke on a sob. "I want them to feel like Maya did."

I smiled then and thought to myself *if only you knew how hard your girl fought.* I swallowed hard and said, "I don't think your girl was as scared as you think at the end, cher. I think she was pissed. She fought like a goddamn wildcat. I think you should know that."

"How do you know?" she asked.

"Hex had a candid chat with the doc over in St. Mary's Parish before we left," I answered. "Got a few of the details – not a lot, but that was definitely the one that stuck out. Maya did *not* go quietly, my love. She fought and fought hard and made the bastard work for it."

She settled down against me and sighed out, asking me, "Did you mean that just now?"

"Mean what?" I asked, frowning. "About Maya? 'Course I did."

"No, the other thing," she said.

I kissed her forehead and said, "Gon' have to help me out here, cher. I don't think I catch your meaning. Just what you trying to get at?"

She pushed herself up and searched my face in the diffuse light and brought her lips to mine, kissing me softly, once, twice, a third time and smiled.

"You did mean it if you don't even realize you said it," she said and settled back down with a sigh that sounded nothing short of contented.

I chuckled, and said, "Well alright, then. I still don't know what you're talkin' about." And I didn't.

She gave me a squeeze and said, "You don't have to, just know that it makes me happy."

"You're baffling sometimes, woman," I said.

She yawned and said, "Right back at you."

I chuckled again, not sure what was up, the girl talkin' me in circles, but if I'd said something to make her happy? Well, then, I was all for it.

CHAPTER THIRTY-EIGHT

A FEW WEEKS LATER

*A*lina...
 Life returned to a sort of new normal that contained what still felt like a gaping and raw wound in the center of my chest with the lack of Maya in it.

Her funeral had been swift, and small, and while I'd been allowed to go – having to stand side by side with her fucking monster of a father as they'd slid her casket into the vault next to her mamma's made me both furious and sick.

La Croix had lurked nearby, and I'd almost wished he would just shoot him – I mean, I didn't really, because that would almost ensure he would go to prison and I'd never see him again and *that* I most certainly *did not* want... but it didn't stop me from all manner of violently righteous daydreaming of all sorts of painful and bloody vengeance.

"Get me out of here," I murmured, as soon as I'd gotten back to him, after crossing the cemetery to where he'd waited for me, sitting on his bike and smoking a joint without a care. The only thing that had kept me in line through the graveside service was knowing he was there. Was knowing that his eyes were on me and that sense of strength he telegraphed through the muggy New Orleans summer day in my direction.

It was such a deep sense that he poured strength into my empty cup in such a steady stream I almost worried he *must* be getting tired… but not La Croix. No, he seemed to have an endless reserve to lend me; but still I felt guilty about being such a black hole sometimes.

I'd returned to work at the bar after only two days. I wanted to get out of La Croix's way so that he could do his thing but at the same time, I feared sitting idle. It was those times I found myself with little to nothing to do that were the hardest for me.

La Croix, to his credit, had gone back to his day job himself. Though he didn't much like me riding the bus to work – he grudgingly relented on it. Still, it didn't matter how late it was that I got out of the bar. He was always there waiting to take me back home.

Then there was tonight… and the first time he wasn't. Instead, Louie waited outside the door for me and I perked up just a bit.

I waved goodbye to Mike and Sandra, and as soon as they were far enough up the sidewalk I turned to Louie and asked quietly, "Is it finally happening?"

He looked at me and looked markedly uncomfortable when he said, "Ms. Lina, now you know I can't tell you that."

I sighed and nodded, "No, I know, you're right," I said. "I just want them to pay so bad."

He gave me a wan smile and put an arm around my shoulders and hugged me tight.

"I know, and if I'm here and the boss ain't, then you know it's only 'cause he's doin' something mighty important, yeah?"

I smiled and looked up and gave Louie a nod.

"I know," I said and then asked, "So you here to take me home?"

"That I am," he said and gave a nod. "That I am."

It was weird riding behind Louie back to the club. He walked me across the street to my apartment building, and I let myself into the lobby. I half expected him to come up and keep me out of trouble but he just gave a wave and said, "G'night, Ms. Lina," and I smiled and said, "Goodnight, Louie," and he jogged back across to the club's small compound.

I went upstairs and fixed myself a snack, settling on the couch to eat and to watch a little tekevision, waiting and wondering, and knowing that this? This would be the hardest part, always, about loving a man like La Croix back.

I closed my eyes and could hear his velvet voice in the dark... calling me his love.

He hadn't even realized he'd said it, which meant the world to me. It meant that he meant it from the bottom of his heart, from the depths of his soul. You never said something like that by design; only by accident – and *Goddess help me*, even knowing who and what he was, I couldn't help myself... I loved him, too.

The time and the hours crept by and the more the minute hand crawled around the clock dial, the more anxious I became worrying for him, until finally... *finally*, I heard his key grate in the lock...

CHAPTER THIRTY-NINE

*L*a Croix...
It was frustratin', the reporter to bite on the Bashaw story was a pitbull of a woman who put the investigatin' in investigative reportin', and she was runnin' this, that, and the other through back channel after channel – dottin' her I's and crossin' all her T's before she would utter a fuckin' peep to her editor or whatever.

The local stations had brushed my boy off like he was crazy – but not the reporter over at the Times Picayune. She knew a story when she smelled one and she'd been practically droolin' over the documentation we'd brung her.

Still, them wheels turned slower 'n molasses 'n January and so we had to wait. Shouldn't be much longer now, though.

In the meantime, we had our hired gun to deal with – an' he'd proven to be almost as much of a pain in the ass than pinnin' the tale on daddy dearest.

That there boy up with the Sacred Hearts was one crafty ass motherfucker. He had found our killer out there with one of those paramilitary outfits in Texas. You know the type. God and country, humpin' the stars 'n bars like it was his sister on a Friday night under the bleachers durin' homecoming. They were way out there in the middle of fuckin' nowhere, buildin' their bunkers and makin' ready for the next civil war, or the end of the world, or some shit.

So, the question became, how to get the motherfucker back on our turf?

Seemed our boy out in Florida and his boy up in Kentucky had an idea or three on that and when my burner rang, I'd got to it just in time before it cut off.

"Radar, how you doin' brother?" I'd asked.

"Good, I'm good. You ready to take on Texas Hitboy?" he asked and I grinned savagely.

"My friend, I don't think you know just how ready we are…"

Setting things up was almost too easy after that.

On my end, it just involved greasin' some palms out at that little bar 'n grill I'd taken my little Alina too, the night I'd first taken her on out to my place an' made love to her.

Seems our inside man up north had been trackin' our boy's emails and he'd had a meet set up with a potential client out this way. A little computer magic that way above our paygrade, and dude was bein' diverted from his real meet right into our clutches.

It was a little too easy, you ask me – but I guess I was just an old-fashioned guy that way.

It was me and the rest of my boys all here. Makin' shit look good, the parking lot a healthy mix of bikes and cages – and of course the van if we needed it.

We was on the opposite side of the city from our usual go-to of the Smokehouse and the Atchafalaya Basin, so some of the boys were a little outside their comfort zone… that bein' said, I was right at home. This was my swamp, and my people in it. I had all the control and then some.

Cypress was right along me with the notion, having grown up in the same area of Bayou Black.

By all appearances, it was a normal weeknight at Chaffee's, the jukebox loud, the requisite number of local patrons, and nothin' weird about it. Nice equal mix of man and woman. Fisher folk an' hunters.

We all knew the outsider when he showed his face and none let on that he was the only outsider among us. He went up to the hostess and asked after the name of his client for the reservation; but his client wasn't what he got.

He was brought on over to the booth I'd shared with my little Alina that first night of ours together; and I thought that was fitting. He knew the jig was up as soon as Hettie, our hostess, stopped by the table and he saw me sittin' here. He huffed a laugh and shook his head.

"You ain't Crowley," he said in a thick Texas drawl.

"Have a seat," I told him. "Let's talk."

"Alright, now," he slid into the booth across from me. "Who are ya, and why you got me here?"

I slid a picture of Maya and my girl across the table at him.

"Oooooh," he nodded, tapping a finger on Maya's face. "I remember her. Hard to forget. She was feisty. Kicked me so hard she dislocated my fuckin' knee. That shit still ain't right."

"She did a lot more 'n that," I declared. "She's the reason you fixin' to die tonight, boy,"

He was laughing, *for now*...

"And just what you gon' do in a crowded bar full of people, boy?"

I raised my hand and snapped my fingers. The music cut, and chairs and barstools scraped as everyone stood up at once.

Melodramatic? Maybe, but Hex was right. It sure was a lot of fun the way the smirk was wiped right off his fuckin' face.

The locals started clearing out. Their own faces either grim or expressionless, until all that was left was me an' my boys. Well, me an' my boys minus Louis who'd volunteered to collect my woman and see her safely home.

Jacob Landry, real name, Grayson McIntyre, crossed his arms over his chest and leaned back in his seat.

"Well damn," he said and he was tryin' not to look scared, but the sweat beading at his temple and along his upper lip gave him away.

He looked back down at the picture of Maya and my girl's smiling faces.

"Who's the little ginger snap?" he asked. "Like to feel her wrapped around my cock while the light dies in those gray eyes," he said. "You ever been balls deep when the life leaves one of 'em?" he asked. "Does some amazin' things when the body's strugglin' to stay alive. Ain't nothin'—"

The shot was loud in the confined space of the bar. He blinked, his eyes wide, and looked down at the hole I'd punched in his gut from under the table. I'd heard more 'n enough outta him. Wasn't no sense in lettin' him go on, especially about my girl. That shit certainly earned a man a one-way ticket to Hell.

"You're lucky," I said as he tried to stand up but couldn't. He put his hands over the hole in him to try and stop the bleedin' but that was neither here nor there. He would die. "I'm not much of a shot," I confessed. "If I were, you'd be dyin' a lot slower 'n what you are."

He coughed, blood flyin' and mistin' my face from across the table.

I gritted my teeth and sighed.

"That's gross, man. Keep it to yourself." I pulled the paper band off the napkin around my silverware and calmly unraveled it from around the cutlery.

He looked across the table at me with somethin' like hatred.

"You ain't got nothin' to worry 'bout, my friend. Unlike you, we know how to make a body disappear 'round these parts. Ain't no one ever find you. They can look all they like."

He was chokin' hard now and I smiled.

"Think I clipped a lung. Good thing, too. You like suffocatin' so much, let's see how you like drownin' in your own blood. Yeah?"

He stared at me wide-eyed and made a bunch of noises like he was tryin' to speak, but couldn't. He was a tenacious bastard, I had to give him that. It took him the better part of twenty minutes to die.

"You're a cold piece," Hex said when it was finally clear old boy was done. I looked over to where he sat at the bar and I threw him some chin sayin', "You sittin' there watchin' him die just like the rest of us."

He got up and brought over a glass of my favorite brand of bourbon and sat it down in front of me. He raised his own glass.

"To bein' in good company," he said and I nodded.

I looked at the rest of my club and asked, "Well what'll y'all say to that?"

A rowdy cheer went up and we all drank what was in front of us.

The bourbon went down smooth, the scent of blood heavy in the air and it was a good combination. *Bourbon and blood...* who would have thought?

We did a thorough job cleanin' up after ourselves. Policing our brass, Axe gettin' the slug dug outta his guts just in case his body should be found.

By the time we was done, I don't think Chaffee's had ever been cleaner.

"We got this, boss, if you just wanna head home," Cypress said, he and Axe loading the plastic-wrapped body into the van. I shook my head.

"Nah, I wanna see this one through," I declared. The rest of the boys stayed behind to continue cleanin' up the bar, shuttin' it down for Troy, the owner.

The three of us, me, Axe, and Cy, took the body a way out into the swamp, disarticulatin' it like a deer or a hog and dottin' his ass all along the way. Rubbin' his parts down with stinkin' rotten beef blood, coagulating in a five-gallon bucket.

Gators didn't like fresh meat. They grabbed somethin' fresh, they tended to drag it down into the dark, stuff you up under a log or somethin' and leave you for a day or two to marinate.

This just maybe hastened up the process some, and judgin' by the thrashin' and splashin' out there in the dark, it sure was doin' somethin'.

We stopped up in my place to shower off the blood and change our clothes. Sittin' out on the barge with some fresh beers outta my fridge, fire cracklin' in the ol burn barrel out on the edge of the barge, the fire chewin' through any blood-stained scrap of anything we'd had on.

We talked, had a laugh or two, all as the sun started to rise with the mists off the water.

"Well, fuck," Axe said. "Boat looks like a crime scene – that's for sure."

"I got bleach," I declared and we got to work all over again, now that we could see, to scrub that shit clean.

By the time I rolled up an' parked at the club, it was gettin' well on into morning. I didn't expect Alina to still be up, but when I went and keyed my way on in to her place, she sat up on her couch, lookin' over the back of it at me all wide silver eyes flooded with worry and concern.

"Oh, thank the Goddess!" she declared and scrambled to her feet.

"What you doin' up so late, cher?" I asked with a smile and a light chuckle, pleased as punch that she'd waited up for me.

"Mm," she lowered herself flat footed as she took her mouth away from mine and said, "I missed you, and I was worried about you," she said.

"Aw, you don' need to worry 'bout me none."

She snorted indelicately, "Bullshit – and the day I *don't* worry about you will be your first clue that things are seriously wrong, you understand me?"

I smiled and shut the door behind me, throwing the lock.

"I hear you," I said.

"Good," she said letting out a breath slowly.

"Now tell me, how'd it go? Did you get one of them?"

I looked at her, searching her face and what I saw there? I simply nodded and her shoulders sagged.

"One down, one to go, Maya," she murmured and tears gathered on her lower lashes. I pulled her into me, and she wrapped her arms tight around me and she murmured, "Thank you."

"Anything for you, cher," I said and I meant it.

She looked up at me then, and said words I ain't ever expect to hear really.

"I love you."

I lowered my mouth to hers and kissed her and her arms twined around my neck. I smoothed hands down over her slender body and walked her back toward her bedroom, and she went willingly, letting me guide her, trusting I wouldn't run her into anything.

Maybe I should have said 'I love you, too' but honestly? I just figured I'd much rather show her.

CHAPTER FORTY

*A*lina...

"Turn on the news, Marcus just rushed out to grab some of the papers," Dorian was saying into the phone and I dashed into the living room to turn on the noon edition of the local news.

"...Bashaw is being *rocked* by quite the scandal today, Michael," the woman said.

"That's right, Linda. For any of you tuning in who don't know who Nathanial Bashaw is, he's the local New Orleans city councilman who just announced his bid to take on the race for governor in this latest election cycle."

"That's right Michael. It will be interesting to see what he does now with this article in the Times Picayune bringing several *wild* allegations to light in a sex scandal the likes we've never seen..."

I sank onto the edge of my couch, and looked back over the way of my bedroom door and at La Croix leaning against it's frame. It'd been three or four days since he'd come back so late in the morning and had told me without telling me that Maya's killer had been dealt with.

He gave me a single nod as Dorian asked in my ear, "Are you seeing it? Lina, are you there?"

La Croix gave a nod in my direction and pushed off the doorway going back into my room; presumably to dress.

"Yeah, Dor, I'm here, I see it," I said grimly.

"She did it," he said. "Somehow, she actually did it. She took him down," he said and his voice was faint, the same news report I had in front of my own eyes echoing through the phoneline. I smiled, and I knew it was darkly malicious.

Yes, she did, I thought to myself. *With a little help from her friends...*

"It's almost over," I said and Dorian seemed to snap-too, coming awake on the other end of the line.

"What's that supposed to mean?" he asked.

"It means they need to arrest him and Maya will finally get some justice," I said steadily, and Dorian seemed satisfied with that.

"I mean, it's probably going to take some time – the police or whatever can't avoid it now, but they still have to investigate and all so I wouldn't get too excited, not yet," he said and I had to smile.

"No, you're right," I declared, feigning innocence. "It's a step in the right direction, but I shouldn't get too far ahead of myself," I said.

"I can't fucking believe this," he said. "Oh, shit, Marcus is ringing in, can I call you right back?" he asked.

"Yeah," I said and he said, "Okay, I'll call you *right back,* I promise."

The line went dead and La Croix's heavy tread sounded behind me. I looked up and his lips came down and met mine. I kissed him and with a look like he was committing my my face to fondest memory he said, "Time to finish what I started for you, cher."

I nodded and said, "Please be careful."

"Always," he said and returning my focus to the news report, he slipped out our front door and was gone.

I got up and went over to my favorite window with its built-in window seat and looked down as he crossed the street and strode into the fence line of the clubhouse, disappearing inside the old cinderblock building.

I wanted to somehow, some way, feel something other than

relieved that this was almost over. That the evil shit responsible for a lifetime of pain for my best friend was about to die made me feel nothing but sweet, sweet, revenge and I think I was more worried about the fact that it *didn't* worry me one bit that I felt that way. I mean, I had tried. I really had. I had done everything I was supposed to do for my friend. I had gone to the authorities. I had begged, and pestered, and scraped, and had screamed uselessly into the void…

…and the void had answered.

La Croix had stepped out of the darkness, the darkness personified, and had taken a knee before me like I was some sort of dark queen.

I couldn't blame him for my corruption, or my fall from societal grace.

No, the only thing that blame could lie on was society itself. For being so corrupt and for being so apathetic. For being so cruel for so long, I couldn't resist the pull into La Croix's dark embrace.

At least there I felt loved, safe, and protected like I'd never before. He cherished me, the way I'd never been but for my great-grandmother and my best friend. Both of which were gone now, the latter stolen from me… and that could not go unanswered.

It was my night off, and I gathered my things knowing that I would not see La Croix again, likely until late tonight if not tomorrow.

I needed to do something for myself and for Maya, and so I showered, dressed, and shouldered the straps for my easel and water color set, deciding today I would go to some of mine and Maya's favorite places. For coffee at Café Du Monde to watch the people go by. To our favorite metaphysical bookstore, and finally I would find a place to sit and paint for a while.

A self-care day, she would have called it. I'd found them extravagant, usually, but my priorities had obviously shifted…

I was trying to find myself in the new order of things, and honestly, the thing I worried about the most? That I only seemed to feel right or secure in La Croix's arms.

I knew it wasn't healthy, that it was a co-dependency, but I also couldn't seem to help myself that way. At least, not right now.

"Hey!" I turned and Louie was jogging up the sidewalk behind me.

"Where you goin'?" he asked.

I smiled.

"Café Du Monde, my favorite bookshop, and find a place to paint – why you been put on guard duty?" I asked, shading my eyes until he was in front of me, blocking out the sun.

"Ha, no," he said and I cocked my head and he hung his, his ears turning red he changed that 'no' to a "maybe."

I smiled and shook my head with a bit of a laugh and said, "Well I'm afraid it's gonna be real boring."

He shrugged and told me the truth, because it was Louie and he and I had become friends in a way that we didn't keep secrets. Besides that, he was *really* bad at it.

"La Croix wants somebody with you for a while. Says they knew about you, and they have to know that the news coming out now? That it was probably you even though it was mostly us," he said with a shrug.

I nodded.

"I mean, it *was* sorta me," I said. "I found the papers, and if La Croix hadn't stepped in and handled it, it would have been me – it just would have taken longer."

"Fair," Louie said with a sigh. "So, you don't mind the shadow?" he asked and I laughed and shook my head.

"You're not a shadow," I said. "You're one of my friends. Like a brother I never knew I had. So, come on," I jerked my head in the direction I was going and he made a face.

"No, *you* come on. Let's ride."

I grinned, "Thought you'd never ask."

I mean, it wasn't riding with La Croix, which was quickly becoming one of my most favorite things ever; but it sure beat taking the bus…

CHAPTER FORTY-ONE

La Croix...
We waited long enough for the cover of night to end this.

"*You're good*," the voice declared over the earpiece, and I waved to Hex. It was just me an' him on this.

"*System's down, you have fifteen minutes.*" The voice was steady and sounded almost... bored.

"Thank you, brother," I said and the man on the other end of the line said, "*No sweat, happy hunting y'all.*"

We slipped into the fancy Garden District mansion through one of the back veranda's French doors, and paused inside, listening.

Big daddy didn't have a security detail, being he was only startin' his run for governor and the election and campaigning weren't too far along.

We could hear him out there somewhere on the bottom floor of the house, and Hex and I looked at each other.

Sounded like he was alone, on a call.

We followed the sound of his voice, creeping real quiet like; and then Hex straightened, eyeing me right outside the double doors leading into an office or den or whatever.

I nodded, and he made some intentional noise after I slipped the Glock out of the back of my waistband and made ready.

"Bryan, I'm going to have to call you back," the politician said, and we swept around the corner and into his office.

"Who're you?" he demanded, and I raised my gun before he could get his out of the fancy box sitting on the top of his desk.

Hex smiled and shot me a wink.

Jesus Christ, these citizen fucks were predictable.

"Have a seat," Hex said jovially. "We just want to have a little chat."

Maya's dad had his hands up and sank into his desk chair. I held my gun on him.

Hex heaved a gusty sigh, like he was breathin' in deep somethin' that smelled mighty fine.

"Haaaa! You smell that?" he asked and Bashaw eyed him warily.

"Smell what?" he asked curtly.

"Why that would be the end of your political career," Hex declared.

"Actually," I said. "That would be the end period."

Bashaw looked from Hex to me, his expression going from a frown to one of almost disbelief.

"Now you got your choice," Hex said after making a noise of agreement to what I'd said.

"Either we can do that for you, or you can do it yourself. Either way, it don't matter. You ain't makin' it to sunrise alive."

"You do it yourself, it's guaranteed to be quick and easy," I said. "You leave it to me, you're going to die slow," I said. I stared at him hard, making eye contact, letting the darkness in my soul match what was in my eyes, making it known the truth of my words.

He picked up the pearl handled shiny showpiece out of its red velvet-lined case. I leveled my piece right between his eyes and kept my trigger finger at the ready. I would end him before he could aim it at me, and I made sure he fuckin' knew it.

He glared at me and Hex, but in the end, he did the right thing, putting the gun in his mouth and suck startin' it. Right before he had the chance to pull the trigger, Hex, ever one with a flair for the dramatic, gave him a wink and said, "Maya sends her regards." The blowback and spray up behind him was impressive.

I lowered my gun and sucked in a deep breath, letting it out slowly.

"Heh." Hex huffed the laugh a few seconds later and I looked at him. "I didn't think he had it in him," he said and I looked back at the ruin of the politician in front of us.

I cocked my head as something thicker than blood dropped from one of the shelves and splatted on the rug behind him.

"Me either," I declared, thinkin' now he looked right and proper; the rot of his insides now on the outside for all to see.

"C'mon, I'll buy you a drink," Hex said and I nodded, putting my gun up.

"Make it a bourbon," I said and we turned to go.

We slipped out the way we'd come in and disappeared into the night. Slicker 'n owl shit. No mistakes, no trace left behind. Smooth. Just the way I liked it.

"What you doing?" I asked, when we were back to the bikes and he was dicking around on his phone.

"Checkin' with Louie to find out where he and your lady are at," he said. "Figured you might want to be back in her presence sooner rather 'n later."

I nodded. "You'd be right 'bout that," I said.

He looked over at me and said, "You're good together. I'm happy to see it," he said and I raised an eyebrow at him. He laughed and shook his head.

"No worries," he said. "It ain't doin' nothin' to your badass reputation. You're still the scariest motherfucker in New Orleans."

I smirked at that, and nodded, thumbing the switch to bring my bike to life.

He jerked his head, and I fell in beside him. He had a bead on where my woman was at, and I trusted him to take me to her.

She was laughing when we walked into the place, something Louie said was funny – no doubt. She caught sight of me, and she lit up even more, which made something tight in my chest loosen up. She immediately moved over and patted the seat beside her, her expression becoming careful and guarded.

I slid into the booth and kissed her quick, murmuring in her ear, "Talk about it later, but it's done."

She leaned back and nodded. Something washed over her, her hand gripping mine under the table and a certain energy thrumming through her. When she sat back in her seat, I realized it was relief and it made me put my arm around her as Hex popped off with something or other in response to somethin' Louie said, making the younger brother and my girl laugh again; the kid's ears turning bright red.

"Sometimes you're too easy, boy," I said but a smile was on my face.

"You wanted a bourbon, yeah?" Hex asked.

"Yeah." I nodded, and he tugged on Louie's cut.

"C'mon, junior," Hex said. "Let's go grab our table a round and let these two lovebirds have a moment."

Hex didn't need to tell Louie twice and when I looked at my woman, her fair skin tinged pink across her nose and cheeks, I had to ask her, "What'd you get up to today?"

She smiled and said, "Painting in Jackson Square."

"Aw yeah?" I asked and she nodded.

"I think I captured the Cathedral quite nicely."

"I'm sure you did, cher. I'm sure you did."

I kissed her temple and she said, "Thank you."

"For you?" I said. "Anything."

She smiled up at me and I knew she wasn't thankin' me for complimenting her artwork.

"Should make the news tomorrow," I said, my voice low, after glancing around to make sure I wasn't overheard. She nodded carefully and I warned her, "Might not play out how you think, but just know – I was there and he knew it was from her."

"That's all that I ask, and I believe you," she said.

I caressed her cheek and said, "I wish it hadn't gone down like this. I wish it could have all come about differently, you an' me."

She smiled at me and it held just a tinge of sadness, but the light in her eyes was something to behold.

"I think that things went down just as they needed to," she said after a moment. "I don't think anything from the time she was gone until now happened by coincidence," she said.

"Oh, yeah?" I asked, curious.

"Maya was clever by far," she said. "Vivacious and bold, knowing just what anyone needed just by looking at them. I think she put us together for several reasons – your particular set of skills notwithstanding. She knew people's hearts and minds better than anyone I've ever met and I think she knew that we needed each other as much as she needed us together, you know?"

"You have any regrets about the bargain we made?" I asked her.

She smiled so sweetly then and shook her head, squeezing my hand once more under the table.

"No," she said. "None."

I reached into the pocket of my cut and pulled out the tangled chain of the necklace I'd took from Maya's jewelry box.

"I know you didn't want to take anything of your girl's when we was moving you out," I said. "But with all the things said and done and with her bein' at peace? I think somethin's needed to mark the occasion," I said.

She looked up at me, curiously, as I upended her hand and put the necklace in it. She looked down into her hand and back up at me.

"Maya's?" she asked.

I nodded.

She smiled and took a deep breath and let it out slow.

"Thank you," she said and I nodded.

Hex and Louie returned with drinks and retook the seat across from us. My little Alina smiled and rejoined the conversation, even as she worked carefully to untangle the chain on the necklace that I'd given her. When she'd done it, she had me put it on for her. The gold looked good against her skin, the diamond pendant suspended in its gold ring, bouncing and shimmering with her pulse, sitting perfect in the hollow of her throat.

She laced her fingers through mine under the table once more and I felt powerful and whole.

I knew what it meant to be the king, looking across at my crew. When I went home, I made love to my queen like never before.

"You good?" I asked her in the diffuse light and deepening dark, the glow of the candles against her skin making her positively glow.

She dragged my mouth to hers, her hands to either side of my face and kissed me fierce.

"I'm better than good," she whispered hotly against my mouth and I decided then and there… it was good to be the king.

I wouldn't trade any of what went down for the world to have her in my arms like this.

In fact, I would burn the world. Lay any and all to waste and ruin. I would do anything and then some to have this life right here.

EPILOGUE

*A*lina...

I stood up, running the water and the paper pulp through the screen, taking it over to the folding table and setting it down, pressing and squeezing the water out and lifting the board to flip the freshly pressed damp paper out of the mold and out to dry.

We were home, out in the swamp, and I was working on my passion rather than toiling behind the bar these days.

I was more comfortable out here than back in the city anymore, and I'd cut way back on my hours at the bar. Down to only three nights a week, if I could help it; and most of my money nowadays went into more supplies to keep my side hustles alive.

"Lookin' good, cher." La Croix's arms went around my waist and he kissed my shoulder just the other side of my tank top's strap.

"Phew," I said. "It's hot out here, today. Boy howdy."

He chuckled and held a glass of sweet tea loaded with ice in front of me.

"You spoil me," I declared, leaning way back against him and he brought his mouth to mine.

"Not near enough," he said and I laughed.

"Are you kidding me?"

He shook his head.

"You remember back when you asked when you'd get your great-grandmamma's ring back?" he asked.

I took the mason jar down from my lips and swallowed the mouthful of tea I'd taken, turning around in the circle of his arms. The cord and my great-grandmother's ring were missing from around his neck, where they usually were.

"Yes," I said, a lump forming in my throat as he slowly got to one knee.

"Alina," he murmured, holding the ring up to me, only it wasn't dented like it was.

Tears sprang to my eyes as I blindly set my tea behind me, neither one of us caring when I missed the table and it crashed to the barge deck.

"Baby, what're you doing?" I asked.

"Oh, I think you know," he said with a wicked grin.

"Are you serious?" I demanded.

His smile faded. "You know I don't do shit I don't mean," he said.

"Don't you bullshit me, La Croix," I warned and he remained absolutely and perfectly silent, the gravity of the question in his dark and nearly unreadable eyes… but I knew the trick… I knew all of his secrets, and I accepted him wholly for who he was. Not only did I love this man, I loved this life with him and there really was only one thing more and he was offering it, holding up my grandmother's ring, the silence deafening before he dropped those two little words that I longed to hear.

"Marry me?"

I leaped into his arms, sliding down his body and into his lap, kissing his tattooed face, and wrapping my arms around him as I squealed and cried tears of joy.

"Yes," I promised him and he held me tight.

"Now don't do that, cher," he said, but he was smiling… but I couldn't help myself.

I knew he hated it when I cried, but I was just too happy not to.

"This life ain't somethin' to be so excited about," he tried to warn as he had countless times and I shook my head.

"I disagree," I said. "This life is *exactly* what I want," I told him. "I love you, and since coming into this life with you? I never knew what free really meant. I only *thought* I was free."

He smiled at me then, a rare, full smile and not simply a smirk.

"Now you're gettin' it," he declared and I grinned as he slipped the ring onto my finger.

"Oh no, boy… *now* I've got it," I said and I bit his bottom lip. I laughed, squealing as he picked me up and marched me into the house and out of the sun.

That was alright. I'd found that I thrived better in the dark since meeting him anyway.

ALSO BY A.J. DOWNEY

The Sacred Hearts MC

1. Shattered & Scarred

2. Broken & Burned

3. Cracked & Crushed

3.5 Masked & Miserable (a novella)

4. Tattered & Torn

5. Fractured & Formidable

6. Damaged & Dangerous

The Virtues

1. Cutter's Hope

2. Marlin's Faith

3. Charity for Nothing

4. Stoker's Serenity

5. Justice for Radar

The Sacred Brotherhood

1. Brother to Brother

2. Her Brother's Keeper

3. Brother In Arms

4. Between Brothers

5. A Brother's Secret

6. A Brother At My Back

7. A Brother's Salvation

Sacred Hearts MC Novella

Christmas with the Brotherhood

Indigo Knights

1. Her Thin Blue Lifeline

2. His Cold Blue Command

3. A Low Blue Flame

4. His Wild Blue Rose

5. Her Pained Blue Silence

6. A Cold Blue Call

7. Her Reluctant Blue Cavalier

8. Forged Under Fire

9. Under A Blue Moon

10. Sound of Blue Thunder

Sacred Hearts MC Pacific Northwest

1. Over the High Side

2. Wind Therapy

3. Apex of the Curve

4. Low Sided

5. Eating Asphalt

6. Hammer Down

7. Only Fool Riding

Paranormal Romance (with Ryan Kells)

1. I Am The Alpha

2. Omega's Run

3. Hunter's End

Indigo City Darker (with Jared KingPacal Lain)

1. Triple Threat

2. Double Shot

Standalones

Synchronicity

ABOUT A.J. DOWNEY

A.J. Downey is a Pacific Northwest girl living in an East Tennessee world who finds inspiration from her surroundings, through the people she meets, and likely as a byproduct of way too much caffeine. She specializes in real and relatable romance stories featuring that real-life kind of love that everyone craves.

Stalker Information:

Website
www.ajdowney.com

Sign up for her newsletter at
http://eepurl.com/dkQiIH

Facebook Group - AJ's Sacred Circle
https://www.facebook.com/groups/authorajdowney/

facebook.com/authorajdowney
twitter.com/authorajdowney
instagram.com/ajdowney
bookbub.com/authors/a-j-downey

Made in the USA
Middletown, DE
06 May 2023